KILLER DOLLS

PART THREE

Melodrama Publishing
www.MelodramaPubishing.com

FOLLOW
NISA SANTIAGO

FACEBOOK.COM/NISASANTIAGO

INSTAGRAM.COM/NISA_SANTIAGO

TWITTER.COM/NISA_SANTIAGO

Order online at
bn.com, amazon.com, and
MelodramaPublishing.com

This is a work of fiction. All of the characters, organizations, and events portrayed in this novel are either products of the author's imagination or are used fictitiously.

Library of Congress Control Number: 2016912061
ISBN-13: 978-1620780664
ISBN-10: 1620780666
First Edition: December 2016

Editor: Brian Sandy
Model Photo: Frank Antonio
Cover Model: Nefertiti

Melodrama Publishing
www.melodramapublishing.com

Printed in Canada

Books By Nisa Santiago

Cartier Cartel: Part 1
Return of the Cartier Cartel: Part 2
Cartier Cartel - South Beach Slaughter: Part 3
Bad Apple: The Baddest Chick Part 1
Coca Kola: The Baddest Chick Part 2
Checkmate: The Baddest Chick Part 3
Face Off: The Baddest Chick Part 4
South Beach Cartel
On the Run: The Baddest Chick Part 5
Unfinished Business: The Baddest Chick Part 6
Guard the Throne
Dirty Money Honey
Murdergram
Murdergram 2
The House That Hustle Built
The House That Hustle Built 2
The House That Hustle Built 3
Killer Dolls
Killer Dolls 2
Killer Dolls 3

KILLER DOLLS

PART THREE

NISA SANTIAGO

PROLOGUE

Aoki sat in the driver's seat of an Infiniti SUV with tinted windows and took everything in. She did her best to blend in, wearing jeans and a white T-shirt, her long, silky hair pulled back into a tight ponytail, and huge shades that covered most of her tiny face.

Aoki's life had always been one crazy event after another. This time she had escaped death. When Oscar's goons shot her in the chest and left her for dead in the marsh, it felt like the final chapter in her life was coming to a close. Surprisingly, there was more to read. She was saved and put back together like a bionic woman by an organization. They gave her a second chance, but that second chance came with a cost.

It took her two years to fully recover from her gunshot wound, graduate from The Farm, and make a name for herself. She spent the next three years stalking her target. It'd been a long time, but she was finally back in action and able to locate him. Her nemesis. The pain still burned in her chest. Despite all the betrayal, the lies, and scheming he did, she couldn't take his life when she had the opportunity. She was determined not to make that mistake again.

She sat parked across the street admiring the 6,000 sq.-ft. mini-mansion perched atop a small hill on two and a half acres of land. The place sat far enough away from the Jaguars, Lexuses, Beamers, and Benzes that lined the suburban street, and the homes on either side of the mini-mansion were more than a respectable distance away. The circular driveway surrounded a large white porcelain fountain. It was a beautiful home that anyone would be proud to live in with the perfect family and their perfect lives.

The tree-lined block was picture-perfect with its luxury homes, foreign vehicles, and manicured lawns stretching from one end of the street to the other. The suburb in the Upper Marlboro community was an idyllic scene. The residents were a family-oriented, sophisticated mix of ethnic groups with good careers, promising futures, and well-groomed children. It was a community where families took long summer vacations, threw lavish barbecues in their backyards, and enjoyed in-ground pools and cocktails. The families probably went to church every Sunday and did movie night every Friday. It was the ideal place to raise a family and enjoy the American dream.

Aoki sighed. She was a bitch from the hardcore streets of Brooklyn who grew up with fucked-up, drug-addicted parents. A place like Upper Marlboro, Maryland might as well have been the Land of Oz, for all she knew. But she wasn't some white bitch named Dorothy, and she wasn't from Kansas. She was a ravenous, bloodthirsty killer bent on revenge.

She sat back in the QX80 with a pair of small binoculars and watched as a father of two loaded his precious kids into the backseat of a black Porsche Cayenne. The children looked to be three and four years old. The man looked proud and happy.

Moments later, an attractive woman emerged from the million-dollar home, her cell phone attached to her ear, engaged in conversation and joining her family in the driveway. She smiled at her husband and gave him a kiss on the lips. She was tall and leggy, with long, shiny, black hair, fair skin, and hypnotic hazel eyes. She was dressed attractively in a trench coat, burgundy knit dress, and a pair of pumps.

Aoki frowned as she eyed the woman heavily; she definitely wasn't his type or his style. In fact, she was surprised to see he was married with kids. So much had changed over the years.

A mid-November breeze blew hundreds of fallen leaves throughout the street and across the sidewalks. Just weeks earlier the trees were green and alive, and the air was balmy and cozy. Now the fall weather brought about colors, the trees shaded with red, brown, and gold.

Aoki continued watching the family, and him especially. He looked different and more upbeat, dressed handsomely in an overcoat, blazer, jeans, and brown loafers, sporting a dark goatee and a shaved head. He had changed. He was still handsome, but he looked more sophisticated, shedding his street image to become more of a civilized man—a happily married man. But Aoki knew who he was and what he was about.

Aoki thought about her own American dream. She'd realized long ago that the life she was spying on from a distance would never be hers. She was damaged goods and too far gone to become anyone's wife or mother. She had betrayed the man she once loved and who loved her too. It had done something to her—created a vortex of pure hatred and bitterness inside her.

She couldn't help but wonder what her life would be like if she had made different choices. What if her parents hadn't fallen victim to the drugs and despair? What if she and AZ hadn't fallen out? What if she hadn't believed AZ's lie about Emilio? Would she be married with kids? Would she and Emilio have made it? Would they live in Los Angeles?

She thought about Tisa and Rihanna. They all had made so many mistakes. There was so much death, betrayal, and agony. The pain of the past swirled inside her head like a revolving door.

She watched the family pile into the Porsche. AZ got behind the wheel. He seemed so content with the wife and the kids. Most likely his wife had no clue he was on the down-low. *Dumb bitch!* Aoki had the details on her too: she was an assistant state's attorney for the city of Baltimore.

The happy couple pulled away from their home, and Aoki followed behind them at a safe distance. When they arrived at St. Joseph's Catholic Church, Aoki was taken aback.

"Him goes to church now, ay," she said to herself.

AZ took Randy in his arms while the wife carried their youngest. She watched as dozens of good ol' church folks strutted into the cathedral for Sunday Mass. Today was the Lord's day, but Aoki didn't care about religion or beliefs. She cared about revenge.

AZ had been allowed to live the good life for too long now. His day was coming. He couldn't escape her judgment. He couldn't run or hide from her. Wherever he went, an upgraded and trained Aoki had the skills and the resources to track him down.

She would allow him to live today, but his clock was ticking. She planned on wiping out his whole lineage in six months or less. The bitterness consumed her. She would never forget or forgive what he'd done to her. Seeing him living the good life while she had spent years going through hell fueled her rage and hatred even more.

She was back from the dead—with a short hit list.

Aoki started her car and peeled away from the church, but as she was watching AZ, someone was closely watching and following her.

ONE

Aoki walked into her Manhattan loft a week after departing Maryland, where she'd been stalking AZ. She had studied his routine and knew about his family. She wanted to toy with him, fuck with his head. Everyone believed she was dead. He wouldn't even see it coming. It had been a long personal trip for her. Now it was back to business.

Located in New York City's Hell's Kitchen, her amazing 3,600 sq.-ft loft featured parquet flooring with brick walls, a high, vaulted ceiling with steel columns, a kitchen adjacent to the freight elevator, and large windows with a panoramic view of the city. It had an open concept, and it occupied the entire floor. The place had become her fortress for over a year. Aoki had armed the place with top-notch security cameras and motion detectors, and a few booby traps for intruders or unwanted company. She stored extra weaponry and emergency cash in a hidden room tucked behind a faux fireplace.

Over the years, Aoki had become a deadly and skilled killer and was now one of the best in the business. With a heart as cold as ice, she always got her man or woman, or son or daughter. She didn't have the luxury of discriminating when it came to killing. If The Commission ordered a hit, you either fulfilled the contract, or you became the contract.

The Commission paid her lovely and financed her opulent lifestyle. She drove around in nice cars, wore the best outfits and jewelry, and her home was the finest. The respect and fear she'd garnered had gone international. She traveled the world, saw many things and places, and assassinated many faces, some of them powerful men and women. Her list of kills was extensive and ranged from high-end political figures to violent crime lords, shady (or even honest) businessmen, and unfaithful spouses.

Aoki loved her job. She loved the smell of blood and the power and control. She felt like a god when she was on a mission. They couldn't escape her. Many had begged for their lives, offering to pay her handsomely for redemption, but she was a product of The Commission, and there were no negotiations. She was a one-way street of death and destruction.

Aoki walked toward the window and stared out at her Hell's Kitchen neighborhood. Four stories below her window, the city was buzzing with life. Yellow cabs crowded the streets, and pedestrian traffic strutted everywhere, with the local businesses teeming with commerce. With darkness descending on the city, the local nightclubs were preparing to open their doors for patrons ready to party, dance, and drink their problems away.

Aoki had become somewhat of a recluse, only leaving her loft when she needed to, mostly to shop for necessities. She had been there and done that. The only time she mingled with the nightlife was when conducting surveillance on a target. She spent most of her time in training, in preparation, studying, and staying focused. She vowed to murder her former friend, AZ, and she planned on achieving her goal by any means necessary.

She pivoted from the window and started to shed her clothing. She walked toward the bathroom to take a shower. It had been a long day. At the moment, she was on hiatus from a job. It gave her some time to relax.

She left a trail of clothing on the floor from the window to the bathroom. She turned on the shower and allowed it to get steaming hot. She loved the feel of a heated shower against her skin. In fact she liked it borderline scalding hot. It made her feel alive and strong. One thing her training on The Farm taught her was to tolerate pain. Pain reminded you that you were still alive. Aoki was good at enduring pain; she had been doing so all her life.

Aoki stepped into the steaming hot shower and slightly cringed at the feel of the water cascading against her skin. She lowered her head and closed her eyes. After a minute, things felt natural to her.

She sighed deeply. She was proud of the bitch she had become. After The Commission had recruited her, she had to cut off all ties to her former life, which was pretty easy to do, since her former life was forgettable.

The only consequence to the deal was that it separated her from her friend Rihanna. She and Ri-Ri were once tighter than shoelaces; they were like sisters. After Gena's and Tisa's murders, Ri-Ri lost it, becoming disheveled and a danger to herself. Her sanity started to fade. First, she was placed in Kings County Hospital's psychiatric facility for a 72-hour hold. When the staff saw no improvement, she was transferred to Creedmoor in Queens.

Aoki lingered in the shower with thoughts of her past. Her time on The Farm in upstate New York was an experience she would never forget. It molded her into the perfect killing machine. She had gone through intense training. The Farm's purpose was to transform young minds and bodies into heartless killers for profit.

Aoki remembered when she laughed at the word *assassin*. She wanted to be referred to as a triggerman. Now assassin/triggerman was synonymous with job/career. It was all just work. The Farm had brainwashed her, making her devoid of empathy and caring. The first two weeks were the hardest—the grueling 24/7 training, the intense conditioning, and the mind control. After the first few weeks, the training started to become natural for her. Her old identity gradually slipped away, and a new person emerged with a perfect athletic body.

The Farm bred some of the most dangerous men and women. There were times when Aoki went days without sleep and food. It was boot camp on steroids. She endured ten- to fifteen-mile runs, bloody hand-to-hand combat, and strenuous exercise that could make the hardest Marine cry like a baby.

She became the best on The Farm, and The Commission took notice. She was passing everything with flying colors, and her combat skills and gun handling were off the chart. She was a quick learner, but there was also a switch inside her that made her a killer already. She had the strength, the endurance, and the will to survive. Along with combat training there was language, voice, and diction. That heavy Jamaican accent of hers had to go. In her field you couldn't have any distinguishing traits. Though, when she wasn't working, her native tongue flipped back on like a switch.

Lingering in the shower for an hour, she thought about her first kill—well, her first assignment for The Commission.

＊

Bingo was a violent drug dealer on the rise in the streets of West Philadelphia, and his rivals wanted him gone. The Commission received the request, and Aoki was given the low-level contract to pop her cherry. Bingo was a serious player with an intimidating physique—six three, two hundred and thirty pounds of muscles. The Commission wanted to see how thoroughly she could handle herself.

She observed Bingo closely for a week without him even noticing and learned his routine. He was an unpredictable man who never did the same thing twice, so it was difficult for her to find a pattern, but she did.

Bingo found comfort in Norristown, P.A., a town north of West Philly, six miles outside Philadelphia city limits. There, he stayed with a trusted, long-term girlfriend, a white woman who was both pretty and pregnant. When possible, Bingo would lay his head and find intimacy there. Bingo was a private and shrewd man, so none of his crew knew about his pregnant white girlfriend.

After keeping a close watch on the two-story home, Aoki made her way inside one night to execute the contract. Dressed in black and gripping a pistol with a silencer and a hand-forged steel dagger, she entered the home effortlessly and made her way upstairs. She moved like a shadow inside the home, like she was taught.

The pregnant girlfriend was in the master bedroom watching TV, lotioning her protruding belly, and Bingo was in the shower.

Aoki slyly moved into the bathroom. The shower curtain obstructed Bingo's view of the door, but he was still a careful man, judging by the 9mm on the sink countertop.

She had the element of surprise and used it. Quickly, she drew back the curtain and fired a shot between Bingo's eyes. The silencer and television muffled the sound of gunfire. Before he could drop and make noise, she caught the body and placed him carefully inside the tub with the shower still running. She then drove her dagger into his rib cage just because she wanted to. It happened that quickly—like lightning striking.

Aoki then hurriedly, but craftily, removed herself from the scene, the girlfriend still unaware of what had just happened. When Aoki exited the house, she could hear the pregnant girlfriend's blood-curdling scream.

Aoki was on her way to becoming one of the best, rising up in the ranks quickly with kill after kill, and soon, her skills took her abroad.

TWO

Aoki climbed out of her BMW 650i coupe and walked toward the towering Creedmoor Psychiatric Center in Queens Village, right off Union Turnpike and Cross Island Parkway. Creedmoor provided inpatient, outpatient, and residential services for severely mentally ill patients, and had been Ri-Ri's residence for five years. It sat on more than 300 acres of land and included more than fifty buildings, some of which had been long abandoned.

Aoki strutted toward the front entrance looking classy in a mink coat, curve-skimming dress, and six-inch Christian Louboutin boots, her long black hair flowing.

Aoki knew she was violating The Commission's rules by seeing a friend, but she didn't think it was right to cut off all ties to someone she had been through hell and back with. She had been visiting Ri-Ri in secret since she left training on The Farm.

Aoki waited in a bland room with bar-covered windows while staff patrolled the area like it was the visiting room at Rikers Island. She sat at a table and peered out the window.

Ten minutes later, Aoki spotted Ri-Ri escorted into the room by a female staff member. Dressed in a long white robe, slippers, with hair looking like it hadn't been done since two birthdays ago, Ri-Ri looked out of touch. Besides the death of her mother and sister, the murders they'd committed for AZ and Oscar had taken a lot out of her. Ri-Ri's spirit wasn't strong enough to handle the pressure and had gone 7:30.

A heavyset woman sat Ri-Ri down at the table across from Aoki and smiled at Aoki.

"How she been lately?" Aoki asked.

"Pretty much the same," the lady replied. "You have fifteen minutes with her."

Aoki nodded. Fifteen minutes was fine. She was grateful just to see her old friend again, though the girl sitting in front of her was now nothing but an empty shell. Despite her condition, Aoki liked to see and confide in her friend, even if it was a one-way conversation. It felt like confession at a Catholic church.

"It's good to see you again, Ri-Ri," Aoki said.

Ri-Ri stared off into space, looking removed from Aoki and everything around her.

The damage to her mind and soul was deeply rooted, and Aoki was partially responsible. Tisa had become a liability, and it was risky to keep her alive. Aoki had confessed to Ri-Ri that she had killed Tisa. There was no response from Rihanna. No emotion.

During her visits, Aoki told Ri-Ri everything, from being shot and left for dead to AZ being gay and their beef, to her training on The Farm, The Commission, and the kills she'd executed for profit. Ri-Ri remained still like a piece of furniture. Aoki didn't care; Ri-Ri was a friendly face from her past life and the only family Aoki felt she had.

Her fifteen minutes went by quickly. The heavyset lady came to their table and escorted Ri-Ri away from the visiting area and back to her padded room. Ri-Ri was on constant suicide watch because of the numerous times she'd tried to kill herself. Thankfully she hadn't had an incident in over a year now.

Aoki released a deep sigh, and then she removed herself from the table and then the room. There were always mixed feelings about seeing Rihanna. It was hard seeing her in such a fragile and deteriorating condition. But that was life, and she couldn't change things.

Aoki walked toward her car, and as she moved through the parking lot, she couldn't help feeling that someone was watching her. She stopped her stride and pivoted where she stood, her eyes keenly taking in her surroundings, looking for anything out of the ordinary. The Farm had taught her to have a photographic memory and be able to spot the extraordinary no matter how ordinary it looked. But there was nothing strange and no visible threat.

She continued walking to her car and climbed inside. For a moment, she lingered behind the steering wheel, thinking. She was six months from her twenty-fifth birthday, and that meant she would be able to age out of The Commission, collect her millions that were held in an overseas bank account, and try to live a normal and productive life if she wanted to—or if she was able to.

She was almost a quarter of a century old, and though it was a young age for many, it felt like a lifetime for Aoki. No one would ever be able to comprehend the things she had done and seen. Truthfully, Aoki was becoming tired of the wild, murderous life she had been thrust into. Paranoid, she constantly had nightmares of being murdered or betrayed. Though she was living the good life in her Manhattan loft, she was damaged goods too, maybe far worse than Rihanna.

Not many of her peers from Brooklyn made it to their twenty-fifth birthday, and sometimes Aoki wasn't sure she would. Six months was a long time for her, and anything could happen. Aoki promised herself that after her twenty-fifth birthday, she would never take a life again. She was going to retire and try and make a real life for herself. She was ready to contradict herself and her beliefs and maybe find love again—this time, in a different country.

That whole lifestyle felt like it was light years away, but she thought she deserved happiness too. Yet, she wondered if a woman who had caused so much death and misery could ever find true happiness.

THREE

AZ grunted and moaned. "Oh shit! I'm gonna fuckin' come!" He thrust his way into paradise, feeling the tightness of the glory hole he was in. The erection had felt like his hardest. He was hitting it from the back, gripping the hips, ready to explode like a volcano. The feeling was like no other, satisfying like soul food to a starving man. Sweat poured from his brow. He could feel his ejaculation brewing. He inhaled and exhaled as his balls slammed against the finest piece of ass he'd had in a long while.

"Fuck me!" his lover announced.

AZ continued to grunt. He had needed this, some quality time with his lover. "I'm gonna fuckin' come!" he announced again.

A few more hard thrusts and intense grabbing, and AZ finally let loose, exploding his load into his lover, Baron. It felt like his ejaculation would never stop. It was strong and intense. AZ quivered after releasing his seed, and the two men collapsed against each other on the bed, smiling, their manly bodies entwined with contentment and hard breathing. AZ held Baron in his arms like he was a soft woman.

"That was fun," Baron said.

AZ chuckled. "It was. I always have a nice time with you."

They stared into each other's eyes, like children staring at the stars out in the country. Both of them gleamed with gratification. AZ squeezed Baron tighter into his arms. He loved the way his pale flesh, smooth thin chest, and white ass enticed him.

Like AZ, Baron was in the closet, and there was no way he was coming out. Baron was a successful realtor from a prominent, influential family with a wife and three kids. There was no way his family, especially his father, was going to accept his homosexuality. His father was a concentrated homophobic and thought homosexuality was a grave sin. He had already made several threats that Baron would be written out of the will and disowned if he turned out to be gay.

AZ and Baron had rented a fully furnished condo in the District Heights of Columbia, a few miles from Washington, D.C. The area was private and covert. The lease was in AZ's name. There, they could enjoy each other without their neighbors knowing who they were or what they were about. It was their private paradise not just for sex, but for watching movies together, cooking, and casual talk. It was their second home.

They'd met eight months earlier at a bar in D.C. After repeated moments of eye contact, AZ took the initiative to spark conversation with Baron. They found they had a lot in common and a lot to lose. Baron was a great match for AZ. He wasn't like Conner, eager for love and a relationship, acting childish when things didn't go his way. Baron was no threat to AZ's double life, and the sex was good.

After an hour of relaxing together in the soft king-size canopy bed with high thread-count sheets, AZ removed himself from Baron's tight grasp and started to get dressed.

Baron rolled over butt naked and smiled at AZ. "Are you leaving already?"

"Yeah, it's getting late, and I got a long drive to New York tomorrow."

"You and these constant trips to New York," Baron said. "I'm starting to think you have another lover there."

AZ laughed it off. "Nah, it's just business. And, besides, no one can replace you and that hard white dick of yours. You know I like that white meat."

"You better."

AZ pulled up his jeans and buttoned his shirt. Baron was a breath of fresh air for him. Someone he could confide in and be himself around.

Baron propped himself up against the headboard and watched AZ get dressed. Everything about AZ turned him on. His marriage was a sham—ten years with his wife and she'd never made him feel like this.

Baron removed a cigarette from the pack on the nightstand and lit it. He took a few drags and asked the inevitable. "So, when am I going to see you again?"

"When I get back from New York," AZ replied.

"And when will that be?"

"Sometime tomorrow night."

Baron huffed. He then asked, "How's the wife?"

AZ laughed. "Like you care about her."

"I don't. I only care about you . . . very much. The sex anyway. The sex is what I look forward to."

"Same here."

"My wife is a complete bitch!" Baron announced. "But I'm stuck with her because of my father. And he's an asshole. If he ever found out about you and me, he would destroy me and come after you."

"I'm not worried about your father. He don't know me, and he don't wanna know me."

"That's what I like about you, AZ; you don't take any shit from anyone."

"I'm from Brooklyn; we had to survive out there."

"My Brooklyn bad boy," Baron said with enthusiasm.

"You know it. Anyway, I gotta get home to the wife and family."

Baron sighed. "Same here."

AZ continued dressing, and Baron joined him. Within moments, the two were fully dressed and ready to exit the condo. Once again, they had put the place to good use. But now it was back to reality and back into the closet.

AZ was the first to leave. He kissed Baron on the lips before his departure and climbed into his G-Class Benz and headed home. Baron climbed into his Lexus and did the same.

＊

It was after midnight when AZ came through the front doors of his lavish home. The place was dark and quiet. He made his way toward the steps and ascended to the master bedroom. His wife was curled up under the covers sleeping cozily, her back to the door. He crept into the bathroom and took a shower to remove any scent of Baron from his body. After the shower, he quietly climbed into bed with his wife and went to sleep. His trip to New York was urgent, and he needed his rest.

The following morning, AZ was up early for his trip out of town. His wife Wendy was taking a shower, and it was AZ's turn to get the kids ready for school.

He went into their room with a smile on his face. Randy was three, and Terrance was two. They were the apple of his eye. AZ was a proud daddy, and his two sons made him happy. If he had ever done something right in his life, it was having them.

Their room was decorated with Transformers and Ninja Turtles, his sons' favorite cartoon characters. They slept in twin beds with Transformer bedding, and they were spoiled with toys and games. AZ wanted to give his kids what he didn't have growing up.

He woke up Randy first then Terrance. The two sleepyheads didn't want to get up, but he made them. He kissed them good morning and helped them wash up and get dressed. Years ago, AZ didn't see himself living this life—married with children—but times had definitely changed for him.

While his kids were eating their cereal in the kitchen, he went back upstairs to check on his wife, who was hurrying to get dressed. She was anticipating a busy day ahead. AZ walked into the room and kissed her on the lips. Their kiss was dry; Wendy seemed more interested in getting dressed and preparing for her day at the office than showing her husband any affection. AZ didn't mind. He had gotten all the affection and loving he needed the night before with Baron. Wendy was always busy with her career, bringing her work home.

"Is this trip to New York today that important?" she asked him gruffly. "Because my day is going to be hectic, and I might not be able to pick up the kids from day care. I have three depositions to take care of and a pretrial hearing this afternoon."

"I told you, it is. My partners and I are working on this new development agreement. We have our hands in some prime real estate in Manhattan."

Wendy frowned and continued to scurry around the bedroom, collecting her things and putting together an outfit. She went with a houndstooth skirt suit and black heels, and let her long black hair flow down to her shoulders.

She sighed. "I guess if it's business, then I'll call the nanny and let her know to pick up the kids."

"That's my girl."

"Don't be too late coming back."

"It depends on traffic, babe. You know I have to make this money for us to continue living like this. You like this house, the cars, the clothes, and the gifts I give to you and the kids?"

"You know I do," she said proudly.

"And for that to continue to happen, it takes sacrifices and long hours commuting from here to New York."

"I don't see why you have to invest in property so far away."

"It's where the money is at, and New York is what I know. We can turn over a fortune in New York flipping these low-end properties and getting into this gentrification. Besides, you know I grew up there. I know my shit, babe."

"I know you do, but the kids do miss you."

"I'll make it up to them. Promise."

Another deep sigh escaped from Wendy's lips. She looked at her husband and believed he was doing what was best for the family and their future. AZ had become a prominent businessman in her eyes. His fortune afforded her the life she always wanted growing up. Her income as an assistant state's attorney was okay, but sixty-five thousand dollars a year was a drop in a bucket, considering their lifestyle.

Wendy and the kids climbed into the Porsche Cayenne while AZ watched them from the living room window. He waved goodbye to his family and kept his eyes on the vehicle leaving the residence.

The second they were gone, he got on his cell phone and made an important call. Three rings later, Heavy Pop picked up.

"Tell me you in New York, nigga," Heavy Pop said.

"No, I'm not. I'll be there in about three hours."

Heavy Pop groaned. "Fuck Maryland! I don't know how you can live out there with them uptight country folks, nigga."

"It's not that bad out here."

"To me it is."

"You need a change."

"And you need to hurry ya ass so we can lock down this deal."

"You tell Mateo I'll be in town soon. This meeting is still happening."

"It needs to happen."

"I'll be there. Call you when I'm on the road." AZ exhaled and hung up.

He turned and took in the furnishings of his home. He thought about the lies he continued to tell his wife and his peoples.

AZ packed his 9mm and jumped into his Benz truck. The moment he started the car, he became startled by the radio playing too damn loud so suddenly. "What the fuck!" he uttered, and quickly turned it down to normal volume.

That was odd to him. He never had his radio blasting like that. Lately, strange things had been happening that he couldn't explain.

Two weeks earlier, he had parked his Benz in one place, only to find it parked somewhere else. He had no clue how that had happened. The strange occurrences were making him super paranoid. He felt somebody was fucking with him. Who, he had no idea, but they were playing with fire and would get burned beyond recognition.

AZ looked around and saw nothing or no one strange. He shrugged off the odd radio situation and pulled out of his driveway. He lit a cigarette and made his way toward I-95 North for the three-hour drive to New York.

AZ and Heavy Pop had significantly risen in the drug game and were now the biggest distributors from New York to Miami. Both men had everything they wanted, from wealth to respect to power. But AZ was living a triple life. In Upper Marlboro, he was a husband, a family man, and a prominent businessman. In New York and everywhere else, he was a drug lord whose reputation preceded him. Then, of course, when he needed love and sex, there was Baron.

AZ bought up real estate in low-income areas, created multiple healthy businesses, and invested in gentrification. His wife didn't know that all of his business deals were funded with drug money. When it came to his home life and business, AZ painstakingly dotted his *i*'s and crossed his *t*'s. He had outstanding lawyers to help him with the paperwork and launder his money. He did his homework and took his time in building up both worlds so they wouldn't easily come apart.

Wendy, being an assistant state's attorney in Baltimore, was unknowingly sleeping with the enemy. She helped prosecute violent criminals every day, especially drug dealers, while sharing her bed with a major one. AZ knew if the truth ever came out, it would destroy Wendy's career and break her heart.

✳

With traffic moving well, AZ eased through the Lincoln Tunnel. It was early afternoon, and midtown Manhattan was full of life. He steered his Benz toward Le Bernardin on West 51st Street, parked nearby, and exited his vehicle. He breathed in the city air. Being back in the New York was a good feeling for him. This was his home. His life. AZ had a lot of memories in New York, some good, some bad, and some definitely ugly. But this city had made him the man he was. He beat the odds stacked against him, surviving war and death, and became the man he always knew he was meant to be.

He walked toward the restaurant and dialed Heavy Pop on his cell phone. Two rings later, his friend picked up.

"I'm here," AZ said. "Where are you?"

"We inside," Heavy Pop said.

"Be in there in a minute."

AZ ended the call and walked in the front entrance. The décor expressed a sexy French flair and jaw-dropping design, and the ambiance was lovely, with gourmet cocktails and attractive clientele. AZ informed the maître d' whom he was there to see, and the attractive, pale, well-dressed woman led him away from the main dining area.

Heavy Pop and Mateo were seated beneath a glass chandelier in the private back room sipping on cocktails and having casual conversation. Both men stood up to greet AZ as soon as they saw him. Heavy Pop greeted his brother from another mother with dap and a brotherly hug, and Mateo casually shook his hand.

"It's nice to finally meet you, AZ," Mateo said.

"Likewise."

Mateo said politely, "I appreciate you taking the time to meet me in the city, knowing you're coming all the way from Maryland."

"Business is business, and the drive doesn't bother me, as long as it's worth my time."

AZ locked eyes with Mateo, trying to read everything about him. He'd heard so much about the man who was once an icon to them. Mateo was in his mid-forties and was a major player in the drug game for decades. But things had changed.

All three men took their seats at the table and lounged comfortably. They had their own waitress and all the privacy they needed to discuss business, being removed from the general patrons. Heavy Pop was eager to get things started. He had come a long way too, being shot and almost killed, and now he had a young son and a nagging baby mama.

Each man was well-dressed in high-end fashion in their own way. Tall and lean, Mateo was wearing a sharp black suit with a beige silk tie that screamed Armani, and a gold diamond Rolex peeked from beneath his white cuffs. His hair was trimmed and coiffed, his skin glowed, and he could've easily passed for a Hollywood star.

AZ ordered a cocktail. "I'm surprised to meet with you on this level, Mateo. Your name been ringing out for years now."

"I know, but things and situations change," Mateo replied.

AZ told him, "It's good to see you trying to get back on your feet, Mateo, but I'm curious. You've always been a distributor in the game, not a buyer. You had direct contact with the cartels, and damn near every muthafucka from Boston to the D.C. went to your organization for coke and dope. Now to see you like this, coming to us for your supply, how the fuck did that happen?"

Mateo sat back in his seat and took a sip from his drink. He locked eyes with AZ, knowing if this was ten years ago, he would have been the one doing the interrogation. He answered coolly, "Bad luck and bad investments over the years."

Heavy Pop chimed, "That's the game, right? Up and down."

"In this game, you always got to stay on your toes," AZ said, almost like a low blow to Mateo. "You can't get caught slippin' in these streets 'cuz the wolves will devour you."

AZ and Heavy Pop had the upper hand, with the strong connect and the resources to make Mateo a rich man again.

"Look, I fucked up. I admit it. I caught a few bad breaks throughout the years, and with pussy, drugs, and a wild lifestyle, it was a disaster waiting to happen. I got four baby mamas all filled with drama, and seven kids. I got distracted. I got stupid. I made some bad investments too, lost a ton of money on that record label I started. Then the gun charge took a lot out of me, along with the IRS taking a huge chunk out of my ass, with owed taxes and shit, practically leaving me with nothing when I came home."

AZ added, "Yeah, and then there's niggas saying you got jammed up in North Carolina on some federal raid."

"That's bullshit!" Mateo vehemently denied. "One of my baby mamas snitched that fucker' ratwas! That bitch cost me a lot of business and dried up my lifeline. I underestimated that fuckin' ho. I was flying high on that pure white heroin from Honduras. When that rumor started about me getting raided in North Carolina with over a hundred kilos of cocaine, everyone started to jump ship."

"Could you blame 'em?" AZ asked.

"I can't. But it ruined me. I had a tight ship—connections with the Coast Guard, pilots, and political connections so fuckin' high, I damn near had the president on speed dial."

Heavy Pop laughed.

But Mateo's downfall was nothing to laugh at. He had taken a major hit.

"And what do you need from us?" AZ already knew the answer, but he needed to hear Mateo say it from his own mouth.

"I'm back on my feet, but I just need that extra push. Know what I'm saying?"

AZ nodded.

"We got you," Heavy Pop said.

Instead of manufacturing and distributing, Mateo needed to hustle to build his empire again, and he had the funds. Mateo had heard through the grapevine about AZ and Heavy Pop being legit niggas—serious and moving more "white" than a Russian blizzard.

Mateo had reached out to them via a third party, and once AZ heard the name of the man who wanted to meet, he didn't hesitate. Mateo always came correct, from his understanding.

AZ asked, "So what are we talking 'bout here, Mateo? What do you expect from us?"

"I want two hundred—"

"Kilos?" Heavy Pop asked, looking dumbfounded.

"Two hundred ki's on consignment? That's just too much of a risk for us. I mean, no disrespect, your name rang out, it still do, but let's be for real here—This ain't back in the day, and you've dropped a few levels on the food chain."

Mateo frowned. "Obviously, you got me confused with some fledgling small-timer in this game. And I'm insulted that you would think that of me—that I need shit on credit or consignment. I'm talking cash, and for that amount, I want high quality coke with a bulk discount."

"Damn! Cash?"

AZ gawked at Mateo stoically. It was a tall order. In fact, it was one of their biggest orders to date. "That's a lot a weight, especially for a man that's been somewhat on a decline the past three years."

"Look at me—you know my name, my pedigree, and you know I'm smart. I'm still a man with resources and cash on reserve. You think the government was able to take everything from me?"

AZ didn't answer him.

Both men were in business mode, like sharks circling their prey in the ocean. It was game time. So far, AZ's trip to New York was looking like it was worthwhile.

"It's gonna take us some time to put that order together," AZ said.

Mateo took a sip from his stemmed glass. "I'm cool with that. How long you think?" he asked coolly.

"About a week."

Mateo nodded his head. "And price?"

"Thirty a ki'," AZ replied.

"You can't be serious. For two hundred, I'm gonna need a lower number."

AZ looked at his partner in crime, who said, "Hey, he's getting two hundred. I ain't got no problem with a lower number."

AZ sighed. "Twenty-eight."

"Twenty," Mateo returned seriously.

Mateo and AZ went back and forth with numbers.

Mateo finally offered, "Twenty-three five a ki', and I promise you I'll be a loyal client to you from now on. These two hundred will be gone within no time. I already have something set up."

AZ sat silently for a moment, mulling over the offer, which was almost seven grand under their asking price. He then shook his head, locked eyes with Mateo, and agreed to the deal. Usually, AZ wouldn't have accepted such a low offer, but for that quantity and with Mateo having the cash up front, it was a sweet deal on both ends. They shook on it, and their business was concluded.

Heavy Pop said, "Mateo, I'm curious. What ever happened to the baby mama that started that rumor about you?"

Mateo smirked. "You know, I heard her funeral was very nice . . . though it was a closed casket."

"Damn!" Heavy Pop uttered.

The three men stood up from their chairs, and Mateo made his exit. AZ and Heavy Pop walked out of the place ecstatic.

AZ was already running the numbers in his head. They would get the kilos from Oscar at twenty thousand a key, but at that quantity, and having a good business relationship with Oscar, he was sure they could get them at eighteen a key, leaving them a net profit of $550,000 each for a couple hours of their time. Mateo was promising to move that kind of weight every two to three weeks. That was over a million each per month just from one client. It was a good day's work.

Heavy Pop wanted to celebrate and go to one of the high-end strip clubs in the city, but AZ wasn't in the mood. He decided to drive back to Maryland before rush-hour traffic came creeping. He wanted to spend some quality time with his wife, celebrate with her when she came home. Lately, things had been shaky in his home, and he needed to keep up appearances with her. He climbed in his Benz and made his way back to the Lincoln Tunnel and toward Maryland.

FOUR

AZ wanted to celebrate the deal he had made with Mateo, so when he got back to Maryland, he and his wife popped some champagne and watched a movie. They continued their quality time together in the bedroom while the kids were sleeping.

AZ thrust himself inside of Wendy while he had her pinned against the bed in the missionary position. He sucked on her nipples and grinded between her thighs. He could feel she was moist.

Wendy knew that the deal in the city must have gone forward, since AZ was going caveman on her pussy that night. They hadn't had sex in months, and they barely kissed. AZ was on cloud nine and he wanted to please her. However, she wasn't pleased. He was her husband, and it was simply her duty to give him pleasure. Some nights she just lay there like a doll, simply giving him what he wanted. He grunted, and she didn't.

She lay there with her legs spread and felt his erection pushing in and out of her.

Wendy loved the life that he gave her and the kids, but there wasn't true love for her husband. He was smart, a great businessman, and a wonderful father, but when it came to passion and the intimacy, it just wasn't there. After spending years together, she had grown bored of him and their marriage.

"I love you, baby!" AZ proclaimed, working his erection inside of her.

"I love you too," she replied dryly.

AZ wanted to switch positions, doggy-style. He wanted to explore her forbidden area. Sexing his wife anally would remind him of having sex with Baron.

"Hell no!"

"C'mon, baby, let's just try something new tonight. I can get some lubrication and take my time inside . . . no rush."

"No! Are you crazy? Why not just fuck me regular and get your nut?"

"I thought I would spice up our sex life."

"By fuckin' me in the ass? You already know how I feel about it. It's disgusting! You're lucky I'm in the mood for this much."

AZ released a deep sigh. Quickly, his celebration was transforming into misery and rejection. He loved his wife, and he wanted to fuck her like a beast and, for one night, pretend he wasn't a down-low homosexual who loved a hard dick too. He wanted to be normal with his wife. Anal sex with the wife was normal, right?

Just like that, AZ's penis became flaccid.

Wendy saw this and removed herself from the bed and donned a long robe. It was official. Playtime had ended. "I need to use the bathroom," she announced matter-of-factly. She walked out the bedroom, closing the bathroom door shut.

AZ lay naked on the bed looking flabbergasted. The other night with Baron had been much more satisfying than this shit, and he craved to see him again. *Maybe I should have celebrated with him instead,* he thought.

He puffed out disappointment as he stood up and threw on a pair of basketball shorts and a T-shirt. He left the bedroom and went into the boys' bedroom to check up on them. Both his sons were sound asleep. They looked peaceful in their beds—like little angels in cartoon pajamas curled up under the sheets, probably having sweet dreams. What did they have to worry about? They were spoiled and protected. They were innocent. He could see himself in his sons.

AZ closed their door and went back into his bedroom. Wendy hadn't come out the bathroom yet. It sounded too quiet in there. He placed his ear to the door and heard nothing, not even water running. He then knocked and asked, "Wendy, you okay in there?"

"I'm fine!" she snapped. "Just leave me alone for now!"

He assumed she might have had a rough day at the office. Being an assistant state's attorney for Baltimore could become a stressful job. She had to deal with it all—crime, politics, and bullshit. She also was a beautiful woman, and AZ considered, maybe, she had to put up with sexual harassment on the job. He'd once told her that if she had any issues with work that she could come to him. For anything. He would take care of it. Wendy just shrugged him off. She saw AZ as a meek businessman from Brooklyn with no clout in her city. He was a nice guy, and she felt that he could be just a little too amiable for her line of business.

AZ pivoted and walked away from the door. He picked up the remote control to the 60-inch flat-screen mounted on their bedroom wall and powered it on. CNN came to life across the screen. The anchorman talked about a crisis overseas, somewhere in Lebanon. AZ paid little to no attention to the broadcast. He could care less about what was happening ten thousand miles away from him. He had his own problems at home.

Sitting at the foot of the bed, he suddenly remembered noticing that Wendy had taken her cell phone into the bathroom with her. He wondered why. What was going on? What was she up to? There was something going on with his wife, and he wanted to know what it was.

FIVE

Cristal slowly submerged herself into the soothing bath. The hot water in the porcelain tub was doing its job, caressing her body, soothing her nooks and crannies. Her body was aching from head to toe. She closed her eyes, wanting to relax and take her mind off her troubles.

Mary J. Blige's "Be Without You" played through the wireless speakers in her bathroom. Mary's music was another soothing technique to help her heal and get better. She listened to the lyrics and sang along. Mary was therapeutic in so many ways.

She released a deep sigh and sank deeper into the comforting water. She felt safe for now, with a loaded 9mm within her reach by the tub and the door locked.

Not long ago, they'd almost cornered her. They had come for her unexpectedly. She'd thought she had always been careful covering her tracks and staying off-grid. Obviously, she was wrong. They had always been watching and were close on her tail.

The Commission never forgot, and they never gave up. With GHOST Protocol on her ass too, she had to be twice as cautious.

Cristal continued to linger in the warm tub. The umpteenth song from her Mary J. Blige playlist was playing. Her mind transported her to her days in Brooklyn when she once was innocent.

She was now alone in this world, her entire bloodline having been wiped out by someone she'd once considered a close friend. Tamar was dead now, but the lasting effects of her sadistic actions were carved into Cristal's mind. The Farm and The Commission did her more harm than good. They taught her how to destroy lives, and in reverse, she had destroyed her own. Almost everyone in her crew was dead—Lisa, Mona, Tamar. Sharon was smart enough not to take up EP on his invitation to The Farm, and had become a cop in the NYPD.

Thinking about it all brought tears to Cristal's eyes. She wiped them away quickly and got out of the tub. She dried off and knotted the towel around her. She went to the mirror and looked at herself. She was a bad bitch, but her soul had been torn apart, and at times she doubted she would ever be whole again.

But then Daniel came into her life and changed her views. The way he loved her was magical. He made her laugh, think, and smile. He gave her a reason to want to live—to separate herself from her past.

Damn, she missed him so much. She yearned for his touch and his kisses against her lips and skin. The way he enlightened her to different things was gratifying. Daniel was the love of her life. It was torture knowing she would never see him again. But she had figured out a way to hear from him again.

Cristal went into her bedroom, got dressed in yoga pants and a hoodie, and opened a dresser drawer, where she kept several SIM cards and cell phones. Each phone was untraceable. Along with the cell phones was a GPS jammer. She knew that phone calls could be easily traced the minute a caller picked up.

After she placed a SIM card into a cell phone, she stepped outside into the fall weather and started her mobilization. She had to be mobile, so the call could bounce from tower to tower. It was worth the hassle. She had been calling Daniel lately, but not saying a word to him. She just wanted to hear him answer the phone and hear him breathe.

"Hello? Who's calling?" he'd ask, but she would never say a word.

All this effort was to keep him safe. She didn't want anything to happen to him. She couldn't see him and feared they were watching him closely, and when she called him, they couldn't find her location. As long as they couldn't find her, Cristal thought Daniel would be okay.

After a few calls to him without her saying anything, he started to wonder if the person on the other end who remained silent was actually his very complicated and very dead girlfriend.

"Hey, if this is you, I hope and pray you're okay."

During the following phone call a week later, Daniel talked about his summer without her, and how much he missed her. He started to talk into the phone normally about his day, his future, his hurts and pain. He thought he was going crazy, yet it was comforting to him. Daniel always felt that there was something more to Beatrice and her death, and he wanted to believe that it was her calling and remaining silent on the phone. He took a chance and began speaking freely like it was Beatrice AKA Cristal.

Cristal listened to him silently. Though it was a one-way conversation, she felt engaged. She took that as a sign that their love was real, transcending logic, death, The Commission, and GHOST Protocol.

SIX

The late Bishop once told Cristal, "Never stay in one place for too long, don't make any friends, only pay cash, stay humble, and most important, keep a low profile. Avoid confrontations and law enforcement by any means necessary."

Cristal had followed his rules, and it had brought her this far. But life on the run, away from everything she once knew, was hard. She had a high contract on her head—a million dollars each from The Commission and GHOST Protocol, two of the most dangerous and influential organizations anyone could tangle with. There was no telling how many people they had killed over the years, and now Cristal was on their hit list. She had pissed them off by publishing her *Killer Dolls* novels under the pseudonym Melissa Chin. Cristal told all of The Commission's dirty secrets—She didn't care—and her books became international best-sellers, even making *The New York Times* list.

Fuck 'em, she told herself. There was no way she was going to die by their hands and not be heard. And she was definitely heard through Melissa Chin's voice. She wanted to out them, feeling they were evil and corrupt murderers. Now these organizations would stop at nothing to destroy her. Since she didn't have any family left, it was harder to track her down and kill her. The only family she had left, the only one she loved, was Daniel, but he was three thousand miles away.

She felt her location in the state of Washington had been compromised, not by killers for hire, but by the residents. Though she kept to herself and minded her business, always dressing low-key and not making friends, she was still a pretty girl with a nice shape, and she would attract the men in the town. They would flirt with her while she passed. They found her to be so beautiful and intriguing. White, black, it didn't matter, they all started to chase her, and it was making the native females jealous. The more she resisted their flirting, catcalls, and flowers, the harder they tried. Cristal tried her best to fit in, but she wasn't one of them. She would never be. She was a newcomer in town, and her beauty became her kryptonite.

Cristal thought Everett, twenty-five miles north of Seattle, was a large enough town to not stand out in. With a population of 105,000, it felt perfect. But five months later, she was having issues. Candice Richardson was the name Cristal went by in Everett, where she worked at a local bookstore to pay her bills. Her story was that she was from New Mexico and had no family. A local girl named Megan Davis disliked her very much. Megan's fiancé, Paul, took a liking to Cristal, and he found himself going into the bookstore regularly and trying to strike up a conversation with her. She would continually ignore him, but to no avail. Paul made it known that he liked Candice. Megan became jealous and confronted Cristal at her job.

"You want to have relations with my man?" Megan griped. "We're Christian people in this city, and we don't take kindly to your kind coming here and corrupting our men, you jezebel!"

Cristal coolly replied, "I don't want your man."

"He sure wants you!"

"That's between you and your fiancé, ma'am. He or you aren't my business."

"You stay away from Paul. You understand me?"

"I don't want him, and *he* needs to stay away from *me*."

"Stay away from my fiancé or else. Believe me, you don't know what I'm capable of."

Cristal was far from worried about some Western small-town bitch. But it wouldn't be fair, and it wouldn't be worth it.

Megan turned and stormed out of the bookstore, leaving Cristal feeling needless in town. It was time for a change.

Some nights, Cristal returned to the reasonably priced one-bedroom basement apartment she'd rented from an elderly lady, lock her doors, and cry. She would wonder how she'd gotten herself, and her friends, into this life. Her mind almost always went to Hugo and their unborn child. It was all so very sad and tragic. She thought about her sexual relations with EP, the man she'd once trusted and loved. Now he was dead, too, no doubt taken out by The Commission for his sins against them. The night she had met him at that party in Manhattan and thrust herself into his world had sealed her fate. She was doomed but refused to give up.

She took long baths and tried to free her mind from all her worries. The solitude around her was the only comfort. Sometimes she thought about becoming an old lady one day. Perhaps she'd be sitting in an old folks' home under an assumed name, telling her stories to the residents, capturing their attention about the life she once led, if they would believe her. Then she'd envision the horror of some young, paid punk creeping into her bedroom at night, slitting her throat, and making her choke on her own blood. It was a haunting vision. To her, it was a sign that it would never end until she was dead.

Cristal donned a long, blue robe and sat on her bed, no TV, no radio, the blinds drawn to create darkness in her apartment. She feared a sniper's bullet from afar penetrating her window and striking her dead. Nowhere to run, nowhere to hide, she knew there would always be an assassin waiting to strike. Not long ago, she was that assassin who always got her target, no matter how or where.

It was time to leave Everett and relocate someplace more secluded from civilization. People started to notice her, when she simply wanted to be invisible. This place could never be her home. In fact, wherever she went would never be home or become a long-term residence.

That night, she packed her bags, and left the rent underneath her landlady's door and made her escape from Everett. But first, she left Megan Davis a parting gift—four flat tires on her Ford Taurus—a "fuck you very much."

Cristal boarded the Greyhound bus to the Midwest and didn't look back. Once again, it would be a new place, a new start, and a new identity.

*

Cristal leaned her head against the bus window and stared out at miles of virgin land extending in every direction. It almost seemed endless. It was dark, the sky was filled with stars, and the I-84 freeway was open, with no traffic.

As the bus moved smoothly, Cristal thought about her late Grandma Hattie. She missed her cooking. She thought about her cousins, aunts, and uncles—three generations of her family were slaughtered that fateful night in her grandmother's apartment. She felt responsible for their deaths. The guilt she felt was so overwhelming, it sometimes crippled her with regret and pain.

If EP hadn't come into her life, there would have been no Farm, no Commission, her friends and family would be alive, and she would still be calling Brooklyn her home. By now, she might have been pregnant with a hustler's baby, going through the regular baby daddy drama that a Brooklyn bitch goes through. She would've been in her grandmother's kitchen tasting her sweet potato pies and cornbread, laughing it up with family, and running the streets with her crew.

EP had come into her life and promised her so much more, and she believed him. And, for a moment, things did get better. The skills she'd acquired and the places she'd seen were all because of business dealings for The Commission.

Then, just like that, it all changed.

Cristal could feel the cold from the outside as she continued to lean her head against the window. Mostly everyone on the bus was sleeping or busy with a book, tablet, or smartphone. Even the lady next to her was dozing off with music playing into her earphones. Conversation had been nonexistent. Cristal wasn't sociable, and neither was the lady she was seated next to, which was the way she liked it.

As the bus continued to roll into the night, Cristal's mind began to wander deeper into her past. She thought about her first contract hit with The Commission. It was a close friend of hers, a man named Pike. He once was a basketball star, and someone she had a crush on for a long time. Unfortunately, The Commission wanted him dead, and that was her breakthrough into the business. Killing someone close to you meant that you had the stomach for the business.

Cristal and her crew made the hit look like it'd come from a rival crew, so the cops and the hood didn't suspect the girls. That day changed her and her crew forever.

A few tears trickled from her eyes and down her face as she continued to gaze out the window into the vast darkness of highway and sprawling land. Everything around her felt so still. Yes, this was going to be forever—being armed, watching over her shoulders, and knowing that death could be right around the corner for her. One slipup and she would become The Commission's next victim.

SEVEN

The two men walked side by side on Oscar's rooftop pavilion, forty-five stories high with an extraordinary view of Manhattan, mostly Midtown and the West Side. Oscar's rooftop pavilion was luxury at its best. It came with a bar and a cascading pool.

Oscar, dressed in gray fleece lounge pants and gray sneakers for the November season, was nursing a cocktail while conversing with AZ about business. One couldn't tell he was a notorious drug kingpin for the Gulf cartel. His appearance was always simple, but with the snap of his fingers, he could move tons of drugs into the country and have dozens of people mercilessly killed.

"Two hundred kilos is a lot of product, AZ. Are you sure you're able to handle that amount?" Oscar asked him face to face.

"I'm sure," AZ replied confidently.

"Business has been good between us so far. You understand, you ask for more than you can handle, it can rock the boat," Oscar said.

"Oscar, you should know me by now. I'm always on point and came this far by being smart, not stupid. I'm a businessman, and when I see opportunity, I'm going to take it."

"Opportunity—it can be the thing that can get one killed in this world of ours, if they're not careful."

"I'm careful."

"Only time will tell, my friend."

It had taken some time, but AZ was able to repair the fractured business relationship with Oscar that Aoki had almost destroyed. They were businessmen, and anything that made money made sense to a major drug connect. Oscar had the product, and AZ could move it.

AZ refused a drink. He just wanted to stay focused and keep it moving.

Heavy Pop stood off to the side peering at the bird's-eye view of the Hudson River. Being just the wingman, he always let AZ do the talking and the negotiations. If AZ could get the two hundred kilos from Oscar, the two of them would be making money hand over fist. They were already making millions, but with Mateo as a client, they were on their way to becoming gods.

Oscar stopped walking and took a sip of his cocktail. He was pondering AZ's request. Two hundred kilos was nothing to him. His cartel moved tons of kilos daily, but he had to ask questions and remain attentive. Three of his henchmen, a strong statement of his power, were planted in the background, being seen and not heard.

"A new client is asking for this order, I assume," Oscar said.

"Yes," AZ replied.

"And how is this client able to afford two hundred kilos of my product?"

"He's the plug to the game. He's been around.

"Have you vetted him?"

"I did," AZ lied.

"And his name?"

"He's from California and looking for an expansion."

"Sometimes an expansion can mean war."

"I'm careful, Oscar, and he's paying in cash."

"And his name?" Oscar asked him once again.

"His name is John G., short for John Getty, and his organization out West is called Blaque," AZ lied.

"Blaque, huh?"

"Yes."

Oscar started to walk around his pavilion again with AZ alongside him. AZ didn't know why he'd lied. He felt Mateo's name rang out for good and bad reasons. Two hundred kilos was a difficult deal to simply walk away from. AZ just wanted to do some business and continue to get rich, but now Oscar was interrogating him.

Oscar asked, "So how did you meet this organization called Blaque?"

"I've known them for years; they're an underground network out West, a faction from the Black Guerrilla Family in L.A. They have the money to move weight, and I have the means. I come to you so we can get money together, like we've been doing, Oscar. You can trust me, and you can trust them. This deal is real legit."

"You can never put too much trust in one man, or one organization."

AZ nodded. "I understand."

Oscar stood silently for a moment. He then turned and locked eyes with AZ. "I'll give you the two hundred kilos to implement this deal, AZ. But I warn you to be very careful. Trust no one, and remember, you and me, we're simply in business together—supply and demand. We're not friends. You only buy from me directly because you've established yourself in my eyes. But as quickly as a boat floats, it can sink too."

AZ nodded. He understood completely that Oscar was a man you didn't want to upset. He was an apex predator, one of the men on top of the food chain in the drug game. The man had teeth sharp enough to shred his enemies with one bite.

"I understand, Oscar, and believe me, I'm not trying to get on your bad side. I want to continue making this money the right way. I've been careful and smart about this deal."

"Slow and steady wins the race. I'm sure you've heard that before."

AZ nodded.

"I'll have your two hundred kilos ready by week's end," Oscar said.

AZ smiled. "I won't let you down."

"I know you won't. You've been loyal to me and smart, unlike your friend Aoki. Learn from her mistake and never bite off more than you can chew. She fucked me, so I fucked her."

Hearing Aoki's name put AZ into a place of resentment. It was clear to him that Aoki had been murdered with the order coming down from Oscar personally. But what was done was done. That was several years ago, and AZ had moved on with his life.

"We're done here," Oscar told him firmly.

"Thank you, Oscar. I appreciate this."

Oscar didn't reply. He took focus on the picturesque view of the city from above and kept quiet.

AZ walked away from Oscar and went toward Heavy Pop, who had been patiently waiting for the meeting to end. AZ looked at his friend, and the smile on his face indicated that Oscar had approved the deal. Heavy Pop smiled lightly.

One of Oscar's henchmen escorted the duo out of the building.

"We on it," AZ said to his friend.

"When can we expect the shipment?" Heavy Pop asked.

"By week's end."

"Same as before?"

AZ nodded.

They climbed into his Benz truck, and AZ started the ignition. He told Heavy Pop, "I had to lie to him somewhat."

"Lie about what?"

"Who our client for this deal was."

"You didn't tell him it was Mateo? Why not?"

"He was coming at me, grilling me about this deal. And you know Mateo's name ain't been the best on the streets lately."

"I know, but you shouldn't have lied to him, AZ."

"We making him lots of money, right? So why should he care who we deal with on these streets? This is our business."

"Yeah, but we wanna stay on his good side."

"And when he starts counting a lot more money coming from us, we're definitely gonna stay on his good side."

"Yeah, okay. I'm hungry, nigga. What you wanna eat?"

"How about some steaks?" AZ suggested. He wasn't rushing to get back to Maryland, where he felt unwanted.

"Now you're speaking my language."

AZ drove away from the towering building in the city and headed toward a bar and grill on Ninth Avenue. There, the two men dined on large steaks and potatoes and continued discussing business.

✳

The box truck pulled into the two-story warehouse on River Street in Williamsburg, Brooklyn. Once inside, the rolling gates came down, giving the men inside privacy for the drug transaction. Two young black men exited the box truck and walked around to the back, where they were greeted by several of Mateo's men and Mateo himself. He stood near the vehicle dressed in a dark suit, eager to see what he was paying for.

"Where are AZ and his partner?" Mateo asked.

"They'll be here soon," the driver answered.

"I guess you're their scouts, huh?" Mateo said. "Making sure everything is copacetic before we do this?"

"Something like that," the other man replied.

The driver of the truck jumped up on the back of the vehicle and lifted the door open and revealed over three dozen large barrels filled with machine oil. Dozens of tightly packaged kilos were concealed on the bottoms of the barrels. He then put on some large rubber gloves, reached into the barrel and retrieved a kilo for Mateo to evaluate.

Mateo stared into the back at the product and nodded. "Nice!" he uttered.

As if on cue, AZ and Heavy Pop entered the building. They greeted Mateo with a handshake.

AZ said, "We held up our end, now it's time for you to do the same."

Mateo nodded to his men, and several large duffel bags were dropped at AZ's feet.

AZ squatted toward the bag and unzipped it. Inside, there were bundles of crisp hundred-dollar bills wrapped into ten-thousand-dollar stacks and totaling 4.7 million dollars.

AZ was very pleased. "Now that's how business is done," he stated proudly.

"We're good?" Mateo asked.

"Oh yeah, we're good."

With that said, both men went their separate ways, one rich with cash and the other rich with white gold. They planned on doing business together again in the future. AZ felt good about it; whatever doubts he had about Mateo ended with the millions in his possession. A large percentage went to Oscar, but he and Heavy Pop would still clear a mint. They couldn't help smiling, knowing there was more to come with Mateo becoming a force on the streets again.

As AZ left the building with Heavy Pop, somebody from a nearby rooftop was taking pictures of them.

EIGHT

oki sat at the window seat of her favorite Jamaican restaurant, Patti Joy, in Jersey City, enjoying her solitude with a plate of oxtail, rice and beans, and a sorrel drink. It was mid-afternoon, and the place was sparse with customers.

It was a beautiful fall day. Thanksgiving was right around the corner, but Aoki didn't care for the holidays. She had no family or friends to enjoy them with. She had been alone for years, indulging herself in her work. Usually, she spent the holidays taking someone's life, cleaning her weapons, or stalking AZ. This year, she simply just wanted to relax.

Her work as a contract killer was becoming more dangerous and taking a lot out of her. Yes, the work was exhilarating and rewarding. Her body count was high, and the money afforded her a life of luxury. Yet her mind and soul were taking a beating, and there was no telling what lay ahead when The Commission wanted her to kill again.

She took a sip of her sorrel drink and reflected on the last job she'd completed a week earlier, a three-man job in London.

*

Aoki received her orders and a ticket to the UK. She landed at Heathrow Airport twenty-four hours later, since The Commission had given them a week's timeline to complete the job. Packed light, she moved through the terminal with her carry-on and stayed focused. She looked like a woman traveling on pleasure. Eyes shifted her way, and the UK men took notice of her sexy physique in tight jeans and crop top under a wool coat.

It wasn't Aoki's first time in London. She took in their accents, their Estuary English, and their love for tea. Aoki had her own accent and differences, and when she spoke, she too stood out. She wanted to fit in, so she had to change her dialect, like they'd taught her on The Farm, and speak proper English. Agents had to know how to camouflage themselves in any situation. Aoki did her best to become invisible. The last thing she wanted to do was look like was a wide-eyed tourist with a strong Jamaican accent and bring unwanted attention to herself.

She exited the busy terminal and got into a cab. "Where to?" the driver asked her.

"Corinthia Hotel."

"Fancy gaff," the driver said.

"Just take me there." Aoki wasn't in the mood for talking.

The driver made his exit from the airport and merged onto the M4 motorway toward London. Aoki had five thousand pounds on her and the instructions.

She soon arrived at the front entrance of the Corinthia Hotel London, a five-star hotel on Whitehall. She climbed out of the taxi and paid the driver the fare. It was a 500-pounds-per-night hotel, but The Commission was footing the bill for everything. The ornate Victorian building with glass-domed lobby was a two-minute walk from Embankment tube station, and six minutes from Trafalgar Square. Her upscale room had it all: flat-screen HDTVs, Nespresso machines, a suite bathroom decorated with marble and rainfall showerheads, along with 24-hour butler service and a private furnished terrace. It was a far cry from Brooklyn.

Aoki stepped out onto the terrace and took it all in. London was a beautiful city. The sun was setting, draining away the light and gradually transforming the city into nightlife. Aoki had no time to get caught up in the beauty and the culture of the city. She was there to do a three-man job, one of her most challenging contracts yet. She had to scope out her targets and come up with a foolproof plan.

As she lingered on the terrace, she suddenly heard a knock at the door. She turned and went to see who was knocking. She was waiting for her connection to make life to her assignment.

As she approached the door, someone slipped a thin manila envelope underneath. She picked it up, tore it open, and removed the contents. There were three glossy pictures of three different men and their accompanying details. All three men were white and successful in their careers. The Commission wanted them executed for the multi-million dollar Ponzi scheme they had masterminded, stealing five hundred twenty million dollars from very powerful men. Their names were Thomas Cell, a banker, Henry Hutton, a prominent lawyer, and Jonathan Bowen, a high-ranking public official.

Aoki studied their faces and details, committing everything to memory. She then destroyed the information. She couldn't risk anything getting into the wrong hands. She had to be untraceable, a ghost in the city.

Her suite was quiet and relaxing. She ordered room service and champagne, and dined alone. She then undressed and took advantage of the bathroom, submerging herself into the large white tub with the soothing hot water and small TV embedded into the wall. She closed her eyes and took a deep breath.

As she was getting comfortable, her cell phone rang. The call came from an unknown number. Aoki answered.

A female voice spoke on the other end—her contact. She was blunt with no formal greeting. "In an hour, you will meet your handler at the Silver Cross bar on Whitehall." The call ended abruptly.

Aoki ended her soothing bath and threw on a pair of tight jeans, a chic T-shirt, put her hair into a long ponytail, and donned her leather jacket. She stepped out of the hotel suite, stepped into the elevator, and pushed for the lobby. Aoki was like a robot—showing no emotion and remaining focused.

Two young white boys got on the elevator from the floor below hers. They tried to flirt with her, like it was their right to do so.

"Where are yeh from, beautiful?" the boy on her left asked. His accent was thick, and he couldn't stop staring at her. There was something about him that she instantly didn't like.

Both boys were dressed like they came from money—old, inherited money.

She remained quiet.

He continued to talk to her. "I fancy ye're from the U.S," he said.

She remained silent.

He added, "What's the matter? Moggy got y'r tongue?"

The other boy laughed at the comment.

Aoki remained silent and deadpan. She had no time for little boys. But the one on her left was relentless with his tongue and his vulgar approach.

He said, "Yeh don't fancy compliments when yeh get 'em, huh?"

Aoki cut her eyes his way. Her look could definitely kill.

"Just making some conversation," he said and shrugged.

The elevator reached the lobby, and the doors opened. Aoki was the first to step out, saying to them while moving from their presence, "Go fuck yourself!"

Her harsh comment left the two boys befuddled, with the other boy saying, "What the fuck is her problem?"

"I guess she's not getting enough dick in her life. She might be one of those lesbians, y'know, a carpet-eater." He laughed.

The other shouted, "Ugly black bitch! You know who you just snubbed?"

Aoki stopped dead in her tracks and spun around, glaring at the two young boys walking away. They were uppity and ignorant, probably always getting their way in life and suffering no consequences for their rude behavior because daddy had money and power. She figured they were related.

She marched their way with her fists clenched tightly and ready to react. She followed them as they walked toward the hotel bar, which was swelling up quickly with customers. They took a seat at the bar. She purposely bumped into the boy with the rudest mouth, spilling his drink onto his sweater vest, staining it.

Turning around and seeing that it was Aoki, he hollered, "You clumsy black bitch! Watch where ye going!"

"Excuse me. I'm so sorry," Aoki apologized.

"You owe me a drink," he demanded.

She smirked and simply walked away. He cursed at her, but she ignored him, walking farther away from his verbal onslaught.

Aoki had what she needed from him. She had pickpocketed his cardkey. She planned on paying a visit to him real soon. But, first, she had work to do.

She walked to the Silver Cross bar, a large split-level traditional pub situated in the heart of London with its spacious dining area and flagstone floors. Patrons were having a good time, ordering drinks in rounds and laughing and chatting.

Aoki stood near the entrance and looked around. There were too many faces and too much activity. She had no idea what her handler looked like, but she was sure he or she knew her identity. She stepped farther into the pub and soon felt a nudge from behind. She quickly pivoted, and a man motioned his head toward a corner booth.

She didn't say a word and walked toward a lone stranger having a beer in the booth. She took a seat opposite him and looked into his eyes. They were cold and callous, matching her own. He was a lean and handsome man with a grayish goatee, wearing an expensive suit and a diamond Cartier watch. No doubt he was the handler and connected to The Commission.

The man took a sip of his beer and then placed a set of car keys onto the table. He said, "There's a black sedan parked around the corner, an AMG E63 S Mercedes-Benz. Take the keys, open the trunk, and take out what you need."

Afterwards, he removed himself from the table and from her sight, disappearing into the crowd of lively drinkers at the pub, leaving Aoki seated alone with the car keys. She snatched them up and made her exit.

She strutted outside, turned right, marched around the corner, and placed the key into the trunk and opened it. Placed inside the trunk was a small black duffel bag. Aoki unzipped it and found a small arsenal of guns and knives inside. She pulled out the bag, shut the trunk, and casually walked away.

She went back to her hotel room and placed everything in the bag onto the bed. The most impressive weapon was the OA-93 that was fitted with an M4A1-style collapsible stock. It was sleek, effective, and deadly. It also came with a suppresser. Aoki had two choices to carry out the contract—pure bloodshed to send a message, or subtle and unnoticed.

*

The lawyer and banker were easy to track down. They were self-assured men with egos as big as the Grand Canyon, and they both enjoyed their money, success, liquor, and pussy. They were known to frequent the nightclubs together, spending their stolen cash like water. Aoki knew every move of the banker and the lawyer, but the high-ranking official had gone off the radar and was difficult to track down.

Jonathan Bowen was a shrewd man in business and frugal when it came to his money. The man didn't go out. He didn't do nightclubs or restaurants. He wasn't a whoremonger like his friends. He wasn't married and had no kids. He was pretty much a forty-three-year-old recluse with international political connections and ties to organized crime in London. He was almost a ghost.

Aoki methodically did her homework on Jonathan Bowen, but he proved harder to track, maybe even harder to kill. Fortunately for her, she finally located him. He was staying on the top floor of the Crowne Plaza. He had the entire top floor to himself and employed a fleet of security. It was like Jonathan knew she was coming for him.

Aoki knew he needed to be the first on her list, before the two baboons. Once word got out about their deaths, Jonathan would heighten his security detail and most likely disappear into obscurity. So Aoki did reconnaissance of the hotel, the staff, and the security—that was the easy part.

The day she planned on attacking him, she hacked her way into the hotel's computers and phone lines using a Trojan horse virus and listened intently for evidence of her target's exact location. The Farm had taught her to know everything about her target and learn how to control him from a distance. Learn their habits, their interests, and their routines, and study the people around them. If you know their social life and the company they keep, then you know your target.

Aoki hacked into his hotel invoice and found he ordered room service around the clock. Jonathan had a ravenous appetite. He loved food and his wine. That would be her way to get to him. A paranoid man still had to eat.

She stole one of the female staff uniforms and played the part of a docile worker. When the room service order came in for his room, she intercepted the meal cart and rigged it for her own purpose. She coolly stepped into the staff elevator and pushed for the top floor, using the staff cardkey she'd stolen to access the top floor. The elevator wouldn't budge without that key—another added security measure taken by her target. Aoki kept calm. One of the reasons The Commission had reached out to her for a difficult job was because they knew she had no fear and was a bold bitch when executing a hit.

The doors slid open, and Aoki pushed the meal cart into the carpeted hallway and toward the hotel door, where an armed guard stood watch.

He frowned at her. "Where's the regular girl?" he asked.

"She's out sick," Aoki said on beat in a heavy English accent.

Aoki was poised and ready for him with something special. She was hoping he didn't cause a problem. He stood six four with a stocky build.

"I have his order and definitely his favorite today," she said. "Prawns and pasta."

"Sounds good," the guard returned.

Aoki attempted to lift the cover to show him everything was legit, but he took her word. He patted her down, making sure she didn't have any concealed weapons, then escorted her into the room.

Once inside the lavish room, Aoki counted four armed men in black. But her target was nowhere in sight. She was sure, though, he was somewhere close. Jonathan Bowen had many enemies, not just The Commission, but the mafia and former business partners he'd embezzled money from. For that reason, he spent a fortune on top-notch security to protect him.

"Hey, boys," she greeted affably in her fake accent. "Where's your friend?"

"What's under the tray?" one of the bodyguards asked.

"His food. What you think?"

"Lift it and let us see."

Aoki smiled. "Okay."

She lifted the cover, and it happened. She ducked down, reaching underneath the cart, and extracted the 9mm pistol with the silencer at the end. *Phew! Phew! Phew! Phew! Phew!*

She let loose rapid fire, slamming bullets into the men, and watched them fall like bowling pins. They were all dead in a matter of seconds.

When the smoke cleared, Aoki was the last one standing in the room. She scurried around the suite, gun in hand, and methodically searched for her mark. She found him cowering on his knees in the bathroom, hiding in the shower.

When Aoki walked in, he yelped out like a bitch, "Please, don't kill me! Don't do this!" his hands stretched out in front of him, shivering with fear.

Aoki aimed at his head.

"Please, don't do this! I'll pay you whatever. I'm a rich man."

Aoki had nothing to say to him. She released several bullets into his head and chest, and he collapsed against the tiled floor, blood pooling around him. Then she hastily made her escape from the hotel and disappeared before the police came.

*

A few hours later, Thomas Cell and Henry Hutton came staggering out of Core Bar on Queens Street. The beer and liquor had their hormones raging, and they were on the prowl for some young females for sexual gratification. They spotted a beautiful young woman with chocolate thighs in a miniskirt staggering across the street from the bar. Thomas spotted her first and proceeded her way, and Henry followed. The two men pretended to be concerned.

"You okay, miss?" Thomas asked.

"You had enough to drink tonight, I see." Henry grabbed the petite beauty by her arm and guided her into a more private area. "C'mon, let us help you. Come with us. You'll be just fine."

Both men looked at each other, and they were thinking the same thing—the fun wasn't over yet. The young girl soon found herself in the backseat of their lavish vehicle with Henry trying to feel up her skirt and Thomas behind the wheel. Not only were they crooks, but they were perverts too. Henry squeezed her smooth thigh, kissed her neck, and cupped her breasts.

"Save some for me," Thomas uttered.

"From the looks of things, she definitely has plenty to go around."

Thomas laughed. He peered at his partner violating the young beauty in the backseat via rearview mirror and started the car. He was getting hard just watching his friend lick on her body and feel on her crotch and tits.

The girl was totally wasted and probably wouldn't remember a thing the next day. Henry was trying to undress her, eager to take a peek at her goodies. He undid his trousers and removed his hard member, jerking himself off while fondling the girl. "You have a very nice mouth," he told her.

She chuckled at the comment.

Henry placed his hand around the back of her head and attempted to guide her mouth into his lap. He was aching for a blowjob. At first, it seemed he was about to get his wish. She opened wide and leaned into his lap.

"Yes, I want yeh to feel me. If you do a nice job, I'll probably give you a bonus," he said. "We're bleedin' rich men, yeh know. We can take care of you."

Thomas hesitated in pulling the car away from the curb. He found himself transfixed by the perversion taking place behind him. He could see her thighs opening further with his friend's help, and the girl's mouth about to wrap around his friend's hard cock. The tinted windows gave the men the privacy they needed, and the late, chilly night made the area around the pub sparse with people.

What Henry expected to be pleasure abruptly turned into pain and agony. He felt a quick slice at his genitals and then saw the blood. Aoki had cut him deeply with a scalpel. The blood was real, and so was his screaming. She had nearly sliced off the tip of his dick.

Before Thomas could react and help his screaming friend, Aoki thrust another sharp blade into the back of his neck and twisted it deeply. He shuddered violently behind the wheel and felt his body stiffening. It only took seconds for him to die.

Henry was still screaming out in agony. His hands were coated in blood, and he was in absolute shock. He looked Aoki's way in panic. He was horrified as he sat paralyzed from the sheer pain between his legs and his blood spilling all over the backseat.

"Aaaahhhh! You cut me!" he exclaimed. "Aaaaahhh! Oh shit!"

He desperately tried to stop the bleeding by frantically clutching his dick and balls, wanting to put his family jewels back together again, but there was too much blood.

Aoki hated perverts. She wanted him to feel some pain. Then she wanted him dead. It would have been fun to play around with him, but he was a contract kill, nothing personal. She plunged the scalpel into his eye and throat repeatedly, and he slumped against the door and died screaming.

This killing reminded her of the day she had killed two men in similar fashion in Brooklyn. Her first contract kill was for AZ. She was doing a favor for a man she once considered a friend. Now Aoki had graduated into something much more devious. Killing someone with a knife turned her on. She loved the up-close approach. She could feel the blade sinking into their flesh, and she could see their body react from the pain.

For a few minutes, Aoki lingered in the bloody backseat with the bodies in the car. She was hot and sweaty with mixed emotions. She took a deep breath. The Commission was going to be proud. She was also hoping that this was it. She had killed for the organization for a while, and her twenty-fifth birthday was approaching. Aoki had enough blood on her hands from all the murders she'd committed to fill up a blood bank twice over.

She wasn't afraid of being caught. The world around her felt still. There was no sound. No traffic.

She looked at her victims and smiled. "It's been fun, boys, but I need to go."

She cleaned herself up and stepped out of the car. The Commission had instructed her that they wanted the bodies found on the streets. She'd done her part. Now it was time to go back home. She couldn't wait to step on US soil again.

*

The flight was crowded for the lengthy plane ride back home. The 747 ascended from the stretch of runway at Heathrow Airport and quickly soared into the sky, London fading from view. Aoki sat comfortably at her window seat and closed her eyes with the shade closed. She had no desire to look back.

She smiled to herself, though. She had left something behind in the hotel for the staff to clean up. Right before she'd checked out, she took care of the two spoiled brats who had disrespected her in the elevator. She had slipped into their large suite in the middle of the night and waited for them. When they arrived, she attacked them both. They were no match for her. With both boys bound to their beds, she stabbed them repeatedly.

NINE

Aoki ordered herself another plate of oxtail. There was nothing more fulfilling than a tasty Jamaican dish. She liked to linger in the Jersey City restaurant alone, feeling that the place was a safe haven for her. She tried to move unpredictably, knowing that having a routine could get her killed, but she just couldn't quit this good Jamaican food. Their dumplings were almost to die for.

She finished her meal at Patti Joy, paid the bill, and stepped out into the nippy weather wearing a short navy blue coat. Tired of the cold weather, she dreamed of the day she would permanently escape to Jamaica with her millions of dollars. She wanted to buy a beachfront home, drink ginger beer, eat beef patties and coco bread, and find a man to love her. She climbed into her car and headed back to the city.

Aoki stepped into her Manhattan apartment and instantly knew that she wasn't alone. In the dark she felt her presence near.

She asked in a cool tone, "How long yuh waitin' fih me?"

"A while, but I'm a very patient woman," she replied.

Aoki turned on the lights and saw Muriel seated in a chair with her legs crossed, smoking a cigarette.

"It's what dey teach us, right?"

Aoki's handler was in her late thirties, beautiful, and blessed with long blonde hair and long, shapely legs. She was from a small town in Ukraine that the world had forgotten—an impoverished and distant place, where she had seen her family starve and the women raped repeatedly by sadistic men. Her home was torn apart by civil war and violence. She too had been raped when she was a young girl, but Muriel rose up from it kill-by-kill and became a cold professional killer with deep roots in The Commission.

Many men were threatened by her, but Aoki wasn't. They locked eyes. Muriel saw a lot of herself in Aoki. They had both come from a place of pain and anger and were survivors.

Muriel stood up, showing off her height of six one, plus the height of her boots. She was an Amazon of a woman wearing a simple knit skirt suit. She never desired fancy. She extinguished her cigarette into the chair she was sitting in, staining the material, and handed Aoki another murdergram.

"Me love dat chair," Aoki said.

"Buy a new one. This one is very important. I wanted to deliver it to you myself," Muriel said in her thick Ukrainian accent. Though she was Aoki's handler, Muriel didn't come around often.

Aoki took the package. Another assignment so soon after the London job. She hadn't even received congratulations for a job well done. She looked reluctant for a moment, but it was a fleeting feeling. She was bred to kill. She didn't need any rest.

"Who dis time?"

Muriel dodged the question. "She's a special one, and you need to be careful."

Aoki opened the package to find an 8x10 photo of a pretty young woman. She knew the girl from somewhere but couldn't put her finger on it. Aoki read the name of her target: Cristal Monroe. Then it dawned on her that the girl was an agent. She had been trained on The Farm too, but now she was on The Commission's list to be killed.

"She ah agent, like me so."

"She's a threat that needs to be taken care of."

Aoki nodded. "Me will do it."

"She took out several agents in North Carolina."

"Me hear 'bout dat."

"She's trained with our organization and GHOST Protocol, so don't get too cocky. Kill this bitch and come back home."

Aoki was somewhat impressed that Cristal had also worked with the competing agency. She had so many questions that she knew Muriel wouldn't answer.

"How she ah work for GHOST too?"

"Ten weeks," Muriel said, giving her the deadline and ignoring the question.

Aoki was somewhat taken aback by the timeline. Ten weeks was a lifetime for a skilled assassin to execute a hit. "For de job?" Aoki said. "Special bitch, huh?"

"You find her, you kill her quickly. We have a lot invested in this job. No fuckups."

Aoki nodded.

Muriel made her way toward the door, Aoki following behind her.

Before walking out, Muriel turned around and stared at Aoki. She repeated, "You have ten weeks to get the job done."

"What 'bout me retirement?" Aoki asked out of the blue.

Muriel didn't say a word. She pivoted and walked out of the place callously like she was bred to do.

Aoki sighed. She didn't fret; another job meant more pay, more respect, and another kill under her belt. She stared at Cristal's photo and went through the information The Commission supplied on her last known residence, her weapons of choice, and her likes and dislikes. Aoki had to read her like she was a book. Where would she go? Where would she hide? What would she do? Cristal didn't have any family left to do surveillance on or vet for information, since they were all dead. Nor did she have any attachments, except an ex-boyfriend named Daniel. The file said Cristal hadn't had any contact with Daniel since his graduation day.

Aoki knew there was some way to track her down. There was something or someone. That someone was Daniel. She studied the picture, stared into Cristal's eyes like she was hypnotized, and continued thinking. The Commission believed that Cristal hadn't been in contact with her ex in months, but Aoki felt they were wrong somehow. It was shown that Cristal was deeply in love with this man.

The agents had fucked up the job at the graduation ceremony. It was a bloodbath, and Cristal managed to escape. Aoki wasn't going to allow that to happen again. Now it was her contract and her responsibility. The Commission wasn't going to accept failure. Failure meant death for her, and she didn't have plans to die, not when she was so close to retirement.

Aoki took a seat and continued thinking like she was Cristal. "Where yuh at?" she asked out loud. "What yuh gwan do?"

Aoki had all day to think about Cristal. She figured her target would still be in the States, as opposed to going overseas. Why go international when either way her life was in danger? Cristal would only stand out in Europe, Asia, and the Middle East. Aoki figured Cristal would want to blend in as much as possible. Maybe she had gone South and taken residence in a small town.

Aoki figured if Cristal was keeping in contact with Daniel it would have to be subtle. Daniel would put her on the fast track to finding Cristal, who would want to keep close tabs on him just in case his life was in danger via The Commission.

At least that's what Aoki would do.

TEN

AZ held the star-key pendant with a cushion-cut yellow diamond in his hand and admired the stones. It was an impressive piece with an 18-inch platinum chain.

"You have very good taste," the saleslady stated.

"It's for my wife."

"She's going to love it. I know she will."

He smiled as he continued to inspect the key. The price tag was over $20,000, but the cost meant nothing to him, since he had just netted millions from his latest drug transaction, and there was much more money to come. He wanted to buy something special for Wendy, and there wasn't anything more special than an expensive gift from Tiffany in New York, which would be his last stop before he got on the highway and headed back to Maryland.

"I'll take it." AZ handed the pendant back to be boxed and wrapped.

"Wonderful."

Wendy had been busy with trials and pre-trial hearings lately. The cases were continuous for her office—drugs, murders, rapes. Being an assistant state's attorney in Baltimore was a strenuous job, but it was also rewarding. Wendy wanted to put away the bad guys and looked to one day making her city a better place to live. She had a high conviction rate and was known to be a pit bull in a skirt in the courtroom. Her team of paralegals and investigators were good. She put a 110% into every case she prosecuted. She wanted to become a voice for the victims and advance to one day become a prominent judge.

But her marriage with AZ was failing, and AZ wanted to spice it up with gifts. That always put a smile on her face and made her feel giddy.

"How would you like to pay for the item? Check or charge?" the lady asked him.

"Cash," he said.

AZ removed two ten-thousand-dollar stacks and placed them on the counter before adding another $5,000 to the pile for tax and tip.

After the extravagant purchase, he climbed into his truck, started the engine, and pulled out of the parking lot with the signature blue box with the white bow on the passenger seat. He couldn't wait to present the necklace to his wife.

*

Wendy had a love for finer things in life. Money and material things were what moved her. No matter how heated their arguments or how nasty the things they said to each other, AZ knew he could always smooth things over by buying her expensive gifts.

The year before, he'd bought her a Porsche Cayenne for her birthday. She was floored when she stepped outside to see her brand-new car with a large pink ribbon wrapped around it. She jumped for joy and threw herself into her husband's arms and planted kisses on him that nearly left his face dripping wet. She'd screamed and broken out into the "whip and nay-nay dance" in front of her family, looking like she was performing at the Apollo Theater.

"I love it! I love it! I love it!" she'd screamed out.

AZ placed the keys into her hand, and Wendy took off toward the car like she was running in the NFL Combine and thrust herself behind the wheel like a child on a new bicycle. Her eyes gleamed with more excitement seeing it was fully loaded with leather seats, moon roof, XM radio, and more. She continued to holler with joy. It was her new toy to play with. The fact that her friends and family were around to witness the blessing gave her something to gloat about for months to come. That new car made Wendy forget about her intense argument with AZ a week earlier.

Wendy wanted AZ to spend more time with the kids. She felt he was ignoring the boys and their well-being. He was always gone—New York, New Jersey, D.C.—leaving his family in the rearview mirror. It was growing tiresome to her. She had her career too, and their sons were growing up fast. With him traveling regularly, home was becoming a burden to her because she needed him there to help.

Wendy was juggling home and working on a major criminal case in Baltimore. She was trying to prosecute two defendants who had committed a violent rape during a home invasion in East Baltimore. The victim, a thirty-year-old woman, was badly beaten and left for dead. Two black men took off with over ten thousand dollars in property and her innocence. What seemed like an open-and-shut case was now edging on difficulties, starting with one of her primary witnesses not being able to remember their faces. Plus, the presiding judge had denied admission of some vital evidence for the prosecution. Her days at the office were growing longer and longer, with the continuous paperwork and court hearings, and the babysitter was making a fortune from them.

The couple had gotten into an argument that night, upon AZ returning home from New York. He cursed her out. She slapped him, and he was tempted to punch her in the face, but he kept his cool and didn't explode on her. For a week, she ignored him and acted like he didn't exist, but the new car on her birthday changed her entire mood.

With gifts like cars, jewelry, clothes, and shopping sprees, she would warm up to him and become the best wife on the planet with sex and home cooked meals. Six months earlier, Wendy had become "Suzy Homemaker" for him, treating AZ like he was a king. She wanted him to purchase a vacation home in the Bahamas. It would be her escape from the madness of her job. And it was something that her mother and sisters kept on whining about; what was hers she shared with family.

AZ did it with no problem. He put down a hundred thousand dollars on a sunny three-bedroom beachfront condo in Nassau, Bahamas. It had a comfy king-size bed, and the bay windows allowed the soft Caribbean morning light to penetrate the rooms. Wendy fell in love with the place. He loved it when she was kissing his ass.

*

AZ headed toward the Holland Tunnel and then jumped on the New Jersey Turnpike with a beam inside him. It had been a good day so far. His business relationship with Oscar was booming, and he had his best friend by his side. He and Heavy Pop were the drug trafficking dynamic duo. It was all about the money, and he was making plenty of it. It felt good to be back from the dead and to thrive in life. He and Heavy Pop were like the last men standing from his hood, with B Scientific and other hustlers like him nothing but a memory in the ghetto.

Traffic on the Turnpike started to slow down coming into Trenton, New Jersey. For another five miles, cars and trucks crawled bumper to bumper. AZ sighed. It was going to take longer for him to get home. But it was Jersey, and it was expected. The radio was a bore, and he was about three hours away from home.

He pulled out his cell phone and decided to make a call. Baron was on his mind. The man's phone rang twice, and then he picked up.

AZ smiled upon hearing Baron's voice. "Hey, what you doing?"

"I can't really talk right now," Baron replied nonchalantly.

"Oh, I just wanted to see you. I'm on my way back to Maryland. Thought we could link up."

"Probably tomorrow."

"Okay, that sounds cool. We'll talk."

AZ hung up feeling somewhat slighted. He wanted to feel Baron's hard white flesh against his. There was something special about this pale white boy that created an erection so hard on AZ, it was almost painful to go a week without seeing him. He was just a booty call; some dick on the side when AZ needed some sexual healing. But things were getting interesting between them. AZ went from seeing Baron once a week to twice a week. Yes, he loved his wife, but he was a gay man who loved to pitch, and catch too.

What was it about men that stirred a burning lust in the center of his belly? He was a married man with two kids, but still he was a drug kingpin on the down-low. For so many years, his secret had been safe, especially with Aoki dead. No one but his male lovers knew of his taste for men.

Could he ever go without dick? He'd tried. The year he'd met Wendy, it had been seven months since he'd been with a man. Having thrust himself into the drug world, his violent rise among the wolves in the game permitted no time for love. He was focused on business and making his money. Wendy was supposed to be his female hope—the woman who corrected him and gave him a family.

They'd met at a fundraiser for breast cancer at the Lincoln Center in Washington D.C. Though his business was spreading poison on the streets, AZ wanted to make some difference with his money, and he wanted to rub elbows with a few political figures in D.C. He was well aware that in his line of business it was always good to have some powerful friends. AZ wanted his money to have limitless reach, and he was willing to contribute to various fundraisers, campaigns, transnational investments, and charities in the area. He wanted to induct himself into the business world and cement himself into the lives of folks that mattered. There was also the occasional blackmailing of someone of influence in case he got into a legal jam. AZ had to think three steps ahead of trouble. He had pushed his pawns farther onto the board, and now the pieces that mattered were moving right behind them.

That night at the D.C. fundraiser, he locked eyes with Wendy from across the room. It was a fleeting glance for her, but his gaze lingered. She looked radiant in her black lace corset dress and Gucci heels. There was something about this woman that attracted his attention. She seemed relevant in a room full of politicians, lobbyists, rich businessmen, and high-end lawyers. She was able to hold a conversation and match wits with the best in the room.

AZ approached her. Dressed handsomely in a Tom Ford suit with a price tag of seven thousand dollars, he exuded wealth. He couldn't remember the last time he'd stepped to a woman and initiated the conversation. The ladies always approached him. But there he was, tapping his future wife on her shoulder and sparking up a conversation with her.

Wendy liked what she saw, and there was chemistry between them. The bonus for AZ was finding out that she was an assistant state's attorney for Baltimore. He saw her position as a major advantage for him.

After a few dates with him, she fell in love, and AZ saw opportunity and a future with her. Not only would being with her cloak his homosexuality, but he could get inside her head and know her world. With Wendy being a prosecutor, AZ felt he had one up on the law. She believed he was a real estate developer. Why not? He had the knowledge and the wealth of the business. Together, they were a power couple.

A year later, they were married, and she was pregnant.

Now, almost four years later, he had become highly suspicious of her. He had a feeling she was stepping out on him. She had been secretive and cold, and it was taking more and more gifts to keep her happy. There were phone calls at night that she claimed were work-related, but AZ's gut told him otherwise.

She was a busy woman, but he didn't believe she was this busy. Someone else had her attention because it damn sure wasn't him. Yes, he had Baron on the side, but it was just dick, he felt, and he didn't want his wife dealing with anybody.

✻

When AZ arrived home later that evening, there was no Porsche in the driveway, indicating Wendy wasn't home yet, and the kids were still with the babysitter. He walked into an empty house with his gift in hand.

✻

Wendy spread her legs across his lap, clutched his shoulders, and slowly lowered her throbbing pussy onto his large erection. The penetration was slow and filling. She liked when he took his time and made every second of their time together matter. She could feel every inch of him inside of her, the tip of his penis almost feeling like it was rooted in her stomach.

He thrust upwards into her, and her body jerked then quivered in his grasp. The young thug was blessed in so many ways. He focused on her soft, round tits as she rode him in the backseat of his Yukon. Her pussy was creamy and tight. He cupped her buttocks with his hands and sucked her nipples.

In an exhale, she chanted, "Fuck me! Fuck me! Fuck me!" her voice dripping with desire as her body was being ravaged. The constant friction happening inside of her was taking her to the next level.

Their intense bumping and grinding started to fog the windows to the truck. He continued to push into her as their bodies bent sexually in the backseat. They had all the privacy they needed in the parking lot, his dark tints shading their nastiness.

Her legs twisted around him as she was placed on her back into a new position with her thug lover on top of her like a sexual ornament. He gripped her neck, gently choking her as she felt her orgasm brewing.

"I'm gonna come!" she screamed out.

Her thug lover groaned while still moving inside her. He squeezed her tits, danced between her thighs, and painted the perfect picture of sex, his dick being the paintbrush.

Wendy's husband had been absent from her mind since their rendezvous began over an hour earlier. Home was trouble, and her career was a hassle. Her affair with Justice felt like the perfect diversion from her unraveling criminal case. The rape victim was scared and becoming uncooperative. She first had refused to take a rape kit at the hospital and give her deposition. Wendy had to constantly fight with her witness, and it was becoming tiresome.

Wendy came so hard, her body felt drained from the endless explosion. Justice did what a man was supposed to do—sexually please his woman, a department AZ had been lacking in for a long time.

Her cell phone started to buzz. The first call was from her paralegal. She left a message. The second call came from AZ. She ignored him too. She wasn't ready to snap back into reality yet.

"That was really good," she said to Justice. That dick put a smile on her face.

"I'm glad you liked it."

They started to collect themselves and put back on their clothing.

Justice was a twenty-two-year-old thug Wendy had met in the nightclub. Looking her best in her hip-hugging dress with her long black hair flowing down to her shoulders, she immediately caught his attention. He offered to buy her a drink, and she accepted. The two got to conversing, and she was feeling his style, forgetting that she was a married woman.

Though Wendy was an assistant state's attorney, she had a forbidden weakness—she loved herself a thug. Wendy was an educated woman with degrees from Howard and NYU, but deep down inside, she was a hood rat from the projects of West Baltimore who hid her ghetto style well.

"He's been calling," she said, referring to AZ as she saw his missed calls on her cell phone.

"Why do you stay married to that cornball nigga? It's obvious you ain't feelin' him like that, and he don't have the time for you."

"He's my kids' father."

"And I got two baby mamas, but I don't fuck wit' them like that."

"It's complicated."

"You like his money?"

"I love nice things."

"And you don't think I can buy you nice things?"

She smiled. "You're cute." And then she kissed him on the lips. "But I have to get home to my husband." She hadn't realized how much time had passed.

Justice looked so envious, he was turning green. He really liked Wendy. She was different and fun to be with, and her beauty was breathtaking. It pained him that she had to go home to an asshole named AZ. The things Wendy told him made AZ look like an easy mark. Maybe he and his crew could roll up on AZ and take from him one day when the time was right, since that's what his crew did—rob muthafuckas for everything they had.

Wendy climbed out of his truck and walked awkwardly toward her Cayenne, a gap between her legs. His big dick had left an indentation inside her pussy and put a smile on her clit. She started her car and then needed a moment to get herself right. She pulled down the sun visor and checked her image in the small mirror. Her lipstick was a little smeared from sucking Justice's dick, but besides that, she was still looking flawless. She applied an extra coat of lipstick to her lips and puckered them in the mirror. She smiled.

Wendy pulled into her driveway and released a deep sigh. She had the kids in the backseat and a plastic bag of Chinese food in her hand. AZ's car was parked in the driveway too. She wasn't excited to see her husband.

Wendy put on her "at-home face" and said, "C'mon, kids, let's go."

The kids jumped out of the backseat and ran toward the front door, as Wendy trailed them. The house was quiet. She figured AZ to be in the bedroom or in his den. She decided not to disturb him. She set out the Chinese food on the kitchen table and made her kids a sizable plate for them to enjoy.

As she was about to eat an egg roll, she heard AZ say, "Where were you?"

She turned around and saw AZ coming into the kitchen. He looked relaxed and comfortable in some sweatpants and a T-shirt, and appeared to have been home for quite a while.

"I was at the office," she lied.

"I called, and your assistant said you weren't there. In fact, you left hours ago, she told me. And you haven't been answering your cell phone."

"Well, it's been a very busy day for me with this case. I'm doing a lot of running around and been in and out of court. My primary witness to this case is inconsistent, and I think this judge is against me, AZ. So excuse me if I'm doing too much because you're always out of town on business."

He said calmly, "I just wanted to know where my wife was for several hours. Is there a problem with that?"

"And how was your trip to New York? Do I blow up your cell phone when you're doing business out of town?"

AZ frowned. "New York was fine. Simply business."

He turned to his two sons and smiled at them. They always knew how to brighten his heart without doing anything. Their presence alone exhilarated him. He kissed them on their foreheads and took a deep breath. Whatever his boys needed, he felt fortunate to be able to provide for them. They were living the life of luxury, and he was going to continue to do whatever it took to keep giving his family the best that money could buy.

"It's been a long day. I don't feel like arguing with you, and I need a bath. Are you going to watch them while I'm upstairs trying to relax?" she asked with an attitude. "I deserve it."

"I'll be here."

Wendy pivoted and marched out of the kitchen.

AZ watched her leave with nothing else more to say. Though she was a busy woman, her reason for being late and not answering her cell phone didn't appease him. Her gift was in the bedroom. He was ambivalent about whether he should give it to her or not. He loved her, but something definitely was off.

AZ sat at the table with his kids and enjoyed their time. Life on the street could be grueling, bloody, and violent, but being home with them was his antidote to sweep his mind from the evil he did in the drug game. Whatever troubles he had out there, he didn't bring home.

An hour later, AZ walked into the bathroom, where Wendy was submerged in a soothing, warm bubble bath. She was enjoying her wine, her music, and her solitude. For a minute, he stood in the doorway quietly and observed her. Any man would be so lucky to have her, and he felt blessed with her. She was beautiful, the mother of his two beautiful kids, and a career woman.

He walked into the bathroom, startling his wife a little. He took a seat at the edge of the tub and presented his gift. "I'm always thinking about you, even in New York," he said. He handed her the blue box.

Already, Wendy was smiling from ear to ear. She loved the surprises. She knew it was expensive and tasteful. Her husband always came correct. She tore off the bow, opened it up, and was in awe at the Tiffany key necklace inside. Her eyes lit up like the North Star. "Ohmygod!" she uttered in disbelief. "Ohmygod! It's so beautiful, AZ. I love it!"

"I knew you would." AZ removed the necklace from the long case and clasped it around her neck.

Wendy stood up from the tub, dripping wet with bubbles, and hurried toward the mirror like the necklace would disappear if she didn't look at it in time. Naked and wet, standing in front of the bathroom mirror, she gleamed with joy. It was a magnificent piece, one that would rouse envy among other females. She couldn't wait to show if off.

"Ohmygod," she uttered the phrase excitedly once again. "I love it so much. Thank you!"

"I'm glad you like it."

She threw her arms around him and pushed her naked frame into him, dampening his clothing, and kissed her husband like a woman should.

"Come and bathe with me," she suggested, taking AZ by his hand and pulling him toward the tub. The sparkling diamond key dangled slightly over her naked breasts like a Christmas tree ornament.

"I'm okay. You enjoy your time alone."

"You sure, baby? I can make you feel really, really good tonight. You definitely deserve it."

"No, I'm good."

She smiled. "Thank you," she said once again.

AZ wasn't in the mood for sex. He wanted to make her happy. He wanted his family to be happy. He wanted the best of both worlds to continue.

Wendy couldn't wait to broadcast the news about her new gift. She retrieved her cell phone from her purse, dipped herself back into the tub, and dialed her mother.

"You won't believe what my husband just bought me while he was in New York," she exclaimed with vigor.

AZ disappeared into the bedroom, but he could still hear his wife's voice echoing from the bathroom. She was happy, he was happy. Still, he couldn't shake the feeling that she was hiding something.

ELEVEN

AZ lowered his head and sighed, feeling replenished as the warm shower cascaded down on him and relaxed him. He lingered inside the running shower for twenty minutes collecting his thoughts.

He thought about Wendy and his marriage. The other day he had gone through her cell phone looking for proof of her infidelity, but there was nothing. Her text file on her iPhone was always at no messages, and her call history showed a few missed and received calls from a private number.

It made him extremely jealous that there was a strong possibility that his wife was stepping out on him. He didn't know with whom, but he planned on finding out.

He stepped out of the shower and toweled off. The house was quiet. The kids were sleeping, and Wendy was in their master bedroom. AZ was about to turn the shower off, but he didn't. Something told him to keep the water running, to give the impression he was still in the shower. He knotted the towel around his waist and walked softly down the hall toward the master bedroom. The bedroom door was ajar, and from the hallway, he could see his wife seated on the bed in her panties and bra. Her cell phone was clutched to her ear like her life was on the line.

"I miss you too," she proclaimed to someone. "But this is becoming harder to do. I have a life, and I have a family."

AZ listened intently. He could feel his blood boiling. Enough was enough. He pushed open the door and charged into the room.

Wendy, caught off guard by his abrupt entry into the bedroom, stood up from the bed and looked at AZ like he was an intruder.

AZ ran over and snatched the cell phone from her hands and shouted into the phone, "Yo, who this?" He assumed the caller would hang up immediately once he heard AZ's voice.

But the caller returned, "Nigga, who you?"

"I'm her fuckin' husband!" AZ shouted.

"Yeah, I know, and I'm the nigga that's fuckin' your wife."

"What, nigga? I'll kill you, nigga!"

Justice shouted, "Nigga, you can't kill shit. You don't know me, nigga. I can be your worst nightmare."

"Listen, you ignorant muthafucka. You don't know me, and you don't know who you're dealing with or what I'm capable of doing to you. I will murder you, nigga! Stay the fuck away from my wife!"

AZ hung up. He glared at Wendy, who stood in front of him looking dumbfounded. "You fuckin' this nigga?" he screamed.

She didn't see the hit coming and had no time to respond to his accusation. AZ raised his hand into the air and came across her face with a backhand slap, sending her flying across the bed. She landed on the floor.

It wasn't over yet. AZ stormed across the bed, and more violence ensued. He landed several powerful tight-fisted blows to her face and body. Wendy found herself cemented to the floor, crying out hysterically and begging for him to stop. But rage consumed him. It seemed like there would be no end to his wrath.

He snatched her up from the floor, though she could barely stand. "You fuckin' cheatin' bitch!" he screamed. He wrapped his hand around her slim neck and slammed her into the bedroom wall so hard, the hanging pictures rattled and fell off. The impact left a gaping hole in the sheetrock.

Wendy, gasping for air, desperately tried to defend herself. She clawed at AZ's eyes and face, and she kicked and screamed.

AZ was exploding with anger. He squeezed and squeezed, feeling her slim neck crushing from his strong grip. Her eyes started to shut, and she felt herself fading. Her life was on the line. He punched her once again, and the blow almost sent her into unconsciousness.

Wendy knew if she blacked out, she wasn't going to wake up. Frantic and hurting, she had one move left to execute. She lifted her knees forcefully between his legs and kneed him in the groin.

The blow sent a shockwave of pain through AZ's body, and he immediately released his hold from her neck and folded over in pain. He fell to his knees and clutched his groin. "You fuckin' bitch!" he cried out.

She had her moment back. She ran away from him and hurriedly reached for her cell phone and quickly dialed 911. She only had seconds to survive, since AZ wasn't going to stay down for long.

"I'm gonna kill you, bitch!" he yelled.

"Nine-one-one, how can I help you?" the operator asked.

Wendy screamed into her phone, "My husband is trying to kill me!"

AZ was back on his feet, now shaking off the pain. He didn't show any signs of remorse or that he was calming down. His eyes flared up with redness and more fury. He glared at Wendy like a bull seeing red.

"Ma'am, what's your location?"

"I'm at—" Wendy ran toward the bathroom, and AZ gave a heated chase. He madly tried to grab for her, and almost had her in his reach when he tripped over something and stumbled, giving Wendy a second to slam the bathroom door shut and lock it.

AZ violently threw himself against the door with his shoulder, wanting to knock the door off the hinges. "Open this fuckin' door, you bitch!"

"No! Leave me alone, you fuckin' bastard! You're going to jail tonight! Look at what you did to my face! Ohmygod!"

Wendy still had the 911 operator on the phone, and she advised her to stay locked in the bathroom and that the cops were on their way. Wendy didn't know how much time she had left.

AZ was working the door, kicking it and slamming his weight against it.

"How dare you fuckin' cheat on me? You know who the fuck I am? I guess you fuckin' don't, you bitch, so I'm gonna have to fuckin' show you!"

It didn't take long for two marked squad cars to arrive at the residence. The kids, who had been awakened from their sleep by the disturbance in their parents' bedroom, were in awe at their daddy's violence and scared out of their minds. Even his sons couldn't calm him down, and they opened the door for the cops.

"Daddy's beatin' up Mommy," Randy said to the cops.

The police charged upstairs and stormed into the bedroom and caught AZ still trying to break down the master bathroom door. He cursed at the cops and yelled for them to get the fuck out of his house. They went to restrain him, and AZ fought back, but four against one was a losing battle for him. They threw him to the floor and restrained him.

It was finally safe for Wendy to come out the bathroom, and she slowly did. When she saw her husband lying on his stomach, handcuffed and restrained, she wanted to attack him.

She went for him, yelling out, "You fuckin' bastard," but two officers came in between her and AZ. In tears, her face was swollen, blood trickled from her mouth, and she was trembling with anxiety. The worst, though, was that her two young sons had to witness the violence.

AZ was escorted in handcuffs out of his million-dollar home and shoved into the backseat of the police car, with his neighbors watching it all from a short distance. AZ shook his head as he slumped in his seat. He knew he'd fucked up.

TWELVE

The following morning AZ was arraigned in a Maryland court for domestic abuse, battery, and resisting arrest. His $500-an-hour criminal attorney Robert Goldstein was right by his side handling his case. AZ was ready to fight this case and return home to his family, but with his wife being an assistant state's attorney, things were looking bleak for him. He stood in front of the judge looking cool and collected, while his attorney did all of the talking.

The prosecutor, Mandy Luigi, a fiery redhead with an intolerant attitude, wanted to throw the book at AZ. Wendy was a friend of hers, and she was pushing for AZ to never see the light of day. Mandy asked Wendy if she wanted to get a restraining order against her husband, but Wendy refused to do so. The prosecutor was shocked. Yes, AZ was her husband, but her face was a mess.

AZ's lawyer told the judge, "Your Honor, I request my client be released on his own recognizance. He's a highly respected businessman, a family man, and this is an unfortunate incident that took place. It was an argument with his wife, and things simply got out of hand."

Mandy Luigi shot back, "Simply out of hand? The defendant nearly beat his wife to death, Your Honor, and I request he be remanded without bail." She glared at AZ like he was scum.

"This is a domestic abuse case where the defendant has no prior incidents," the judge said to the prosecutor. "This isn't a capital murder case. I'm setting bail at twenty-five thousand."

"My client would like to post bail immediately, Your Honor," Robert Goldstein said.

The judge nodded.

And just like that, AZ was out of jail. He thanked his lawyer and shook his hand. He was ready to return home, see his kids, and hate his wife. The case wasn't a concern to him. Knowing his lawyer, he would either get it dismissed or have it dropped down to a simple misdemeanor. AZ was sure there would be no jail time, especially when Wendy was not pressing charges or testifying against him.

Wendy felt guilty. The way AZ had almost beat the life out of her made her think she was the only one in the marriage cheating. She regretted calling the cops. Now her peers were in her business, and gossip about her marriage started floating around. Wendy had always been a private woman and known to be a hard ass in the courtroom. This domestic violence incident made her look weak. Her face was bruised and swollen, her marriage was in shambles, and her private life was put on display.

*

AZ arrived home in a cab late that afternoon to an empty house. The kids were gone, and Wendy was nowhere around. He was angry and bitter toward her. He went into the bedroom and looked around. The hole in the wall looked crazy, and there were specks of his wife's blood on the carpet and on the wall.

AZ went into his closet. He needed to change clothes. He didn't plan on staying home for long. He needed to go out and get his mind right. He wanted to stay away from Wendy. He marched back and forth in his bedroom getting himself ready. He showered and shaved.

As he stood near his bedroom window buttoning his shirt, something caught his peripheral vision. AZ couldn't believe his eyes. It was someone from his past. It was Aoki, or it looked like her. She was supposed to be dead. He swiveled his head toward the window to get a better look, and from a distance, she seemed to be gazing up at him with a deadpan stare.

He took off running out the bedroom, hurried down the stairs, and shot out the front door like a bullet searching for that bitch. But there was no one. His front yard was empty. Was he seeing things? But Aoki looked so real outside his window. It looked like she had been watching him intently. But she was dead, wasn't she? Oscar had assured him of that.

He composed himself and decided that it was all in his head. He turned and walked toward the front door. Just as he was about to step into his home, Wendy's car pulled up into the driveway. AZ frowned. Before she could step out of her ride, he went back into the house and slammed the door behind him. He trekked up the stairs and went into the bedroom, where he continued to get dressed.

Wendy walked into the bedroom looking nervous. Her face was a wreck, but her eyes still looked strong and unwavering. She'd cheated, yes, but what he did to her was unforgettable. "We need to talk," she said civilly.

AZ frowned and acted like she wasn't there. He gave her the silent treatment while getting dressed. The only question he had for her was, *Who was the nigga on the phone?* He threw on the last touches to his wardrobe and walked by her like she was invisible.

When he left, she marched behind him, demanding he stop and talk. He got into his truck, started the ignition, and drove away from her in a rush, leaving her pouting on her front steps, her arms crossed over her chest.

Away from his wife and the house, AZ decided to call Heavy Pop and give him the 411 on what had happened. Since Wendy refused to give up her lover, AZ was determined to find him. He had plenty of resources and was hell-bent on using every last one of them to find the culprit.

"This clown-ass nigga is fuckin' my wife, and I want him dead," AZ proclaimed to Heavy Pop.

"I'll be down there first thing tomorrow, and we gonna handle this nigga," Heavy Pop said. "You know his name?"

"Nah, I don't, but I already said too much over the phone. When we meet in person, we'll talk."

"No doubt."

AZ hung up. He was sure Heavy was coming down. They were brothers, and if he had problems, then Heavy Pop had problems, and vice versa. Together, they'd been through thick and thin, to hell and back, and there was no problem they didn't handle together.

AZ navigated his Benz truck to the nearest bar in town, a place called Brick Top, twenty minutes from D.C. Inside, he took a seat at the bar and ordered Hennessy and then stared up at the mounted TV with the night's game about to start. There were a lot of basketball fans in the place to watch the Wizards play the Celtics.

AZ didn't care for the Wizards or the Celtics. He downed his Hennessy quickly and signaled the bartender for another one. He threw that back quickly too. He released a deep sigh and took in his surroundings. Here, he was just another face mixed in with the growing evening crowd. No one knew he was a drug dealer, gay, or a man with marital problems. He was just a man sitting at the bar with his drink.

He loved Wendy. He didn't share what was his. To him, it was about control. Another man coming into his family was intolerable. He thought about his sons. He trusted no nigga, and his wife creeping around was a serious problem. There was no telling who the man was and what his agenda was. He could be using Wendy to get to him. AZ was desperate to know the dude's name and his whereabouts to get ahead of the problem before it got ahead of him.

During the madness of cheering and shouting of basketball fans, AZ heard his cell phone ringing. Baron was calling him. It was perfect timing. He took the call into the bathroom to hear him better. AZ was excited to hear his voice. Baron had some free time and wanted to see him tonight. He was willing to meet AZ at a motel in an hour. AZ didn't hesitate. He was ready to release himself, and his handsome white boy was the perfect remedy.

AZ walked back into the bar to find the place silent, with fans and patrons shaking their heads. The Wizards had lost by two points. AZ, however, planned on winning by any means necessary—in court, on the streets, and with his love life.

THIRTEEN

Cristal collected her three-dollar tip from the cluttered table and stuffed the cash into her apron. She collected the dirty dishes and sent them packing to the young Latino busboy that always had a smile on his face and a nice word to say. Three weeks into her new job, she was adjusting just fine. Her boss and coworkers were friendly, and the customers were polite and generous. Waitressing at a small diner in Idaho Falls, Idaho wasn't a strenuous job like she thought it would be. The same customers came in every day to order their usual, and she refilled cups of coffee, smiled regularly, and kept conversation with everyone at a minimum.

Idaho Falls was the epitome of a growing small Midwest town. With a population of 58,000, it had the perfect conditions for Cristal to blend in. It wasn't too big of a metropolis where there was a lot happening, and it wasn't so small that she stood out like a sore thumb; it was just right. Crime was low there, and so was the cost of living. And almost everything was closed on Sundays.

The diner she worked in was a quaint place, the prototypical rail car diner with good ol'-fashioned-style food, near the historic downtown, where Yellowstone Avenue had lots of eateries, wineries, shops, and art centers popping up.

*

The day Cristal arrived, she walked into the diner for some coffee and a sandwich. At the time, the place was sparse with customers during the late-morning hour. She sat at the countertop looking unassuming. She was famished after a long trip from Washington.

She quietly watched the cook prepare her sandwich as it grew on the plate and sipped on her hot coffee. She had noticed the "help wanted" sign placed on the window. Becoming a waitress was a different job to her, but she was a different person.

Cristal had now changed her name to Julie Norman. Julie Norman was from Detroit, and her reason for moving to Idaho was love. She'd followed her boyfriend to the place with the hope of getting married, having a family, and starting over someplace new and away from Detroit. She was happy and in love, but her boyfriend suddenly had a change of heart. He left her a week after they'd moved to the town and took everything she owned. Now a broken-hearted Julie was stuck in a different city far away from home, with no money or a place to stay. It would be the story she told people if they asked what brought her to Idaho.

Cristal ate her meal slowly and lingered inside. She managed to strike up a conversation with the owner and told him her sob story. He was a white male, average height, clean-shaven, and well-spoken. Being a Christian and a church deacon, he wanted to help her out. He asked if she had any experience in waitressing, and she told him no. He decided to try her out anyway. Then he told her that her meal was on the house and gave her fifty dollars for a cheap motel room. She was to start early the next morning.

The people in Idaho Falls were nice and caring. Their lives were typical: work Monday through Friday, recreational events on Saturday, and church on Sunday. They looked out for each other, and some folks had known each other all their lives. The only downfall to the city was that it also attracted tourists who visited the nearby Yellowstone and Grand Teton National Parks. The last thing Cristal—or Julie—wanted was to run into a familiar face. But the odds of that happening were slim.

The diner owner and church deacon, Mark Morrow, helped Cristal get a small room with a thin window near his church place for cheap. She had to share a bathroom in the hallway, but it was cool. The place couldn't get any more inconspicuous and modest than that.

✳

Her shift was almost over, and her day's total in tips was thirty-eight dollars. She took a seat at the countertop and rested her feet. It was slow, and they were closing in another hour. Hector was finishing up a customer's order, a simple cheeseburger and fries, and Mark was mopping the kitchen floor. Though he was the owner of the diner, he worked like he was an employee, and Cristal respected that.

Sheriff Harrison waltzed into the diner. Sheriff Harrison stood six one, had been sheriff for four years, and was a young, slim white man with a narrow face, a dark goatee, and piercing blue eyes. He threw his authority around like someone shoveling snow after a blizzard. His uniform was meticulous from head to toe, and for some reason, he took an interest in Cristal, or Julie as he knew her by. From day one, he'd been subtly interrogating her like she was a terrorist.

Cristal frowned at his presence.

"Hey, Mark," Sheriff Harrison said. "Things good tonight?"

Mark smiled and nodded, waving a quick hello before going back to mopping the kitchen floor.

Sheriff Harrison then shot his sharp eyes at Cristal and said, "Coffee. Black. You know how I like it."

Cristal removed herself from the stool to pour his coffee. She set the cup on the countertop in front of him and walked away.

Sheriff Harrison's eyes lingered on her as he took a few sips. "So, Julie, what part of Detroit are you from again?" he asked impulsively.

It'd been three weeks of this shit—his random questions and lingering stares. She considered him to be a racist cop.

"I'm from Greektown," she replied casually.

"Greektown, huh? Sounds like an ironic place for Detroit."

"It's home."

"Lots of coloreds in Greektown?"

The word *coloreds* coming out of his mouth made her skin crawl. She thought he was a bigot stuck in the fifties and sixties. She was surprised he didn't walk around with a swinging noose in his hand.

"It's Detroit, home of Motown," she replied sarcastically.

"Yeah, that boy Berry Gordy—that's his name, right?—definitely made a lot of money off of colored talent." He smiled.

Cristal sighed and shook her head, knowing this man wouldn't last one minute in Brooklyn, or anywhere else on the East Coast. The wolves would have definitely torn him apart for his racist attitude. She stood in front of him with a straight face and asked, "Is coffee all you want?"

"Yes."

She placed his two-dollar check on the counter and walked away.

He took a few more sips and then he asked, "This boyfriend of yours, why did he leave you stuck here in the first place?"

"Because he's an asshole."

"What was his name again?"

"Is that really relevant, Sheriff? I'm trying to forget the past."

"I guess not. I'm just making conversation with you."

Keep cool, she thought.

Mark looked at Julie and knew she was upset. It was obvious to him that Sheriff Harrison had become the local bully to one of his waitresses. Mark couldn't understand why. Julie was a sweet girl and becoming one of his best workers. Hector saw the upset look on his coworker's face too. He'd been living there for three years now, and the sheriff had never come at him with questions like that.

"Hey, Sheriff, we're about to close soon. Do you want anything from the grill before Hector shuts it down?" Mark asked, interrupting the harassment.

"No, I'm okay. I'm not hungry tonight."

"Okay."

The sheriff stood up and reached into his pocket to pay for the coffee, but Mark quickly shrugged him off. "No, Sheriff. It's on the house."

"It's a wonder how you stay in business when you keep giving out free meals, Mark."

Mark smiled. "The Good Lord keeps me in business."

"Amen to that." The sheriff spun toward the exit and marched out.

Cristal exhaled with relief. The farther away he was, the better. She managed to say, "What's his problem?"

Mark answered, "He's just a young and lonely man, that's all. That badge is the only thing he has in his life."

"He needs a girlfriend," she said respectfully in front of Mark. What she really wanted to say was, "He needs to find some business and stay the fuck out of mine," but Mark ran a clean and decent diner and didn't like cursing in his establishment.

"I guess so. That and Jesus."

Cristal smiled. She respected Mark a lot. In a way, he reminded her of Daniel. They both were kind, smart, and always knew the right thing to say. Damn, she missed Daniel.

Mark went back to cleaning the kitchen and prepping for closing. Things were normal again. Every night things were quiet and normal. Idaho Falls was Mayberry for Cristal.

She grabbed her coat and got ready to leave.

Sheriff Harrison sat in his police car near the diner with a direct view of Julie moving around inside. He pressed a small pair of binoculars to his eyes to capture her face in closer distance and watched her readying to leave work. His view stayed glued to everything she was doing inside. He was intrigued and wanted to know everything about her. Where did she come from? What did she like to do? What were her likes and dislikes?

He went into the diner almost every day and asked her questions because he had a huge crush on her. She was black and pretty, which was uncommon in a place like Idaho Falls. But he wasn't a ladies' man and didn't know the first thing about talking to a beautiful woman. He'd spent his life alone, in a small town. He would get nervous around Julie, and so he did what he was known to do best—ask questions roughly and looking like he was interrogating her, when he simply wanted to know more about her.

Sheriff Harrison wasn't a racist, though he came across as one. He didn't know anything about Julie's past, or black people. And he didn't know how to go about asking her out. His parents were racists and hated what the blacks were doing to their country: taking good jobs meant for whites, thrusting themselves into leadership positions; fuelling terrorism; and tearing America apart with crime, disease, poverty, and ignorance. To them, President Barack Obama was a Muslim terrorist who was ruining the lives of good Christian white folks in America.

Harrison had been fed this ideology since he was a little boy. His parents made sure that their beliefs were his too, but he saw himself as different. He started to despise their values, and felt himself becoming more intrigued by black people and their culture. In his eyes, they were creative and talented. But part of his parents' negative lingo stuck with him. It's what he was used to hearing in his household.

Sheriff Harrison watched Julie leave the diner with the others. It was a brisk night, and she was bundled up in a long quilted coat and boots. Idaho winters were known to be brutal. They were long, white, and cold—twenty degrees or less on a daily basis, and blizzards were common.

Julie climbed into Mark's 2002 Ford Focus, and they drove off. The sheriff decided to follow them.

*

Cristal walked into her sparsely furnished room. All she had was a mattress, a wobbly table, a couple of chairs, and a small arsenal of weapons hidden for her protection. Just because she was in a different place didn't mean the threats to her life weren't still out there looking for her. She was a wanted woman by two deadly organizations, and she knew she would be forever looking over her shoulders. She went from being the hunter to being the hunted.

After working at the diner, she spent time at home reading a book, training her body, fortifying her place from top to bottom, and taking a long-needed shower. She lived in a simple town, so she adjusted into simple living. She didn't go out to any clubs, take long walks around the neighborhood, or shop at the local malls. The less exposure for her in public places, the better. She barely spoke to her neighbors, and she did her best to avoid law enforcement. She wasn't a fugitive from the law, but she moved like she was.

Over the years, Cristal went through many names, many alter egos, and many risky situations. To say that it was an exhausting way to live would be an understatement. Living a normal life was so foreign to her. Once or twice a month she called Daniel for the one-sided phone calls. She had to be spontaneous. If anyone was tracking him, she wanted to throw them off. She always used different pre-paid phones, and her location was always different.

She dialed Daniel from a private number, and after three rings, he picked up.

"Hello?" he answered.

She remained silent.

Immediately, Daniel knew who was calling. "Hey," he said, his voice sounding a bit keyed-up. "How you been?" he asked, like he was going to get a response. Sometimes he would completely forget and catch himself. "I know you don't talk, or can't talk, but I miss you so much. Me, I'm doing fine. When I finish Hopkins, I am going for my PhD. But you probably don't want to hear the boring stuff. You remember how we used to talk all through the night and how you would love my body massages? Damn, being with you was so much fun."

Cristal sank herself into the bed in the dark, silent room and just listened, her 9mm close by. It was satisfying to hear his voice again. She managed to smile and almost lost herself with him just talking. She felt as long as she remained quiet, it gave nothing away. This was the only good thing in her life, just listening to him.

"I will always love you," he proclaimed. She wanted to tell him that she felt the same way.

FOURTEEN

Tracking down the boyfriend wasn't that difficult. First, she checked the vicinity of Johnson C. Smith University, where he'd graduated from, and got word that he was now at Johns Hopkins University for his master's. It turned out that he lived in a small apartment a short walk away from the heartbeat of Baltimore.

Aoki was in town and went to work. She knew by now that Cristal would be far gone from Daniel and living a new life under a different name, having been trained to keep a low profile and cover her tracks. The United States was a big place, but Aoki was hell-bent on finding her, even if it took tracking her down from state to state. Aoki came up with a better idea, though; one she knew would bring Cristal out of hiding and right to her.

She became Daniel's shadow; wherever he went, Aoki was there. From work, to school, to his apartment, she was there stalking him. Daniel had no idea he was being watched.

Within a week, she knew almost everything about him. He lived a quiet life. His routine was basic, and his appearance unassuming. He didn't own a car, so he walked everywhere or used public transportation. Anywhere outside of Maryland, he used a cab. He was uncomplicated, making him an easy target for Aoki.

He didn't go out, didn't do nightclubs, didn't travel, and he had a very small circle of friends he would socialize with, which was mostly other medical students. He enjoyed his espresso and muffins at the nearby Starbucks. If he wasn't at work or school, he spent most of his time at home reading and studying. He owned one television, and it was rarely on. When it was, he watched CNN, MSNBC, C-SPAN, or FOX to keep up with politics. He didn't have a girlfriend and didn't seem interested in a new love. He seemed content with his life.

Aoki was watching him, and he was a boring person to watch. Knowing his schedule like the back of her hand, she implemented her plan, which was to kidnap him and use him as bait to reel in the bigger fish. Watching him around the clock was the tedious part, but now the heat was about to turn up. She waited until she knew he would be away from home long enough for her to break in and bug his apartment with small cameras in critical areas.

Once inside, Aoki looked around his apartment and couldn't find anything even remotely interesting. No porno, nude pictures, or vices whatsoever. This guy was a real snooze button. Once the cameras were installed, she linked the footage to her smartphone.

＊

Daniel entered his dark apartment and turned on the lights. He was tired, it had been a long day at work and then school, and he simply wanted to get some sleep. He placed his book bag in a nearby chair, pulled off his coat, tossed it on the couch, and went into the bedroom. The lights went on, and suddenly his world went dark.

Aoki was waiting in the shadows, poised by the door in all black. The moment Daniel came into her view, she thrust a syringe of etorphine into his neck, causing his vision to quickly blur and his legs to go rubbery. He could no longer hold up the weight of his upper body. Seconds after the opioid was pumped into his flesh, he collapsed on the floor. Now he was in Aoki's hands.

Ice cold water to the face jolted him awake. He shrieked and looked around his surroundings frantically. He tried to move, but he was tightly bound to a steel chair, restrained by rope and handcuffs. Another shocker to him was, he was in his underwear. So many questions flooded his mind. The room he was in was cement, dim, and cold. It was eerie all around. Daniel was terrified.

"Yuh speak to her, don't you?" Aoki said.

"What?" Daniel said. "Speak to who?"

When Aoki made herself visible to him, he looked at her in terror. He had no idea who this woman was. He'd never seen her before. What did she want with him? It had to be a misunderstanding. She had the wrong man. His worried gaze stayed glued to her every movement, or tried to. She taunted him by circling him slowly and leisurely touching him—her hand on his shoulder, grabbing the back of his head, her manicured nails digging into his arm. He constantly fidgeted and cringed.

"Yuh afraid of me?" she asked.

"I don't know who you are."

Aoki stood over Daniel in her red bottom pumps and her sleek and sexy black jumpsuit, but she had ill-will written all over her. She stared at Daniel and fed off his fear. The man was literally trembling in the chair. She laughed. It was exhilarating for her to see him terrified. He wasn't a man, he was a victim, and there was only one use for him. She stared at him like he was prey. It would have been easy to torture him to extract something, but she knew he didn't know anything about Cristal.

"What is this? Why am I here?" he asked.

Aoki extracted the cell phone from his clothing on the floor and held it up. He was still clueless.

"When was de las' time yuh talk to yuh girlfriend?" she asked, her thick accent almost incoherent to him.

"Girlfriend?"

"Cristal."

"Cristal? Who is Cristal? You mean, Beatrice? She's dead!"

"Yuh lie!" she hollered.

"It's not a lie!"

"She calls and she simply listen to yuh."

Beatrice had never spoken a word on the phone, and he never knew where she was or when she would call him. Daniel was stunned by the information this woman knew. He swallowed hard, panic consuming every part of his body. He had no idea where she was holding him. There was no help, no rescue party for him. He did not want his life to end like this.

Aoki stared at him, and her chilling look made him want to pee in his underpants. Cristal had him caught up, and now his future looked bleak.

The fun was just beginning. Aoki wanted to play games with Cristal, and that started by fucking around with her man and her mind. She wondered how Cristal would react when she couldn't hear Daniel's voice any longer. What would go through her head? Would she come for him? Whatever Cristal would do, Aoki was going to be ready for her.

Yes, the fun had just started. Now it was time for everyone to sit back, strap themselves in, and enjoy the ride.

FIFTEEN

Lisa cursed the bumper-to-bumper traffic on I-95 South. Brake lights extended for miles because of a three-car accident six miles ahead. She hated sitting in traffic. She wanted to get where she was going and handle her business, but it looked like she would be sitting in traffic for another hour.

"Fuckin' people need to learn how to fuckin' drive! Fuck!"

It was a cold day, and the heater was on blast. Lisa's seven-year-old daughter, Alice, was strapped securely in her car seat in the backseat. Alice was growing up fast and looking more and more like her father every day. She was sleeping, thank God. Lisa was tired of listening to her complain. Between that and the thick traffic, she felt like she was going crazy.

Lisa's sanity felt like it was on thin ice. She was going to break soon if she didn't get what she wanted. AZ wasn't answering his cell phone, and it was maddening to her. She hated the drive from New York to Maryland, but what she had to say to Alice's father couldn't be said over the phone. Besides, he wasn't fucking picking up, so she wanted to confront him in person and see how he was living.

How dare he move to Maryland, far away from his firstborn, to go play Mike Brady with that bitch? Wendy—what kind of name was Wendy? It sounded like a shady bitch's name. Lisa wanted to get to AZ's early before his wife came home. She didn't want Wendy putting her two cents in her business.

Lisa was living the good life because of AZ. She lived in a three-bedroom apartment in Williamsburg, Brooklyn, and rent was three thousand a month. She drove around in a two-year-old Honda CRV bought brand-new, and received nearly ten thousand dollars a month in child support. Her clothes and furniture were always up-to-date, but it still wasn't enough for her.

AZ could never give her enough, especially when he had a mini-mansion in Maryland, nicer cars, and was there for his wife and sons. He needed to be in Alice's life more. Hers too. But how could that happen when he was living nearly two hundred miles away?

It burned her up inside how good he was living with that bitch and her kids. No bitch from Baltimore should be living an extravagant life with her man—oops! her baby's father. How dare he put a bitch on and give her the good life? Wendy wasn't from Brooklyn, she was from Maryland. In Lisa's world, you looked out for your own first. Second, she was in law enforcement. Though she wasn't a cop, she was a prosecutor, and Lisa considered that to be sleeping with the enemy.

Lisa was going to be a nagging pain in AZ's side until their daughter turned eighteen. Even after Alice's eighteenth birthday, she didn't plan to leave him alone. This time she wanted a house. She was tired of living in the condo, Alice was a growing girl and needed a backyard, grass, to a swing playground. Lisa was tired of Brooklyn. She wanted to experience living in the suburbs, either Queens or Long Island. Lisa found the perfect house on the market in St. Albans, Queens. It had three bedrooms, two bathrooms, a garage, a backyard, and a front yard, and was listed for $500,000. AZ had to get her this house, or else!

*

Lisa's Honda CRV came to a stop in front of the mini-mansion. She took a deep breath and then frowned. The sight of the lavish home made her angry. The place was impeccable, looking like the cover of a real estate magazine showing off lavish homes. This was how she wanted to live, and she was determined to get her house. If Wendy had a home like this, then she deserved one, too.

She got out of the car and unstrapped Alice. They marched toward the large and beautifully designed entry doors. She balled her fist and banged on the front door with force like she was the police. She saw AZ's truck in the driveway, but no other car. She was hoping Wendy wasn't home, but she was ready for her, though, if she wanted to try and come in between them.

It was no secret that Wendy and Lisa couldn't stand each other. They'd met a handful of times, and each time there was yelling and cursing at each other. AZ desperately tried to keep the peace between the two, but it was impossible.

It was a windy day, cold and cloudy, with Christmas right around the corner. Lisa wondered what AZ was going to buy his daughter. She expected something in the price range of five thousand dollars or more. Alice wanted diamond earrings and the new Jordans.

Standing in her new boots that came with a price tag of six hundred dollars and her hair done up perfectly from a costly salon, Lisa held Alice's hand in hers as she waited for the front door to open.

Lisa had coached her daughter into giving her daddy the sad face, the drooping eyes, and the pouting lips. She was coaching Alice on how to get what she wanted in life. It started with having her daddy spoil her, and as she grew older, it would be how to get men to buy her whatever she wanted. Alice was too young to know about sex, but she wasn't too young to know about the finer things in life and where they came from.

The day Lisa spread her legs for AZ, she knew he was her meal ticket. AZ was a fledging drug dealer at the time, but she saw ambition in his eyes and refused to let him go without some kind of perpetual profit from him. When she found out she was pregnant with his child, she jumped for joy.

The front door opened, and AZ appeared in front of her and his daughter.

Lisa quickly blurted out, "I was calling your phone. Why didn't you fuckin' answer?"

AZ was taken aback by their presence. "Lisa, now is not a good time for you to be here."

"Nigga, please. I came here because of your daughter. When was the last time you saw her, huh? I drove from New York in traffic and you is not about to turn me around, nigga!" She marched inside. There was no way she was going to stand outside or leave until she got what she had come for.

AZ sighed with frustration. Lisa was an aneurysm waiting to happen.

"Where's your wife?"

"She's not home."

"Good. Because I don't need that bitch in our conversation."

AZ managed to smile down at his daughter, and Alice smiled back. She was always happy to see her daddy. Alice's puffy pigtails and big brown eyes made her adorable. The fact that she was a spitting image of him made her irresistible.

"Hey, beautiful," he said to her.

"Hi, Daddy."

"C'mere."

AZ lowered himself to the floor, propping himself down on one knee and opened his arms, and Alice ran into his arms. He hugged her and gave her a kiss on the cheek.

"You are looking prettier and prettier every day," he said.

Alice smiled brightly.

It's what Lisa wanted to see—AZ loving his daughter affectionately and treating her first in his life.

AZ picked up his little girl and swung her around in the air, and she laughed and giggled.

"We need to talk, AZ, fo' real this time," Lisa said, shattering his brief moment with his daughter.

AZ knew that when Lisa wanted to talk about something, there was always drama, jealousy, or money attached to it. "What, Lisa?" he asked dryly.

Already, he was bracing himself for what she had to say. He knew she wanted something—how big, he didn't know yet. He stopped playing with his daughter and placed her small feet back onto the floor.

"Your daughter needs a bigger place to live. We need a house."

"What?"

"Look how you living with your other two kids and that bitch. You don't think Alice wants to live like this too?"

"What's wrong with the condo you have now? It's spacious enough."

"It's too small, and Alice needs a backyard. What, you don't think your daughter deserves to live in a house too? Nigga, she's your firstborn, and she should always get the best."

AZ shook his head left to right, sighing in disbelief. "I give her the best, from ten thousand dollars a month in child support, and taking care of you too. Alice doesn't want for anything. You're just being fuckin' greedy!"

"Whatever your two kids have here with that bitch, she needs to have too. And you can afford a house for her."

"You mean for you."

"I'm not even tryin' to argue wit' you, AZ. I came here to talk civilly and shit, not fight."

"How much is this house?" he asked, knowing she had one already picked out.

"Five hundred thousand," she answered coolly.

"You must be out your rabbit-ass fuckin' mind! You seriously think I'm gonna pay that much for a house? For you?"

"It's for your family," she argued heatedly. "For your fuckin' daughter!"

"She's fine, Lisa. Stop using her as an excuse. She already has everything she needs. My daughter is not a justification for your greed."

The two started to argue, with Alice standing right there, which wasn't anything new. Alice stood to the side, her eyes revealing sadness and ache. She rarely saw her daddy, and when she did, he was always arguing with her mommy.

"You need to stop treating your own flesh-and-blood daughter like she's a fuckin' stepchild. She's your firstborn!"

AZ could make a lot of money if he got a dollar every time she used the expression "firstborn." He was sick and tired of hearing it repeated.

Lisa got closer to him, yapping her mouth wildly with everything foul and crazy.

In the midst of their argument, the front door opened, and Wendy and the boys walked in. The moment Wendy saw Lisa standing in her living room arguing with her husband, a hard frown splattered across her face. She was already having a bad day from work to home. Seeing Lisa, she knew her day was about to become even worse.

"This bitch here," Lisa exclaimed.

"What is she doing here, AZ?" Wendy asked composedly.

"I'm here to have a talk with my baby father. That's what I'm doing here. You have a problem with that?"

"Yes, I do. Matter of fact, I want you to leave my house, and leave my husband alone."

Lisa's blood was boiling. The word *husband* made her skin crawl. Every time she got close to Wendy, she wanted to rip her face apart and beat her to the ground. She was the reason for AZ not taking care of his daughter and moving to Maryland.

"I'm not going any-fuckin'-where," Lisa said, glaring at Wendy.

As the women hissed at each other, Randy and Terrance clung to their mother's legs and stared questioningly up at the hostile lady. The boys didn't know anything about their half-sister, Alice.

Lisa shot a look down at the two boys and spat, "You so worried about them two little niggas, catering to these two muthafuckas, and treating your firstborn like a muthafuckin' stepchild, when them two little niggas don't even look nothing like you, AZ. How you know them your babies?" She stood there looking smug.

The house became silent.

Then she added, "You treat these little muthafuckas like they're the Holy Grail. Well, they ain't. You need to start treating Alice better than these two little niggas. Nigga, did you even get a DNA test done? They probably ain't even your kids."

Wendy had heard enough. Her hands turned into fists, and she reacted without any thought to it. She swung at Lisa, and the punch landed to the side of her face. The blow was shocking, but it wasn't enough to take Lisa down. She had come ready to fight.

A fight ensued. Fists went flying at each other.

Lisa quickly had the advantage. She was a bull seeing red, knocking Wendy around in her own home. Though Wendy had twenty pounds on Lisa, Lisa was a beast with her hands. Lisa never became civilized, had never stopped fighting, while Wendy hadn't thumped anyone in years. The only fighting she did was in the courtroom.

Wendy went crashing to the floor with Lisa on top of her.

"You fuckin' bitch!" Lisa hollered. "Don't fuck wit' me, bitch."

The punches to Wendy's face continued. Wendy desperately tried to lift herself from the floor and shield herself from the onslaught, but Lisa was like a lion tearing apart her prey. Once her teeth were fixed into flesh and she smelled blood, there was no stopping her.

Lisa had Wendy's long hair knotted into her fist, and she had control, bringing on pain with hair-pulling and punches.

The kids started crying.

AZ ran toward the brawl and attempted to break it apart. "Get the fuck off her, Lisa!" he shouted.

Lisa was ready to fight him too. She glared at AZ. "Get the fuck off me, nigga! Don't fuckin' touch me!" She pulled out a knife.

Now, he was ready to go get his gun and make a statement. Did Lisa forget who he was and what he was about? "You gonna show out like this in my home and in front of my kids?" he barked.

Lisa's shirt was torn and her hair disheveled, and Wendy was a true mess too, her face bleeding, her hair everywhere, and her outfit ripped. Both ladies were breathing heavily.

AZ stood in between them. "Leave, Lisa, before I make you leave," he growled through clenched teeth.

"So this is how you gonna do us? Huh, nigga? This is how you gonna do me and your daughter?"

Alice was in tears, and Randy and Terrance were screaming and hollering, clinging to their mother's leg tightly like they were being pulled away.

"You're a disrespectful bitch!" AZ exclaimed.

Lisa started to shed a few tears. What had hurt her most was AZ turning against her. What was more painful was seeing him protecting Wendy and her two kids, and he didn't come to comfort his daughter. She was crying too.

AZ reached for his two boys and put them into his arms. He turned to his wife. "You okay?"

Lisa took a deep breath. She had seen enough. The rage and antagonism she felt quickly transitioned into soreness and abandonment in the pit of her stomach. She went to Alice and took her hand. "C'mon, Alice, let's go. Fuck your father!" She marched toward the exit, pulling Alice along forcefully.

Alice glanced back at her father with the saddest eyes. AZ swallowed hard as he locked eyes with his daughter, a mirror image of himself. He wanted to say something, but he stayed silent.

"I'm calling the cops," Wendy said. "You see what that bitch did to me?"

AZ heard her, but he wasn't listening. Alice had his undivided attention; she was still his heart. He loved her deeply, but her mother was so complicated.

SIXTEEN

AZ wanted total annihilation of his wife's side-nigga. He couldn't sleep much because he was constantly thinking about the affair happening right under his nose. He was so busy in New York, putting together a multi-million dollar drug deal, someone else swooped in and fucked his wife.

He was rising faster in power, but he was losing stability at home. Nothing he tried—sex with Baron, business, exercising—could completely free his mind from Wendy's betrayal. He wasn't going to feel right until he got the name and location of the man she was fucking. Wendy was being stubborn, protecting her lover tooth and nail.

They argued incessantly, and the kids were witnesses to their drama. Wendy wanted him to forgive her, but at the moment, he couldn't. She had betrayed him, and he didn't take betrayal lightly.

The incident reminded him of Aoki. Though it was a long time ago, the memories of the friendship they once had, his feelings for her, his revealing his homosexuality to her, and her stabbing him in the back were vivid. He never wanted to go through that feeling or situation again.

He'd thought Wendy was different. Because she was educated and a prosecutor, he figured her to be the perfect woman for him. Their pillow talk was him inquiring about the law, hypothetically putting himself into situations and having a prosecutor's point of view. He would ask questions, and she didn't hesitate to answer. Each day, he grew wiser and wiser about litigation, procedure, and certain indictments, as he prepared himself for what-ifs. Though he was careful, there was always the possibility of the DEA kicking down his front door and taking him away in handcuffs in front of his family.

AZ's home office was quiet. The boys were out with the babysitter, and Wendy was working feverishly on her rape/robbery case. Supposedly. He sat in his high-back leather chair and threw back a few shots of dark liquor as he contemplated his next move. Life on top could be exhausting. He felt he always had to be three or four steps ahead of everyone, from Oscar to the streets, his business, the DEA, and even his wife.

He had gone through Wendy's cell phone records meticulously, looking for a number that was out of place. But with her being the assistant state's attorney, many different phone calls were coming in and going out, so it was like trying to find a needle in a haystack.

Wendy wasn't stupid. She knew how to hide her irregulars. That's why he hired two goons to follow her nonstop. He wanted to know where she was at all times. He couldn't take any chances. Did the man she was fucking know where they lived? Had he ever been to the house? Did he fuck his wife in his bed? The thought of it refueled AZ's anger and made him sick to his stomach.

*

Heavy Pop drove to Maryland, and the two met at AZ's home. Though Heavy Pop had been to AZ's mini-mansion in the Maryland suburbs several times before, he was still impressed. After AZ told him about Wendy's affair, the next day he drove straight there ready for things to pop off, but Wendy wouldn't give up the name or location of her lover.

The two friends sat in AZ's stylish office, downed a few drinks, and shared ideas. AZ spilled out his frustration like an erupting volcano. Heavy was the only one he could talk to about his problems. Though they were close, AZ still kept his homosexual lifestyle a secret from him, fearful that Heavy Pop wouldn't understand and would turn against him. There had been times when AZ wanted to reveal his secret to Heavy, feeling he could trust him with it and their friendship would stay intact, but he would always have second thoughts. Homosexuality was still considered taboo in the ghetto, and if word got out, AZ knew it would open up another can of worms. So he decided he would take his secret to the grave. He wasn't going to make the mistake so many others had made by coming out of the closet and hoping things would be the same. In reality, widespread knowledge about AZ being gay would create a tailspin in the game.

AZ told his friend about the fight between his wife and his baby mamma.

Heavy Pop found the incident amusing. "Lisa has always been a firecracker."

"Tell me something I don't know. I was ready to shoot that bitch."

After that, AZ went on to talk again about Wendy's affair. There was no way AZ could escape it.

"I know you love her, AZ, and she's the mother of your kids, but knowing this, do you still trust her?"

"I don't know."

"Push comes to shove and she needs to be dealt with, could you do it?"

"She's an assistant state's attorney, well-connected politically."

"And you're a fuckin' drug kingpin. What if the day comes when she finds out who you really are? Then what? Are you trying to run for mayor or something?"

"She's been an advantage to me since the day we met, Heavy. I know what I'm doing. The information she's provided over time has been helpful to me."

"And your relationship with her can harm you too."

Heavy poured another shot of Hennessy into his shot glass and threw it back, feeling the dark liquor tingle in his throat. He leaned back in the plush chair and lit a cigar. He inhaled and savored the flavor; there was nothing better than a Cuban cigar.

He had always been the voice of reason with AZ. The men had grown wiser since their hustling days in the Pink Houses. Their survival almost made them feel invincible. Seeing death made them take nothing for granted.

"I'm no slack, Heavy. You know me. If I need to handle things, I will."

"I know, but don't let her become another Aoki. You already know how that shit went down. Wendy's a lovely woman. I like her. But at the end of the day, is she loyal to you, her husband? And this affair she's having, it's already telling you what you need to know. What if she decides to divorce you and have her lawyers and her peoples start investigating you?"

"I deal with that problem if it comes. But I'm on top of things. I have two of my men following her closely. Where she goes, they go. If she takes a piss in the bathroom, I'm gonna know what color it was."

"Married life. A nigga like me will always stay single, because married life is more treacherous than the street life."

They shared a laugh.

AZ enjoyed having his friend around. For once, he didn't have to travel to New York to enjoy a cigar, a few drinks, and good conversation with him. The comfort of his home office was just fine. It was safe to talk. Once a week he had it swept for any bugs.

An hour later, AZ received a phone call via a secure line from his henchmen following Wendy.

He answered, anticipating some good news. "Tell me something good."

Heavy Pop lifted his heavy frame from the chair to get some circulation going in his legs as AZ conversed on the phone. He walked around and looked at numerous pictures AZ had of them when they were younger on the walls of his office. The glory days back when Brooklyn was all they knew, and the street life and selling drugs was survival of the fittest. It still was, but now they had "Pablo Escobar dreams" about the street life.

Heavy Pop's eyes lingered on a picture Heavy's Pop aunt took of them back in the day. They were sixteen-year-olds with cornrows. Heavy Pop had a huge baby face, and AZ was skinny like a broomstick. AZ had his arms around Heavy, and they were showing off their herringbone chains and cheesing for the camera. The boys were happy and inseparable like brothers. It was around the time when Rich Deal put them on his crew and threw them out there to hustle drugs. They'd bought the chains with their first drug proceeds and had felt like kings with their new bling. It was amazing that AZ still had the picture. Heavy Pop wondered if he still had his herringbone chain.

The phone call was brief. AZ hung up and smiled. "I got a name."

"You do, huh."

"Justice," AZ said.

Heavy Pop chuckled. "How ironic. Well, let's go give him some Justice," he said with a cutting smile.

AZ wanted to know everything about Justice, the man who had his wife's attention.

*

Heavy Pop found out Justice was born in Brooklyn, but built his reputation in Baltimore and was a serious figure in Maryland. He was a Blood, an OG whose name rang out, and a drug dealer, but nowhere near the level of AZ and Heavy Pop. He was a three-to-four-kilo-a-month gangster and drove a Range Rover and a Benz. He was tall, bald, and handsome with green eyes, and he always dressed in the finest attire. He had several baby mamas and a reputation with the ladies. A year earlier, he was the prime suspect for two murders in the city. Two men were gunned down on the East Side, but murder charges were never processed due to lack of evidence and no witnesses coming forward.

AZ was baffled. How did his wife and that hoodlum drug dealer ever hook up? Meanwhile, he'd been hiding his own lifestyle from her, thinking she wouldn't accept it. What the fuck?

SEVENTEEN

Justice climbed into his black Range Rover in his boot-cut jeans, leather coat, and beige Timberlands. He was sporting a diamond earring, pinky ring, and a long platinum diamond link chain with a diamond-encrusted Jesus head pendant. From the East Side to the West Side, there was no argument that Justice was making money in Baltimore.

Talk was spreading that he was fucking a high-end bitch, a city prosecutor at that. He boasted about Wendy to his friends and associates, not considering that he was putting her job at risk. She had quickly become his favorite bitch. Damn, the things she could do! She was an undercover freak, and smart too. She had her own money and was far removed from the ghetto chickenheads of Baltimore.

He started the ignition to his truck. Then he pulled out his cell phone and scrolled down to Wendy's number. He couldn't stop thinking about her. He desperately wanted to see her tonight. She had been ignoring his phone calls for almost a week. He had left messages, but she hadn't called him back. He knew it had to be her husband getting in the way of them seeing each other.

Though he'd had a few harsh words with the nigga over the phone, he didn't feel threatened by him. In fact, he was thinking about having him killed. With AZ gone, Wendy would undeniably be his. He didn't want to share his favorite bitch with anyone, not even her own husband.

Justice felt that it was time to put the murder into motion. First, he would talk to Wendy about it, see how she would react. She hated the man anyway, so why wouldn't she be down with killing him? She was a prosecutor, so she could easily cover up the crime. He had the perfect guy to call—Matrix, a white boy from D.C. He was expensive, but he was really good. They said that his victims only saw him coming when he wanted them to, and that meant a slow and painful death.

Justice lit a cigarette and attempted to call Wendy again. His call went to voice mail again. He exhaled in aggravation. Usually, bitches couldn't stop calling him, but he couldn't stop calling her. He couldn't stop thinking about that pussy. She had him tripping. Was he sprung?

He had a lot on his mind, not just Wendy, but his competitors in Baltimore. The game was fierce, and the snitches were overwhelming. Running a drug crew wasn't easy, with envy out there, stretching for miles.

He tossed his cell phone in the passenger seat and sighed. West Baltimore was bustling twenty-four/seven with drugs, bitches, parties, violence and crime, even police passing by on the humble. Justice sat on the corner of W. Preston Street and Druid Avenue in an $80,000 truck with no concerns at all. This was his territory. He could park wherever he wanted and do whatever he wanted. He could walk around Baltimore with a handful of hundred-dollar bills and was sure no one would rob him or come after him.

"Fuck that bitch!" he uttered out of frustration.

He decided to text her: YO, I'M CALLING U. WHERE U AT? YA HUSBAND GOT U IGGING ME? TELL THAT NIGGA HE DON'T WANNA SEE ME. I DON'T GIVE A FUCK ABOUT HIM. I JUST WANT YOU AND THAT FAT PUSSY ON MY DICK TONIGHT. HOLLA AT YA BOY. MISS YOU.

Justice waited for her to reply.

Unbeknownst to him, AZ was reading the text. The man fucking his wife was becoming a lot more disrespectful. AZ texted back from Wendy's phone: I SEE YOU, NIGGA! JUST WAIT AROUND AND WE'LL HAVE OUR TALK. I PROMISE YOU THAT! FACTS!

Oh shit, Justice thought. But he didn't cringe. He laughed. "Nigga got balls. He don't know me." He texted back: NIGGA, YOU FUCKIN' WIT' DEATH, MUTHAFUCKA. ASK BOUT ME. I'M NO SUBURBAN, RICH PUNK HIDING BEHIND HIS WIFE'S PHONE. I'M THE REAL THING, NIGGA. DON'T DIE BECAUSE OF SOME PUSSY.

AZ texted: LOL, AND YOU'RE ABOUT TO DIE BECAUSE OF SOME PUSSY. MY PUSSY, NIGGA. I TOLD YOU, SHE'S MARRIED. AND I SEE YOU BOUT TO DIE NOW NIGGA ON THAT CORNER IN THAT RANGE ROVER.

"What?" Justice quickly swiveled his head around, looking for him. He pulled out his pistol, his heart thumping loudly against his chest. But it was too late. Before he knew it, he was staring down the barrel of a 9mm.

Justice was wide-eyed. "Yo—"

"Fuck you, nigga!"

Bam! Bam! Bam! Bam!

Justice's face exploded violently, and he lay slumped in the front seat with four shots to the head.

AZ hurried back to the car with the smoking gun in his hand but not before reaching into Justice's vehicle and grabbing his cell phone.

Heavy Pop sat behind the wheel with the vehicle idling.

AZ swooped into the car and exhaled. *Damn, that felt good.*

Heavy Pop sped away.

Baltimore was going to be shaken up by the news of Justice's murder. He was somebody major in the city, or at least the ghetto.

"Fuck that nigga!" AZ said.

EIGHTEEN

AZ walked into his home with a bright smile. Although he was still brooding inside, it didn't show at all. In fact, he walked over to Wendy, who stood in the kitchen, and hugged her from behind. With his arms wrapped around her, he said, "I love you, baby."

She was so shocked by his action. It felt like he didn't want to let her go. Where did the sudden mood change come from?

AZ rocked his wife in his arms and said, "I'm sorry. Let's start over."

Whoa, she thought. *Start over.* Yes, she wanted to start over. She didn't want to fight and argue with him anymore. She wanted her marriage to work.

AZ kissed her, and she kissed him back. His smile was warm, and the affection he showed was becoming irresistible. AZ became a little frisky in the kitchen. He touched her tits, kissed the side of her neck, and smacked her butt.

Wendy laughed. After everything they'd been through, she wanted to have some peace with her husband.

"Let's go upstairs and have some fun," he suggested, his hands and lips all over her. "The kids are in the living room watching cartoons."

She giggled like a schoolgirl. She could feel AZ growing an impressive hard-on. All of a sudden he scooped her up.

"Ohmygod, AZ, you gonna make me fall."

"I got you."

He carried her up the stairs and into the bedroom, where they undressed. Their naked bodies took comfort on the bed.

AZ thrust himself inside of her as they fucked in the missionary position. He only wanted to think about his wife. Tonight, no Baron and no Justice. It would be just husband and wife making sweet, passionate love in their bedroom.

Wendy held her husband tightly and shuddered beneath him when she came. She closed her eyes and gasped. She was still wondering what had come over him. They hadn't had sex this good in a very long time.

Afterwards, they cuddled. She lay nestled against his unclothed physique with a satisfied smile, and they engaged in some pillow talk. It felt like the good old days.

*

The next morning, Wendy was up early and getting dressed for work. AZ was also awake. She could hear him singing in the shower. Something was up. He never sang in the shower. Was it good or bad?

AZ offered to cook her breakfast. Now it was starting to scare her. What did he have planned?

Dressed in a black blazer, pinstripe pants, halter top, and carrying her satchel, Wendy walked into the kitchen to find AZ cooking eggs. The boys were eating cold cereal. The TV in the kitchen was on the morning news.

AZ turned and smiled at his wife. "Good morning, baby."

"Good morning."

With a very busy day ahead, Wendy didn't have time for breakfast. She was collecting her things and getting ready to bolt out the door when she heard the news broadcast.

"A local drug dealer was shot dead in West Baltimore last night ... "

Hearing that, Wendy spun around and stared at the television, the story immediately grabbing her attention.

AZ stood by the stove and observed her reaction and trying to read her body language.

"Drug dealer Mitchell Gabe, also known as Justice, was viciously gunned down last night on the corner of West Preston Street and Druid Avenue while he sat in his black Range Rover. Baltimore City police have no witnesses and no suspects in custody at this time. They say that Mitchell, who had a lengthy history of drugs and violence, was shot four times in the head last night . . ."

Wendy gasped when she heard the news. He could see the shock on her face. AZ was smiling inwardly, but deadpan on the outside.

Wendy stared at AZ to see if there were any signs of recognition from him, but he displayed nothing. Did he have something to do with the murder? It wasn't possible. She told herself that there wasn't any way her husband could have done this because he was a real estate developer, not a gangster. Plus, AZ had never seen a picture of him, and she had never told him Justice's name. So, no, AZ couldn't have done this. Since Justice was a big-time drug dealer with rivals and enemies, it could have been anyone.

"Is everything okay, baby?"

"Yeah, I'm fine."

"You knew the guy that was killed?" AZ boldly asked.

"No, he just reminds me of someone I prosecuted years ago."

"Oh, okay. Baltimore is a dangerous city. I'm sad that another black man has been killed in this city. The place is going to hell."

Wendy was in a brief trance. She really didn't hear her husband talking. She snapped herself back into her reality and left for work.

AZ smiled, wanting to pat himself on the back. He walked to the living room window and peered at Wendy walking to her car.

Before she climbed inside, when she thought no one was watching her, she started to cry. She wiped away her tears and took a deep breath. She got into her Porsche and drove away.

AZ frowned. *Bitch!*

NINETEEN

Cristal started to worry when Daniel's phone started going straight to voice mail. It never went to voice mail. Daniel was the type of person to always answer his phone, no matter who was calling. He was an easygoing guy with nothing to hide. So why wasn't he answering? He always kept his phone on and looked forward to having her call, though she never spoke a word. Cristal knew something was wrong.

"Julie, pick up for table two," Mark shouted out.

Her boss's voice snapped her out of her daydream. She had her cell phone in her hand and was thinking about Daniel. The diner was becoming crowded for the lunch rush on a Wednesday, with almost every booth and table occupied.

Cristal shoved the cell phone into her apron pocket and picked up the T-bone steak, French fries, and a baked potato meal for table two. It was going to a large man who looked like he was two meals away from having a heart attack. She skated his way, carrying his plate properly, and placed his food in front of him. He smiled up at her and thanked her for the meal. She hurried back to the kitchen to collect three more meals for customers, who had been waiting patiently.

The lunch rush went by rapidly.

Cristal sat at the countertop counting her tips from the morning and lunch crowd. So far, she'd collected forty-eight dollars.

Julie Norman's story had gotten around town, and the Christian folks of Idaho Falls found themselves looking out for her. She was quickly becoming one of their own.

Cristal hated the attention. She hated being someone's charity case. She hated that her hard-luck story had gotten around town to so many folks. Mark Morrow was a talkative man and had spread the word about her, and they came to help, sometimes leaving tips on their table and also letting it be known that if she needed anything, they were there to help.

But what Cristal needed was solitude. She simply wanted to do her job, go home, and hear Daniel's voice.

As if her day couldn't get any worse, Sherriff Harrison glided into the diner and took a seat at the countertop.

Cristal frowned. *Him again!* She was sick of seeing him. She could feel his eyes lingering on her. "Coffee, right?" she asked dryly.

"Yes." He smiled at her.

Cristal poured his cup of hot black coffee and set it in front of him. This time the Sheriff didn't come with a barrage of questions or harassments. He was calm. He looked deep in thought.

"Julie," he started to say, drumming up the courage to ask her out and apologize for his actions that seemed racist, but then a call crackled through his police radio about a four-car collision on I-15 involving a tractor trailer.

"Shit!" He looked at Mark and said, "Excuse my language."

"It's excused," Mark replied.

The sheriff lifted himself from the stool and sighed. Cristal kept her distance from him. She didn't even want to look his way. She was pleased he was leaving.

*

It was a long day at the diner for Cristal. She pranced around her apartment in her underwear. Once again she tried to call Daniel, but her calls were still going straight to voice mail. She was concerned about him.

She was starting to feel uncomfortable at work. Too many folks were asking questions and trying to meddle into her business. They were only trying to help, but she didn't ask for their help.

It was time for a change again, someplace farther away, maybe back to the East Coast. When she looked out of her window and saw the sheriff's car slowly cruising by where she stayed, she knew Idaho Falls wasn't the place for her anymore.

It was time to go.

✻

Sheriff Harrison walked into the diner out of uniform and with a smile on his face. He was dressed handsomely in a black suit, black shoes, and a blue tie. He carried a cheap bouquet of flowers. It was his moment to ask Julie out on a date, and he wasn't going to back out this time. He was off duty, so there weren't going to be any interruptions. The moment he stepped inside the eatery, his eyes whizzed around the place, looking for Julie, but he didn't see her.

"Mark, where's Julie today?" he asked.

Mark approached the countertop, wiping his hands on his apron. He looked Sheriff Harrison in the eyes. "She doesn't work here anymore."

The sheriff was taken aback. "What? She don't. Why? You fired her?"

"She quit on me yesterday. Said she was homesick and decided to go back home to Detroit."

The news was devastating to the sheriff, who suddenly dropped himself into a chair and sulked.

Mark and the other employees noticed his fancy attire and the bouquet of flowers. Mark was curious. "Why the suit?"

"It doesn't matter now, does it?" Harrison replied.

Who knew the entire time the sheriff was sweet on Julie? Well, he was too late. Julie Norman was long gone.

TWENTY

New Orleans was a different from Idaho Falls. It was a larger party city and a warmer place year round. Cristal was in the French Quarter. The area was vibrant with so many colorful people, sights to see, and a variety of food to eat. There was live jazz music in the streets with people drinking outdoors and roaming from bar to bar, their plastic cups filled with liquor. Dozens of folks were loitering above on balconies with elaborate ironwork and hanging from the windows cheering and hollering. It looked like Mardi Gras, but it was late December.

Cristal moved through the party crowd on Bourbon Street looking unassuming in a pair of shapeless sweat pants and white T-shirt, a scarf covering her head, and dark shades concealing her eyes. She had been in New Orleans two days now and was renting a room at the Holiday Inn near the Mississippi River. The bus trip from Idaho to the Big Easy took her four days.

Her first day in New Orleans, Cristal did nothing but sleep. Her hotel room was on the second floor, and she kept the shades drawn; the door double bolted, and the TV off, her small arsenal in the closet. Her cash was running low, but she didn't plan on looking for a job immediately. She didn't want to make the same mistake she'd made in Idaho. If she needed money, there were other ways to attain it.

The city was lively with bars, nightclubs, old-fashioned shops, street performers, impromptu jazz music on various street corners, eateries known for their gumbo, and much more. The town felt eerie to Cristal. It was her first time in New Orleans, and she'd heard so much about it, both good and bad. She'd heard that Hurricane Katrina had changed the landscape to most areas. The culture and the state had a strong belief in voodoo or hoodoo, and black magic was practiced a lot in the city. She passed a few old-style shops with mystical-looking voodoo queens dressed in long white gowns, dark skin, and dreadlocks promising to tell people's future for a price.

The allure was too much for Cristal to pass up. On Royal Street, she walked into one of the small storefronts that publicized reading tarot card and tea leaves for twenty dollars. The shop was bright and had a chilly feel to it. It was filled with all sorts of trinkets and offered a wide variety of items to help people in both learning and practicing spiritual and religious ceremony. Cristal walked farther into the shop and noticed distinctive tribal masks and statues from around the world, symbolizing ancestral connections with the spirit and earth.

A woman emerged from a back room, pushing through the colorful door beads. She was six feet tall with black skin and hazel eyes. Her eyes were almost hypnotic, and it looked like she could stare directly into your soul. Her dreadlocks were rich and brown, flowing down her back, and she was dressed in a long, flowing white robe and slippers.

She held her hand out to Cristal. "You've come to the right place."

Cristal sighed. She had left her belief in God a long time ago. However, something inside of her told her not to dabble in black magic. It was evil. It was dangerous grounds. But she didn't listen. She walked toward the woman like she was magnetic.

"You want your future told?" the woman asked.

"I'm just curious. I really don't believe in this shit."

"That's what they all say, until they see otherwise," the woman said. "By the way, my name is Lady Ida."

"And do you know my name?" Cristal challenged her.

Lady Ida smiled. "I see a troubled soul."

"I bet you do," Cristal replied dryly.

She followed the woman into the back room, which was decorated in velvet and lavender. The room was dim with purple lighting. A small round table with a purple tablecloth and a tiny antique lamp, with tarot cards and tea leaves under a lace handkerchief stood in the center.

Cristal had never seen anything like it. She was nervous. What if it wasn't bullshit? What if there was something true to voodoo and fortunetelling?

Lady Ida walked toward the table and motioned for Cristal to follow.

Cristal took a seat opposite the woman. A twenty-dollar bill exchanged hands. Lady Ida poured some warm tea into a tea cup and insisted that Cristal take a drink from it. She was hesitant at first, not knowing what to expect. It could be poison. It could be something to harm her.

Once again, she thought, *Why am I doing this?*

"It won't harm you," Lady Ida said.

Cristal looked intensely into the woman's face. Her eyes showed years of experience at this kind of thing. She lifted the tea cup and downed the tea. The flavor was mild, with a hint of sweetness. Not bad.

Lady Ida smiled. She made another cup of tea by opening a tin of loose-leaf tea and sprinkling the leaves into a cup of hot water. She was about to exercise her mental creativity. She blocked out all thought. She took a deep breath and tasted the tea. Then she focused on a particular thought. She left a small amount of tea at the bottom of the light-colored teacup. She held the nearly empty cup in her hand and gave it three good swirls and watched the tea leaves disperse around the interior of the cup. Then she dumped out the remaining liquid by turning the teacup over into a saucer.

Cristal had no idea what was going on. It all seemed strange to her.

Lady Ida was extremely focused. She had performed this reading hundreds of times, and each time she saw something different. She waited three breaths before turning the cup back over. She was now ready to begin reading the tea leaves for Cristal.

She saw an abstract pattern. She said to Cristal, "I see a man. He's someone who loves you deeply, and you love him too. He's far away, but somehow you're able to communicate with him. But if you continue to long for him, then you'll put his life in danger."

Cristal didn't admit that she was somewhat taken aback by Lady Ida's reading of the leaves already. The man Lady Ida probably was seeing was Daniel. She didn't know his name, but she could see his image.

"He's a handsome man, but I see him in grave danger."

Cristal remained deadpan. She could be talking about Daniel, and then again she could have had a lot of practice at telling people bullshit and making it come across like it was a message from the universe.

Next, Lady Ida picked up the tarot cards, holding the deck between her hands to warm the energy inside the room, and to focus on Cristal's thoughts, concerns, and questions. She shuffled the cards, and then she cut the cards three times and placed them into one pile. The cards were controlling her, not the other way around. The universe would soon be sending her a message.

Cristal sat still and silent, watching Lady Ida's every move. It looked like the cards were dancing and floating in her hands. It was a neat trick so far. Lady Ida could feel the energy flowing, and the cards were going where they needed to go. She laid the cards out across the table, starting with the center card and working through the houses they sat in. She started to turn over the cards.

Suddenly, Lady Ida jumped back, like a jolt of electricity had struck her. She looked frightened about something.

"What is it?" Cristal asked.

"I'll tell you what I've seen, but it will be an extra three hundred dollars."

"What?" Now Cristal felt it was all a scam. *Does this bitch think I'm stupid?*

But what Lady Ida said next had her in awe.

"There's a lot of blood around you. Death. And I see an older woman named Hattie."

Grandma Hattie. How did she know about her? Cristal now was taken aback completely. How could she know about her grandmother and her tragic death? *What the fuck!* Cristal thought. She reached into her small purse and pulled out three hundred-dollar bills and placed them on the table, and Lady Ida collected her fee.

"Tell me," Cristal said gruffly.

"I see a curse placed on your family. It was a curse placed a century ago by a voodoo priest. Your whole lineage, including yourself, will be wiped out by the hundredth year. I see cousins, uncles, aunts, parents, and grandparents that all die unnatural deaths."

Cristal shivered from the premonition. There was no denying, she did always feel that her family was cursed. Almost everyone was gone from her life, snatched away by violence, and not only those who were brutally killed that fateful Thanksgiving night. She remembered cousins shot down or stabbed by jealous girlfriends, and uncles struck by speeding cars. She lost two aunts in plane crashes in a two-year period. Year after year, there had always been some tragic death in her family. Everyone except for her.

Cristal wanted to know more. "Who put the curse on my family, and why? Is that person's lineage still around? Tell me more."

Lady Ida tried to read the cards again, but she saw nothing else. There was no more to foretell. Strangely, her nose started to bleed, trickling onto the table, with blood droplets landing on the tarot cards. Lady Ida then suddenly became extremely weak. She'd never felt anything like it. It felt like her body had been completely drained of energy. She placed both her hands onto the table and could barely hold herself up.

"You must go!" Lady Ida said.

"No! I need to know more," Cristal demanded. She stood over the suddenly weakened fortune-teller. She wanted answers. Now she did believe in black magic and voodoo. Lady Ida knew things about her that she'd never told anyone else.

Cristal wanted to kill Lady Ida. It could have been done so easily. But she also saw that the woman was in no shape to be roughed up. She did what she was paid to do. Violence wasn't going to help her out.

"I'll pay you five thousand dollars if you can tell me more about this curse and the person who placed it on my family."

Lady Ida refused. "Go!" she instructed loudly.

Cristal glared down at the weakened woman. It looked like she had aged ten years in minutes. There was nothing left there for Cristal. She heaved a sigh and pivoted away from the woman.

As Cristal was about to step away, she felt Lady Ida's icy hands suddenly grab her forearm. Lady Ida, her hazel eyes looking like they were on fire, stared up at Cristal. "If you reach out to him again, he will die! Your actions have already bound him into your fate."

The woman gave Cristal the heebie jeebies. She left the storefront and stepped out onto Royal Street for some fresh air. Cristal told herself that it was all a scam—nothing but an elaborate con. That woman knew nothing about her and was just some fake wannabe fortune-teller trying to run game on her.

Cristal arrived back to her hotel room and opened the bottle of wine she had purchased from a winery shop on Bourbon Street. She poured herself a glass and sat at the table. Everything Lady Ida told her, she erased it from her mind. Today, she wanted to relax.

She took a few sips of wine and dialed Daniel's number. He had to pick up this time. Daniel was safe. She knew it. She had been extra cautious. The Commission or GHOST Protocol didn't have a reason to kill him. She hadn't come around and had stayed away from him.

Once again, Daniel's cell phone went straight to voice mail.

There was no need to worry. He could have just lost his phone. There was no need to panic. Daniel was safe. Her enemies had no reason to go after him. She would get in contact with him again soon.

TWENTY-ONE

Mateo dropped two duffel bags of money at AZ's feet, payment totaling in the millions for another two hundred kilos. Mateo was flipping birds faster than they could breathe.

AZ was expecting Mateo to come around once a month, not every two weeks. "Didn't expect you so soon, Mateo."

"I told you, I'm a true hustler, and your product, it's gold," Mateo said.

"I know it is."

Their location was a protected one in New Jersey, and while they had off-the-cuff conversation, Mateo's men were loading another two hundred kilos of cocaine into a cargo van.

Heavy Pop stood in the background overseeing the transition of drugs and payment. AZ and Heavy Pop didn't need goons. Their pedigree was protection enough, and with Oscar backing them, no one would ever dare to cross them.

"I'm curious, where does it all go so fast?" AZ asked.

"I got clientele spread all over. Did you forget? My name is Mateo, baby, and I was hustling before I was even born. Anyway, why do you care? You're making lots of money from my clientele."

AZ smiled. "Yeah, I am."

"Anyway, I'm gonna need five hundred kilos in two weeks."

"Five hundred kilos?" AZ was shocked to hear such a high number.

"Yes, five hundred. Can you handle that order for me?"

Five hundred kilos was a great number. AZ couldn't just shit that amount of kilos out of his ass. He thought about it for a minute. He then looked at Mateo and said convincingly, "I got you."

"My nigga."

Mateo and AZ dapped each other up.

AZ picked up the two duffel bags and turned around and walked toward his truck, while Mateo climbed into the backseat of his new Bentley Mulsanne. AZ was impressed by the vehicle. He thought about getting one himself.

They watched Mateo drive off in his Bentley, the van loaded with two hundred ki's following right behind.

When everyone was out of sight, Heavy Pop said, "Five hundred kilos, AZ? What the fuck! He thinks we're Pablo Escobar?"

"We can handle this, Heavy Pop."

"I don't know. That's a lot of extra kilos to move around in concealment. And what is Oscar going to have to say about it?"

"Like he always has been doing—supplying us what we need because we keep paying him his money. We haven't fucked up anything. We're good at this. This is us. Look, it's about to be a new year, and things are definitely up for us, Heavy. If Mateo needs five hundred kilos in two more weeks, we're gonna supply him. Has he ever let us down?"

Heavy Pop looked doubtful. "Nah."

"Look, the nigga is legit. Believe me, if I felt something was wrong or had any clue that he was dirty, then he would have been a dead man from the start. I would have put a bullet in his head myself. But he's good, Heavy Pop. We're both about our money."

"Yeah, I guess you're right."

"Nigga, we just made two million plus. Let's go out and celebrate. Let's have us some fun."

"Let's go have some fun then."

*

AZ sat in VIP at Lucky Charms, a club on Manhattan's West Side. Heavy Pop sat across from him, and in between them were six sexily dressed females dancing provocatively, drinking high-priced champagne, laughing and smiling, and bumping and grinding against each other. The hip-hop music blared through the lavish 40,000-sq.-ft. club with two of the hottest DJs mixing everything from R&B to reggae. The full bar was swamped with patrons, and the dance floor was crowded.

Looking preoccupied in thought, AZ sat aloof from the party scene. A curvy, bootylicious, big-breasted video vixen sat on his lap and tried to plant a kiss against his neck, but he shied away from her.

"You don't want me?" she asked him. "We can fuck tonight, if you want."

"I'm good," he said.

She took his hand and placed it onto her breasts. Her flesh was soft, her eyes inviting. She could become his Burger King, but he wasn't interested in that type of meat.

Heavy Pop, on the other hand, was having the time of his life. The girls had him aroused, and he had his eyes on a thick beauty wearing the hell out of a sexy black dress. Her legs were as long as they come, and her long black hair swiveled around gracefully as she danced. Heavy Pop couldn't resist the temptation any longer. He got behind her and started to grind against her.

AZ was thinking about Oscar. He had called hours earlier and got in touch with his general, Pena. He told Pena that he needed to speak to Oscar, that it was important. Pena told him Oscar was busy at the moment, but he would definitely relay the message. Now AZ was waiting for the phone call. Oscar didn't do any business over the phone, only face to face. Five hundred kilos would be his biggest order, but AZ was confident that Mateo would have the full 11.75 million.

Leaving the club at three in the morning, Heavy Pop walked toward his ride with the sexy dressed woman under his arm. They both were giggling and smiling, ready to head back to his place.

AZ wasn't so festive. He still had a lot on his mind, including his wife and kids. He wasn't into pussy or partying.

"AZ, you okay?" Heavy Pop asked.

"I'm fine."

"I know tonight is not the night you choose to be faithful to your wife," he joked.

AZ didn't laugh, and Heavy Pop started to worry about his friend.

A few women lingered near AZ, hoping he would choose them for the night. But AZ was on his cell phone, sending out text messages to someone.

Heavy Pop was curious. "Who you texting?" he asked.

"Business."

"At three in the morning?"

"Money doesn't sleep."

"Take a break. Get your dick sucked."

The girls were open and ready, and they weren't offended by Heavy Pop's vulgar statement. AZ didn't give them a second look. Instead, he replied to Baron's text. The two had been texting back and forth since he was inside the club. Baron was the one who got his dick extra hard.

Heavy Pop said, "You got all this good pussy in your face and you acting like it doesn't exist? Have some fun, my nigga."

Two big-butt beauties tried to flirt harder with AZ. They spotted his Benz and peeped his jewels. The two gold-digging hoes were desperate to put a smile on his face with some freaky shit.

"C'mon, handsome. Let's go have some fun tonight," the girl wearing the short miniskirt with thick thighs said to him, grasping at his clothing and looking into his eyes.

The second club whore tugged at AZ's arm, slightly pulling him toward her direction. Her eyes displayed complete open-mindedness. Her full lips and mesmerizing black eyes could cripple any man and have him succumb to anything sexual.

AZ managed to smile.

"See, I like your smile."

Heavy Pop was watching his friend. Not once did he touch the ladies. He was worried about AZ's state with his family and his tenacity to move five hundred kilos. Oscar had already been leery about the fake "John G." moving two hundred ki's every two weeks. This wasn't 1988 and Oscar felt that was too much white gold for one man and one organization to move. But AZ continued to vouch for Mateo. Heavy Pop felt they were pushing their luck.

"I don't know about you, but I'm getting myself a suite at the Waldorf Astoria, and I'm going to enjoy my night with some sexy company," Heavy Pop said.

His female companion smiled widely. The Waldorf Astoria made a statement as to how rich these two men were. She couldn't wait to drop her clothes in such a classy and prestigious hotel and have sex in a fifteen-hundred-dollar-a-night suite. No man had ever taken her to the Waldorf.

Her two acquaintances were excited too. They wanted to go and continue the party in style. If AZ didn't want them, then they were ready to make it an orgy with Heavy Pop, who seemed man enough to take all three of them down in the bedroom. He was liquored up and horny, the two main ingredients for having a wild night.

"We wanna fuck you," the girls said loud and clear to AZ.

Heavy Pop was already climbing into his Escalade with his cutie pie with the dazzling eyes. He wanted to fuck so badly. He had an erection that felt like concrete in his pants. He squeezed her butt and touched her breasts repeatedly. He knew what he wanted.

Her friends didn't want to be left behind. They continued to pressure AZ until he gave in. Now, it was about to be a party at the Waldorf Astoria.

＊

The suite at the Waldorf Astoria was classy, but tonight, it had transformed into a heated orgy with two men and three butt-naked whores for whom, for the right price, nothing was off limits. Heavy Pop had his hands full with two ladies, as they twisted, bent, and grinded on the king-size bed, wrinkling bed sheets, and making it rock back and forth as Heavy Pop stuck his dick into every hole and crevice the girls had on their bodies. There was lots of moaning and groaning, and they weren't shy. It was freaky like they wanted it to be.

AZ sat naked in an antique oak accent chair, his dick being swallowed whole by the third whore who had a body to die for. She deep-throated him while he sat there pretending he was having a good time. She did everything possible to make him bust a nut, her head rapidly bobbing up and down in his lap, her long black hair flowing around his thighs like a mane. She wanted him to come inside her mouth, but he was thinking about Baron, and five hundred kilos.

She sucked AZ's dick like a porn star while Heavy Pop rammed his dick into the other girl, her face down in the pillow, while her friend toyed with Heavy's backside.

Suddenly, AZ's ringing cell phone made him push the girl away. It was an unknown caller. "Speak," he hollered into the phone.

"It's me, and Oscar wants to meet with you," Pena informed him in his thick Mexican accent.

"A'ight. When?"

"I'll text you the information." Pena hung up.

AZ held the phone in his hand, waiting for the text to come through, while the whore was primed on her knees, ready to finish what she started.

Heavy Pop didn't miss a beat. He continued to pound his fat black dick into the girl while he tickled her clit, causing her to holler repeatedly.

The text came through. AZ opened the text and read the information. The meet was for tomorrow night in Brooklyn. They wanted him to come alone this time.

Why Brooklyn? And why alone? AZ thought.

Damn, he didn't want to look nervous, but he was.

TWENTY-TWO

The dilapidated red-brick warehouse near the Brooklyn Army Terminal had been closed down for years. It was once a shipping and receiving place that employed over two dozen men for over twenty years. It was a job that helped put the workers' kids through college and provided middle-class living for families. Though the place had been closed down for nearly a decade, the building was still in use for something much more sinister. The industrial area was silent due to the late-night hour, and there was no passing traffic or pedestrians.

AZ climbed out of his Benz truck alone. It was the first time he would meet with the drug kingpin without Heavy Pop or Aoki by his side. He was nervous and could feel his heart beating like an African drum. He came armed with a pistol but decided to leave it in the vehicle. Most likely, they would search him from head to toe. Besides, what could he do with a pistol against men with machine guns and assault rifles? The warehouse wasn't a common place for AZ to meet with Oscar. Usually, they had their meetings at luxurious penthouse suites, five-star restaurants, or rooftop pavilions, where Oscar could flaunt his wealth.

AZ took a deep breath and walked toward the rusted steel door that looked like it hadn't been opened in years. He knocked twice on the steel door and waited. While doing so, he took in his surroundings, and trepidation crept inside his soul.

The door opened, and a burly armed guard with a deadpan expression and carrying a SIG SG 552 appeared before him. He stepped aside for AZ to walk into the building. Trepidation continued to swell inside of AZ as he traveled farther into the warehouse. Its décor was rotten and abandoned completely. He stepped on cracked concrete floors, and there was the distinctive odor of rats and rusty nails. There were long forgotten pallets and crates scattered loosely about. There were other men in the area, each one of them armed like they were in a Rambo movie. They all looked at AZ like he was prey.

AZ suddenly found himself feeling like a sheep that had wandered too close to the wolves. But he kept his cool. He wasn't going to show them any weakness. "Where's Oscar?" he said commandingly.

"He'll be out soon," said one of the guards. "You wait."

AZ sighed lightly and stood in the center of the room, surrounded by killers. The only thing he could do was wait and stay calm. He wasn't in control. Standing there, his mind racing like it was in the Indy 500, he suddenly heard a blood-curdling scream coming from a room. It was loud and echoed tremendously. The man's screaming went on for ten minutes, while AZ just stood there not knowing what was going on.

Then things went quiet. Was he dead, whoever it was?

The door to an office opened, and AZ was transfixed by that direction. Oscar stepped out of the room dressed in a bloody smock and rubber gloves. It was the first time AZ had seen Oscar dressed in anything but expensive linen or some showy attire. Behind him, AZ caught a glimpse of a naked man tied to a chair, and there was blood all over the room. The door shut suddenly. Something horrific happened in there, but it wasn't AZ's business. It was part of the game. He just hoped he didn't find himself in the same predicament.

Oscar approached. "Excuse my appearance, for it's uncommon for me to do business this way, but there was a matter I needed to handle personally," Oscar said coolly. He pulled off the bloody rubber gloves and tossed them to the floor. "Pena relayed your message, AZ. You want five hundred kilos suddenly. I'm curious. For who?"

"It's the same client, Oscar. They just increased their order."

"I see. And this client, they're from California, an organization called Blaque, if I'm not mistaken, right?"

"Yes."

"And they go from two hundred kilos to five hundred kilos?"

"Yes."

"You see my problem, AZ, is the sudden increase in your order. It raises some suspicion. As your people say, it raises some red flags."

"You can trust me, Oscar."

"I never trust anyone, and though I respect your loyalty and admire your ambition, trust is a fragile thing. But this organization from California, Blaque, it makes me wonder how loyal they are to you. And it makes me wonder about their ambition."

"Oscar, I told you before that I vetted them."

"Yes, you have told me that. But you see, now I need to vet him and his organization and the information you have given me doesn't check out. I need the contact number he has given you so I can vet this John from Blaque. One of my concerns is an organization growing stronger and starting their own manufacturing operation."

"I understand."

"And due to unfortunate circumstances with me at war with another cartel, I need to have eyes everywhere, and I need to know who's buying what and where. And though you work for my organization indirectly, you are still an employee to me, AZ."

AZ didn't want to say his real name, but what choice did he have? Oscar wasn't going to let him leave until he knew who was in charge of the Blaque organization that wanted to purchase five hundred kilos of his cocaine. Oscar was waiting for a name. He stared intently at AZ. His blood-covered smock was an intimidation.

"Well, John G., I think, is his government name," AZ uttered, still lying. "But the streets know him as Mateo."

"Mateo," Oscar repeated. "Mateo is the one you're supplying?"

"Yes, Oscar."

Oscar was immediately upset. "And you trust that fool? His reputation is trash in this business. And how is he able to suddenly afford such large quantities?"

"I told you, Oscar, I vetted him."

"He can't be trusted. You, my friend, have allowed greed to cloud your judgment."

"Business has been good so far, Oscar. Everything is running like clockwork."

Oscar's look toward AZ was threatening. He stepped closer to AZ. "I don't trust him. You shouldn't have either. Mateo's a snake, most likely working with federal agents."

"Moving that much weight, Oscar, it's unlikely. I mean, he's a hustler like us. He made some mistakes, but he bounced back and got his weight up. He's cool peoples. I know. I vouch for him."

Oscar still didn't look convinced. "I once warned you, AZ, to never bite off more than you can chew. Your jaws are fat and protruding, my friend, and you're not able to swallow, meaning, you'll soon choke to death if you don't spit some food out. Mateo is poison. I don't like him, and I don't trust him."

"You can trust me, Oscar. This deal won't come back on you. I promise you that. I'm loyal to you to the end."

Oscar continued to stare intently at AZ. There was no telling what he was thinking. The man was stoic, and his henchmen were close. One snap of his fingers, and AZ wouldn't leave the building alive.

"You know why I wanted you to come alone this time?" Oscar asked.

"Why?"

"Because you put too much trust into your friends."

"You mean, Heavy Pop?"

"There's an old saying that goes, never let your left hand know what the right hand is doing. And I wanted to see if you would listen to my instructions. You came alone as I told you to this place where many men weren't able to walk out alive, as you can see." Oscar gestured to the blood on his smock.

"I see."

"I will put together this order for you for one reason, AZ, for you to understand that you never bite the hand that feeds you."

AZ nodded.

"Come. I need to show you something," Oscar turned around and walked toward the room that he'd come out of earlier.

AZ followed the kingpin. Though he had relaxed a little, his heart was still beating a hundred and fifty miles per second. He was out of hot water, but the fire was still close.

Oscar turned the knob and pushed the door open. He allowed AZ to step into the dim room first. It smelled of blood and mold, and there was the naked man he had caught a glimpse of earlier. He was bound to a steel chair, his head slumped toward his chest, his body limp in the chair. AZ didn't know if he was still alive. It was hard to tell. His body had been mutilated something terrible. There was blood everywhere, and his fingers, ears, and testicles were displayed on the cold, concrete floor. The spectacle could've made anyone throw up. Bit by bit, they were tearing him apart with an assortment of medieval tools. It was a ghastly sight.

"Fuck!" AZ uttered.

"I guess you're wondering why I am showing you him. His name is Denardo, and he was once a general in my organization. He was like a brother to me, but I didn't trust him. He was good for my business. He was a feared man in my country, and I needed him. But he got too greedy and became power-hungry, and decided to betray me to my enemies, so he could take over my position. Denardo wanted to bite the hand that was feeding him. I took care of him, and I made him a god in our country with money, power, pussy, and respect, and yet he turned on me."

AZ noticed that the man was still breathing after everything they'd done to him. He was a tough muthafucka. There was a fourth man in the room that was tall and dark. He was shirtless, his upper body swathed with tattoos, and he too wore rubber gloves and was covered in the man's blood. His eyes were icy, and he gave AZ the chills. The way this man looked at him, AZ felt like he wanted to kill him too.

"In our line work, you can never put too much trust in one man, or into one organization. If you do, then it will lead to your downfall."

Oscar stretched out his hand, and the tall, chilling stranger placed a Glock 17 into his palm. Then he casually walked toward the tortured soul and stared at him. The inevitable was about to happen. Oscar placed the barrel of the gun to the man's temple, and he didn't even hesitate.

Boom!

Denardo's brains were blown out, and his blood and flesh scattered everywhere. His tormented frame finally collapsed.

Oscar didn't cringe. Murder was something he was used to. His eyes stayed fixed on his gruesome work for a brief moment.

Oscar turned to face AZ. "So, seeing this, AZ, it's a warning. Don't fuck me, because when I fuck you, it will be very painful."

AZ couldn't do anything but nod his head in understanding.

"Mateo is your problem to deal with. I don't trust him. But if he fucks you, you better not fuck me."

AZ knew what he was talking about—snitching wasn't an option for him. "I won't."

TWENTY-THREE

Mateo climbed out of his precious Bentley Muslanne with his cell phone to his ear and walked toward the boardwalk at Far Rockaway Beach. It was a nippy and brutal day, cold like a nun's tits, and the wind blowing at twenty-five miles per hour. The beach and the boardwalk were unoccupied because of the December cold.

Mateo smiled as he walked onto the lengthy boardwalk and replied, "Yeah, that's good to know. I'm ready for that shipment. I'm a hustler, baby. Let's get this money."

He hung up and continued to smile. Dressed in an expensive black parka, renowned as the warmest coat on earth, and his Timberlands, Mateo was snug from the cold and nasty wind.

He approached a man standing alone on the boardwalk. This man was gazing at the ocean and was dressed warmly himself, sporting a long trench coat and a wool hat. He stood with his hands in his pocket, his attention fixed on the waves as they crashed against the shore. He turned to see Mateo coming his way.

"You white boys and y'all cold weather," Mateo said. "We couldn't meet someplace warmer than out here? My face feels like it's about to numb up. Shit, give me the Caribbean, a strong cocktail, and some pussy in a skimpy bikini any day over this shit here."

The man didn't care about Mateo's griping. He was there for one purpose only. He looked at Mateo with icy blue eyes. "You have something for me?"

"Yeah, I got something for you. I always have something for you. When don't I have something for you?"

"When do you meet directly with Oscar?"

"I'm working on that."

"Work faster!"

"AZ trusts me," Mateo said. "He just got my five hundred kilos approved. Now it's just a matter of time before Oscar wants to meet me." The man nodded.

"Right after I meet with Oscar, y'all gonna pull me out?" Mateo asked.

"When the time comes," the man said. "And not before you and Oscar are on first-name basis. Don't forget this whole sting is about catching the big fish. Years back the feds thought they had him, but he wiggled out from under their grasp and made them look like incompetent assholes. That won't happen to us. All the red tape the DEA had to go through to approve all that cash for these clandestine drugs deals—Where do you think those millions are coming from? A lot of good programs have to suffer so that we can finally shut down a notorious drug cartel."

"All the DEA did was recycle confiscated drug money. You actin' like that money was pulled from public school meal programs or some noble shit like that. But I ain't my man."

"Look, do your job and stop being a wise ass!"

"I *am* doing my job—I handed AZ and Heavy Pop to you on a platter."

"We want more. Oscar is a career-changing arrest, and all those involved with taking him down will benefit."

"Look, don't whine to me about upgraded careers when I'm putting my life on the line every day. It was a risk asking for five hundred kilos. You know how fucked-up shit is today. No distributor is going that hard. What if Oscar gets suspicious?"

"You do what we tell you to do."

"And I don't mind doing it, but c'mon, we pushing our luck with these large quantities of cocaine shipments."

"It'll all be over soon . . . one way or another."

"That's what I'm afraid of."

Agent Taylor was DEA, and he was hungry to make a name for himself. He was one of two men that Mateo would report to.

The DEA had had their eyes on AZ and Heavy Pop for a while, and for years the two men had been cautious and smart. It was a risk thrusting Mateo back into the drug game, knowing his reputation was compromised among numerous organizations in the streets after he was busted a few years earlier. The DEA had to come up with a plan to plant him back into the drug game as a mole. So they fabricated a few documents, erased what was needed, and relied upon the cooperation of other snitches and paid informants to cement Mateo's newfound reputation and explain his absence.

Unbeknownst to AZ and Heavy Pop, Mateo's high-priced Bentley had been wired for sound and video. They'd also installed sophisticated surveillance into the box trucks and cargo vans that transported the drugs from AZ. The DEA had loads of footage of AZ and Heavy Pop, and the drugs stored at the DEA headquarters. They could arrest both men for drug conspiracy and indict them on so many charges they would both get life sentences. But Mateo's assignment was to get AZ and Heavy Pop talking about Oscar, and to try and have them set up a meet. They figured if Mateo became a major buyer from the duo, then it would grasp Oscar's attention.

Plan B was to arrest AZ and Heavy Pop, slap them with the RICO act, and have them turn against Oscar. If they were smart men, they would take the deal. The DEA had the two men right where they wanted them—dead to rights.

"Until next time," Agent Taylor said.

Mateo climbed back into his Bentley and lingered behind the wheel for a moment. He liked AZ and Heavy Pop, but he had no choice. The DEA had him boxed into a corner, and if he didn't cooperate, then he was looking at two life sentences. The deal his lawyer drew up guaranteed that he wouldn't do more than ten years in protective custody. When he got out, he could still have a good life. Mateo didn't want to die in prison. He was too handsome to rot away in jail, and he had his kids to think about. It was either them or him, and it wasn't about to be him.

TWENTY-FOUR

The Commission was a billion-dollar organization with clout worldwide. There was nowhere they couldn't go and nothing they couldn't do. Their agenda was to take the ghetto kids, the menaces to society, the unknown and the deeply troubled and transform them from degenerate human beings to trained killers. The Commission molded many young, skilled killers who had nothing to lose and sent them out globally, giving dozens of wayward souls a fresh start at an innovative and diverse life. Nothing like they ever experienced.

No one had any idea who started the Commission, but they were a board of powerful men shaping the world with the assassination of politicians, drug lords, tyrants, millionaires, and warlords. No one was safe from its reach. So it bothered them that there was a rogue assassin, one of their own who had been defying the odds and had cheated death for so long. With the Commission having a reputation to uphold, Cristal needed to die. Aoki was on the hunt, but if they had to, they were ready to send reinforcements.

*

Cristal sat in the warm, soothing tub with her eyes closed and just thinking about her life. Near her reach on the tiled floor was a fully loaded 9mm pistol with the safety off. The split seconds it took to take a weapon off safety could mean the difference between life and death.

The bathroom was silent, but her heart was heavy. How long would she be in New Orleans? Why did she come here? Where would she go next? Maybe she would go abroad and start her life somewhere far away from America. She thought about Australia, China, and Europe, where maybe she could settle in a small northern Italian town surrounded by rolling hills and green pastures and live a life of anonymity.

But it meant leaving Daniel. Hadn't she already left him, though? Why try to hold on to something that was almost impossible to have? If only she could take him with her. How good would that be to once again join the man she had fallen in love with, be able to hold him and kiss him, and to hold hands and walk somewhere peacefully. To laugh and converse, and to make love to him again. Oh, she missed making love so much.

Cristal hadn't had sex in months. It'd been so long, she almost forgot what it felt like to have a man inside of her. She used to love having sex.

Sitting in the tub, soaking her flesh, her body started to ache for it. She positioned herself inside the tub, spreading her legs wider, and then placed her hand between her thighs and slipped two of her fingers in her vagina. She started to finger herself in a repeated pattern, closing her eyes and moaning from her own pleasurable touch. She toyed with her clit, thumbing it gently, and cupped her breast. It was the best she could do for now. There was no denying it, she was in heat—hornier than a teenage boy.

After ten minutes of pleasuring herself, she removed herself from the bathtub and toweled off. She couldn't come. She'd tried, but it was a daunting task. She was used to having dick in her life.

Stepping out of the bathroom, she removed the towel, opened the blinds, and stood naked in the window with the lights on. Why was she doing this? She had no idea. Maybe it was exhilarating teasing some unknown stranger out there who could be watching her from a distance and jerking off to her enticing body. For several minutes she stood naked in the window. It was insane for a marked woman. So why was she doing something so stupid? In Idaho she did everything simple and didn't take any risks in exposing herself. But in New Orleans, she became bored and needed something to do. So she decided to take a chance and do something she hadn't done in a while, which was go out to a nightclub.

*

Wearing a sexy curve-hugging dress with a deep V front and stilettos, Cristal looked truly amazing when she walked into the jazz club. Her place of choice was the Balcony Music Club between Bourbon Street and Frenchman. It was a groovy atmospheric club that offered live performances from famous and up-and-coming musicians. The special thing about New Orleans, especially the French Quarter, was that it was always alive and vibrant with music. Cristal simply wanted to escape and switch things up.

Cristal had a lot of eyes glued on her when she entered and walked to the bar. She ordered a Shirley Temple, a non-alcoholic mixed drink traditionally made with ginger ale, a splash of grenadine, and garnished with a maraschino cherry. Drinking alcohol and becoming intoxicated was a chance she couldn't take, since she needed to stay focused and alert.

Several men approached her and asked for a dance, but she turned them down. None of them was her type, and she was only there to enjoy the show and take in some good music.

But there was one stranger in the jazz club who caught her eye. He was tall and dark with a thick goatee and haunting gray eyes. He was dressed in a gray suit that highlighted his muscular physique. He was a spectator in the crowd as the band on stage played phenomenal jazz. The guitars were strumming excitedly, and the horns were entertaining the crowd. The revelers threw back beers and liquor, and the atmosphere erupted in cheers and loudness. All that was heard was music and joyous shouting.

Cristal stood by the bar watching everything and everyone. She took in the scenery like a hawk and read the individuals close to her. Nothing or no one seemed to be a threat to her. But she had come with protection—knives in her clutch and a small Derringer fastened to her inner thigh under the red dress she wore. She ordered another Shirley Temple and happened to lock eyes with the tall stranger across the room. He smiled her way, but she didn't smile back.

"Is everybody having a good time tonight?" the lead performer shouted into the microphone. He was playing the saxophone, and his talent was magical.

The crowd erupted into cheering and hollering. People's hands were up in the air, and they were jumping up and down.

"Who in the crowd thinks they have some talent to come on this stage and play with us?" the saxophonist asked.

Several spectators wanted to join the band on stage. They were sure they had what it took to play with the band. It would be someone's lucky opportunity. So many people were pushing toward the stage, it almost looked chaotic from where Cristal stood. There was no way she was going to subject herself to the madness and embarrassment. She didn't know anything about playing an instrument, but at one time, before she became a killer, she did want to sing.

Out of the blue, Cristal's handsome stranger climbed onto the stage to join the band. She wasn't sure if he was asked to or if he made it his business to do it anyway. But there he was, standing over everyone and commanding their attention like he was their general. He grabbed a bass guitar and started plucking the strings of the instrument adeptly, falling right in harmony with the band, like the last piece to a puzzle. The audience started to go wild. Here was this spectator playing jazz like he was Charles Mingus.

Everyone started to dance. It was a full-blown party. For fifteen minutes, this man showed off like he was playing center stage at Madison Square Garden. Cristal was impressed by his performance.

If the crowd wasn't already standing, then he would have had a standing ovation. But the applause was deafening. The man dropped down from the stage looking like a celebrity. Everyone, even the band he joined, was praising him with high-fives and a slap on the back. He had lit up the nightclub with his performance on the bass guitar.

He glided toward the bar, where Cristal was standing. He ordered a shot of vodka and a draft beer. He downed the shot and sat right next to Cristal to drink his beer. His presence was alluring, and he was much more handsome up close. She noticed the gold Rolex peeking from under his white cuffs, and the cologne he was wearing smelled expensive. From head to toe, he was sophisticated and masculine.

She expected him to hit on her, but surprisingly he didn't. Instead, he turned to the curvy, blonde white girl seated to the right of him and tried to start a conversation with her.

Is he into white girls? Cristal became annoyed. She wanted some dick tonight, and he seemed like a suitable candidate. She couldn't vet him thoroughly right there, but she was willing to take a chance on him, if he had given her the chance. But the voluptuous blonde with the blue eyes caught his eye more than a beautiful black woman.

It'd been a while since Cristal had let her hair down and looked for some male company. Why tonight though, and in the city of New Orleans? Wouldn't it have been safer to let her hair down and have sex when she was in Idaho or in Washington? Maybe she wouldn't have enjoyed herself. The men there weren't interesting or exciting.

Maybe she was tired of keeping a low profile, running from state to state, and was willing to risk her life for one night of strong, passionate and crazy sex. She was still a woman with needs.

What she thought was a sure thing for the bass player with the pretty blonde turned out to be amusing for Cristal. The white girl blew him off. She had a man. In fact, she was married. She boasted the diamond ring on her ring finger and left him with egg on his face.

Cristal giggled. *Good for his black ass*, she thought.

"So you find me funny, huh?" he said to Cristal.

"Hilarious like *Def Comedy Jam*."

"I'm glad to have amused you."

"Well, I'm amused."

"You know, you're a very beautiful woman," he said.

"Obviously, you thought that snowflake was much prettier than me," she shot back.

"I saw you first."

"And what stopped you from talking to me?"

"Your look."

"My look?" she responded with a raised eyebrow.

"You seem to have this attitude about you."

"Oh, so a beautiful black woman standing alone in a nightclub now suddenly has an attitude, so you approach the white girl thinking she would be an easier fuck?"

"Look, I'm just here to have a good time and meet some pretty women."

"Well, you definitely got their attention with your performance on stage. You're good. You just went to the wrong bitch for some groupie love."

He laughed. "Thanks. I should have been a musician."

"You're better at that than being a playboy."

"Well, can I buy you a drink?"

Cristal shrugged. "I'm only drinking Shirley Temples."

"That's fine with me."

He signaled for the bartender and ordered another shot of vodka and a Shirley Temple. He downed the vodka quickly once again. Then he extended his hand toward Cristal and formally introduced himself. "My name is Kenny."

"Yvette."

They shook hands.

"Now that we've been formally introduced, what brings a beautiful woman like you here tonight alone, I assume?"

"Vacation."

"And where are you from?"

"California."

"Chicago," he said.

She studied and vetted him right there. His accent was for real, Midwest and northern, and he was dressed sharply like a northerner. But the man had eyes like Satan. His hazel eyes were mesmerizing. She tried to look deep into his soul.

"What brings you to New Orleans?" she asked.

"I just needed to escape."

"A life of crime?"

"No, my ex-wife and her family."

"Oh."

"Yes. I was married for ten years, and we have three kids together. My oldest is seventeen. My youngest is ten. Her family is very protective of her—my ex. Long story short, I cheated, her mother hated me, and I went through a nasty, nasty divorce. Two years of hell in courtrooms. She got custody of the kids, I gained a bad reputation, and I needed to escape. So I figured, what better way to escape than come to New Orleans and join the party?"

"Ten years, huh?"

"Yes. Have you ever been married?"

"Fortunately, no."

He laughed.

They had a few more drinks, and the conversation between them continued to flow. Though Cristal felt he'd ignored her earlier, she still wanted to be with him. Her body needed some sexual healing, even if it was only for one night. They both appeared to be damaged souls who had made mistakes in their lives. But hers was more damaging.

Cristal wanted to feel like a woman again. She wanted to be touched, kissed, and fucked a certain way.

As the night wore on, their connection grew stronger, and their conversation became more intimate.

Kenny ended up asking her, "You want to go to your place or mine?"

"Yours," she said without hesitation.

They both smiled and left the jazz club giggling and kissing, before climbing into the backseat of a cab.

＊

There was no time for foreplay. They both wanted the same thing. The moment they stepped inside his hotel room, they pulled each other's clothes off and became entwined in each other's arms.

Cristal had to break away from his lust suddenly and excuse herself to the bathroom. She had to stash the small Derringer she had hidden on her thigh. How would it look when he felt between her soft, inner thighs and felt the weapon? How would she explain that? She didn't want anything to ruin this night. She hid the weapon underneath the sink and exited the bathroom, and they continued where they had left off.

Kenny pushed Cristal's legs back on the bed and took careful aim at her pulsating pussy.

Her legs were spread, knees up, with him hovering over her, she was giving herself to him absolutely, no second thoughts. Her body needed it. And Kenny was well endowed.

"Just fuck me!" she uttered.

He wrapped up his big dick and shoved it inside of her, which made her squirm a little. The friction against her walls was pleasing. He started to grind with a beat. She was wet and her walls were tight. Her pussy was gagging on the huge meat shoved inside of her.

She wrapped her legs around Kenny and ran her nails down his back. He felt so good; she closed her eyes and moaned. His strokes were deep and pressured; she was being suffocated by his dick that was stretching out entirely inside of her.

"Mmmm . . . oh, oh," she moaned loudly.

He stroked his dick furiously into her, and Cristal was loving every minute of it. She had to shut her eyes and block Daniel from her thoughts. She had to escape from her worries and her fears to be able to catapult herself into an orgasm with Kenny. The sensation of his dick moving in and out of her, and the way he rubbed his mushroom tip against her pussy lips and clit, teasing her, made her want to explode.

Kenny took control over her body in the missionary position, and she almost couldn't move with him on top of her. She had to take her control back. She did a sweeping and cunning move on the bed, somehow using his weight against him, shifting her body slightly to the right, and Kenny suddenly was spun over onto his back in a flash, and she jumped on top of him, straddling in a heartbeat. She grabbed his arms and pinned them to the bed.

"Whoa! How did you do that?" he asked, shocked.

He must have outweighed her by a hundred pounds, but still she was able to lift him and rotate him like he was a child.

"You like it?" she asked.

"So you like being on top, huh?"

"I like being in control."

Kenny smiled.

Once again, his large erection found itself inside of her, and she started to gyrate her hips against his pelvis, milking his dick to come. They both moaned and groaned. He thrust upwards into her, pumping and filling her with ecstasy. She released his wrists and placed her hands against his chest and fucked him hard, riding him like a jockey. Kenny was enjoying every moment of it.

"Damn, your pussy feels so good. Ooooh shit. You feel so good on my dick," he said, digging his fingernails into her ample butt cheeks. He carved himself into her deeper, harder, and faster, fucking Cristal with all his might.

On top of him, she wanted to feel heaven for once and use his dick to make herself come. She was soon there.

She moaned, "I'm gonna fuckin' come!"

"Go ahead. Come on my dick!" he said feverishly.

Subsequently, she lay nestled in his arms, her face against his smooth, thick chest, and the aftermath was breathtaking and nourishing.

Cristal definitely knew how to pick 'em. He did her body right and gave it some needed justice. But after tonight, she wouldn't be able to have him again. She would be gone, or he would. There would be no more rounds and no more hooking up because she wouldn't take his number, and she didn't have a number to give.

"How long are you in town for?" he asked.

She told him, "Until tomorrow night," but she wasn't sure herself.

"I wish I could see you again."

"I can't."

"Why not?" he asked.

"It's complicated."

He sighed heavily. "I see."

He gently removed her naked physique from his warm hold and lifted himself from the bed, leaving her sprawled naked against the sheets, peering up at him. His backside was well developed like a professional boxer. He showed off no tattoos and no scars, and his chocolate-covered flesh looked like it was poured perfectly on him.

As he walked toward the window, Cristal kept her eyes on him, not because she saw him as a threat, but he was eye candy naked.

With his back turned to her and gazing out the window, he said, "I had a really good time with you tonight."

"I did too."

"You weren't what I expected," he uttered.

"You weren't either."

"I wish I could really see you again, but you say it isn't possible. I know it's not possible. Life is crazy, the lives we choose and the people we hurt. To see dawn again and to go back . . ."

To Cristal, he sounded like he was babbling. But she was listening. Something was suddenly off about him. She kept her eyes fixed on him.

He continued with, "The sex was amazing. It was something like a last meal for you, *Cristal*."

Hearing her name, she became wide-eyed. She'd never told him her real name. How did he know it was Cristal?

Kenny suddenly spun around holding a 9mm with a silencer at the end of it and fired bullets rapidly her way.

Phew! Phew! Phew!

Cristal quickly leaped from the bed and scurried into the bathroom as feathers exploded from the pillows that the bullets slammed into. She desperately reached for her small Derringer underneath the sink as Kenny charged toward the bathroom and continued to shoot at her. Bullets tore through the door, splintering it.

Kenny shouted, "You can't run from fate, Cristal. It's your time to die!"

Cristal had to think really fast. She stood poised near the door. Naked with her Derringer in hand, she took a deep breath. She was trapped like some rat in a hotel bathroom. The door was locked, but for how long? She only had four shots to take him down, and he had almost a full clip.

"Open this fuckin' door, bitch!" he shouted, trying to bang it down.

The first thing she needed to do was disarm him. Her training on The Farm needed to come in handy. The bathroom door wasn't going to shield her from Kenny forever, if that was his real name.

Phew! Phew! Phew!

He fired three more slugs at the solid wood door, damaging the hinges and making it easier to kick in.

Cristal readied herself and kept count—nine shots fired so far. But how many rounds did he have in his clip? She stood perched on the sink, and when the door was forced open and Kenny came storming into the bathroom, she fired four hurried shots, but they weren't kill shots. Kenny maneuvered himself promptly away from her weapon just in time, but one bullet was able to slice through his shoulder, and another bullet missed his head by inches.

She lunged at him, her first priority to disarm him. She hit him with two punches to the face and was able to knock the gun out of his hand, and into the toilet. But he was still a threat.

Hand-to-hand combat ensued between them. He was big and strong. He lunged at Cristal belligerently, but she managed to sidestep his attack and countered with a snapping kick to his face and then his shoot.

Kenny stumbled backwards, but it wasn't enough to take him down. He glared at her and growled, "You're dead, you hear me? Dead!"

He charged again and swung at her with intensity, trying to knock her head off, but she ducked speedily and slammed a blow dryer into his ribs. He recoiled from the blow, but he didn't fall. He countered with several punches of his own, and Cristal blocked them desperately, but the force from him was staggering.

He was quick too, adept in combat, and there was no way she was going to defeat him with just her fists and hands. She needed to use her wits.

He roared at Cristal and swung crazily, but she moved quickly, and his fists slammed into the bathroom wall and created two gaping holes.

"You're a fast little bitch," he shouted.

Cristal needed to escape from the bathroom. It was too cramped, and he was just too big and strong. He charged again, and this time he was able to wrap his muscular arms around her. He gripped her up tight into a bear hug, seizing her arms and trapping them to her sides, and carried her into the room. He wanted the million-dollar bounty on her head.

She squirmed in his crushing grasp.

"I'm gonna fuck you up!" he shouted.

She wasn't about to give up. She suddenly head-butted him several times, dizzying him, and then she kicked repeatedly into his outer knee with much force, staggering him.

Finally free, Cristal darted to retrieve her small clutch near the bed. Inside it were two small survival knives that could cut someone's flesh fiercely.

Kenny regained his footing. His forehead and nose was bleeding, and she'd almost broken his knee. He was fired up with rage, huffing and puffing.

Cristal held both small knives in her fists, ready to protect herself.

Kenny wanted to punch holes in her flesh and tear her bones from her body. There was no way a woman was going to get the better of him. He had taken down many strong men, either with a weapon or his bare hands. But this little bitch was giving him a run for his money.

"So you wanna play with knives, huh, bitch?" he growled.

"C'mon, muthafucka!" Cristal shouted. Her hard glare transfixed on his every movement, she was ready to show him how adept she was.

They both were still naked and bleeding, their attraction and lust for each other having quickly transitioned into a death match.

He took a few steps closer, crowding her open space. Once again, he charged at her, trying to tackle her like he was a linebacker, but she sidestepped and quickly cut him several times with both knives, ripping open his side and his biceps.

Cristal smirked. "You wanna continue to play with me?"

Now Kenny was furious. She had nicked him good, but pain was his friend, and he was going to show her how a warrior handles himself.

Once again, he began to crowd her, and she stood ready with her knives. He charged at her, and when she went to strike, he dropped to the floor and executed a sweeping motion that swept her off her feet and sent her crashing to the ground.

He stood up and kicked her sides several times, while she was on her hands and knees.

Cristal cried out in pain. Her knives weren't in her reach. She was now on her hands and knees, scurrying toward the bed.

He grabbed her by the back of her neck, elevated her into the air, and hoisted her over his head, rendering her vulnerable to anything. He hurled her across the room like a ball, and Cristal went crashing into the dresser, the room mirror breaking around her, and shards of glass cut into her skin.

He laughed. "I told you, bitch, you gonna die tonight!"

Cristal was dazed and injured, bleeding and winded. Now, it was his turn to toy with her. He grabbed her ankle and dragged her across the room. She tried to resist, but he thumped her in the back and made it feel like her spine had snapped in two. She howled from the pain. He turned her over to see her pretty, young face bloody and bruised, and then he punched her in the face several times.

Cristal wanted to black out. Her mind was trying to go unconscious, but she knew if that happened, then she would never wake up. He was going to kill her.

He wrapped his hands around her slim neck and squeezed. His hands were crushing. She gasped for air and fought vigorously, grasping and clawing at his wrists, frantically trying to prevent her death, but Kenny's hands were clamped securely around her throat like a vise grip. He wasn't about to let loose until he squeezed every drop of breath from her body.

"I've been sent to end you. Too bad, because you have some of the best pussy I ever had."

Cristal didn't have much time left. She could feel her life slipping from her body. Her breathing was becoming thin.

With one hand still grasping at his wrist, she stretched out her other hand across the floor to snatch something frantically nearby to help keep her alive. Fortunately, her fingers came upon one of her small knives on the floor. She grasped the sharp tool, and in one quick shift, she thrust her knee into his groin and slammed the knife into his neck.

Kenny jerked from the blow, and an abrupt rush of pain jolted his body. He immediately tried to stop his wound from gushing blood.

Cristal pushed him off and scurried to her feet. Shockingly, with the blade protruding from his neck, he still wasn't dead. In fact, he stood erect, glaring at Cristal while he pulled the knife from his neck and blood squirted out.

"You sneaky little fuckin' bitch!"

Shit!

"I underestimated you," he said. "You're good. I haven't seen my own blood in almost twenty years. The Farm did you justice, and Bishop, he made you even better. Too bad he's dead because of you."

The mention of Bishop angered Cristal. No doubt, GHOST Protocol had sent him. They were both standing now in the messy room that had been torn apart by their battle.

Blood flowed from Kenny's broken nose, his neck wound, and his body, and Cristal was in bad shape too.

Once again, Cristal primed herself for combat. She had one special move to pull.

"A different life we had, a different time . . . we would have been great lovers instead of adversaries," he said poetically.

He suddenly propelled toward her with a shard of mirror he'd picked up, and Cristal instantaneously reacted when he tried to slice her face apart with the bloody tool. They tangled in quarrel, matching deadly skills.

Cristal then struck him suddenly in the *V* area underneath his ribs, the place where the sternum ends, and she thrust her second small knife into him.

Kenny jerked and grunted, "Ugh," and stumbled backwards. He reached for the second knife protruding from his flesh.

The blade had paralyzed him as he struggled for breath, and then he doubled over and dropped to his knees.

Cristal stood there in silence, simply observing him dying slowly. She had finally defeated him.

"You fuckin' bitch," he uttered before he keeled over.

There was no time to gloat or rejoice. Cristal hurriedly got dressed and collected her things. She made a speedy exit from the hotel and hurried back to her own room to pack and leave town. Somehow they had tracked her down. How were they able to track her to New Orleans she didn't know. She had been careful, or so she thought. But The Commission and GHOST were very resourceful and highly organized.

Her sexual urges had almost cost her her life. Never again. She left New Orleans that same night.

*

Two days later, Cristal settled in the remote Shenandoah Mountain of Rockingham County, Virginia, with no phones, no Internet, no television, and no neighbors for miles. There, she took comfort in a log cabin nestled deep in the cold mountains. She brought in the New Year alone and hiding from The Commission and GHOST Protocol. There, she would tend to her wounds and heal, and she would spread out her arsenal and train in the woods.

Cristal needed to rest and come up with a final game plan for herself. Running and hiding from the agencies was definitely taking a toll on her. There had to be a solution to escape the madness. So far, the only real escape she saw for herself was death. She had really pissed them off, writing books about them, revealing their secrets, talking about her training on The Farm and the people she had killed. It was blasphemy in the eyes of her ex-employer. Her books sold extremely well nationally and internationally, and the pseudonym she wrote under had become a household name in the literary world. And she had killed several of The Commission's men and now GHOST Protocol.

Still, she wondered how they'd found her in New Orleans.

Taking no chances, Cristal rigged the entire cabin and the surrounding area with booby traps. Scattered around the cabin were simple *trous-de-loup*, concealed pitfalls with sharp spikes at the bottom, something she'd learned to do on The Farm. She knew the key areas to step on once she stepped out of the cabin. Also, the ground was rigged with motion sensor lightings. If anyone stepped too close to her cabin at night, the whole area would light up with blinding lights, giving her a few precious seconds to arm herself for attack.

Inside the cabin at night, with the fireplace burning and the area tranquil and silent, Cristal decided to call Daniel once more via satellite phone. His phone rang several times and then someone picked up.

"Hello?" Cristal said frantically.

"Hello, Cristal," a woman's voice answered.

Cristal knew something was wrong. And the woman knew her name. She felt trepidation. "Where's Daniel?" she asked.

"Him busy."

"If you touch him—"

"Me know de routine—yuh kill me."

Cristal felt helpless. This bitch had Daniel, and she had no idea where they were.

"Time ah runnin' out."

The call ended.

Cristal cursed loudly. She had to find him. Her stay in the Shenandoah Mountains was suddenly cut short. It was back to civilization.

TWENTY-FIVE

Aoki had to admit that she had fucked up big time. It wasn't her intention to murder Daniel so soon. He was supposed to be leverage to lure Cristal to her. But something about him bugged her. The way he spoke so fondly and lovingly about Beatrice and their unbridled determination to beat the odds and stay connected had irked her. Why should their love transcend The Commission's boundaries? Girls like them don't get happily-ever-afters. Aoki wasn't afforded that luxury. Fate had stepped in and shut love down for her and Emilio, so why should Daniel and Cristal's thrive?

Human life was of no value to her. Within a day of kidnapping Daniel, she had taken her trusty dagger, stood behind him, then grabbed him forcefully and cut open his throat from ear to ear. He had struggled to stay alive, squirming violently in her grasp, begging and pleading for her not to kill him, but his efforts were in vain. He had gagged and bled like a stuck pig. Still tied to the chair, his body slumped as his life drained.

Immediately, Aoki began to fear for her own life. What had she done? She was so impulsive and fucking stupid.

What she had going for herself was Daniel. All she needed to do was have him speak into the phone to Cristal and then wait for her to show up like a superhero to try to save her man. Now her plan had gone up in smoke. Aoki figured that Cristal was too smart to fall for the ruse that Daniel was still alive. At some point she would ask for proof of life. Aoki didn't have a choice. When Cristal called, she set the trap, hoping that Cristal would take the bait.

She'd heard about the attempted hit on Cristal in New Orleans that left a GHOST Protocol assassin dead in a hotel room. If he'd succeeded in killing Cristal, it would have looked bad on her. And she couldn't look bad. She couldn't fail. The Commission had given her ten weeks to complete her assignment, and time was quickly running out.

TWENTY-SIX

The house was silent, with Wendy and the boys having gone out for the day. AZ was in his private home office, sitting at his desk with a bottle of vodka, trying to take comfort in his leather chair. He downed the clear liquid in the glass and quickly poured himself another. He downed that too. He then leaned forward, placing his elbows against the desk, and clasped his hands together. There was so much going on, from his personal life to the street life. Mateo was still waiting on his five hundred kilos. It'd been several weeks now, and still, AZ wasn't able to deliver. It was making him look bad. He continued to assure Mateo that he would get his drugs.

Oscar had to hold back this shipment due to internal problems with his organization and delivery issues with his trucks and Drug Enforcement Agents. Before the year ended, Customs and DEA agents combined had pulled over three 18-wheelers in separate locations—Austin, Houston, and at the Mexican border—and seized over eight hundred kilos of cocaine altogether with a street value of fifty million dollars. Suffice it to say, it was a major blow to the cartel.

AZ knew the effects of that many kilos being seized would trickle down. He knew there were going to be severe consequences and people murdered behind this shit. There was no way the police had gotten that lucky. There was a snitch inside Oscar's organization, and until the matter was resolved, everything had been shut down. It angered AZ, but what could he do? He simply had to stand on the sidelines and wait for the game to continue.

But that wasn't his only issue. His family life was falling apart.

He poured himself another shot and threw it back. He stared at the paternity test results that had arrived. It sat on the middle of his desk taunting him. He was hesitant to open the package, knowing the wrong results would change his life entirely. He needed some liquid courage.

AZ had swabbed the mouths of his children without Wendy knowing and sent the kit to the lab to be examined after Lisa's impromptu visit. He had to know. Lisa had planted that bug in his head. There was no telling who else Wendy had fucked since they got together. How long had she been fucking that punk, Justice? Could he be Randy's and Terrance's father?

The results were that he was 99.9% not the father of either boy. The news was devastating to him. He couldn't believe it. Reading the results made his blood boil.

"Fuckin' whore!" he growled, tears running down his cheeks.

AZ went through a swirl of emotions—disappointment, hurt, rage, anger. He sat in his chair and downed more vodka. Knowing neither of his sons was his biologically, he felt paralyzed with resentment. All this time he thought he was playing Wendy. He thought he had the best of both worlds by marrying an assistant state's attorney as a lifetime drug dealer who secretly liked men. But in the end, she was playing him—twice pregnant by some other man.

"Fuckin' whore!" He tossed the glass at the wall and watched it shatter.

AZ stood up and walked toward the window. It was starting to snow outside. Whiteness and ice blanketed his backyard. The trees were bare, their leaves having fallen months earlier, and his back and front yard looked barren, just like his life had started to look.

Whatever they needed, and whatever Wendy needed, he had provided for them. He was seething with so much anger, his blood started to feel like acid inside of his body. He wanted to take that same acid he felt inside of him and pour it all over his wife so that bitch could melt and scream in agony. There was no way around his pain. He couldn't escape from it.

He curled his fingers into a fist and plunged it into the window, spider-webbing the glass. He suffered a few minor cuts on his knuckles, but it was nothing compared to what he felt in his heart.

All over his home were pictures of his beloved family, from his home office to the hallways of the mini-mansion to the fireplace mantel. He'd once cherished the pictures of him with his sons, and he now loathed every single one.

Walking into the kitchen, he placed the paternity results on the kitchen island, where Wendy couldn't miss them. He went into his pantry and grabbed another bottle of vodka. He was going to try and drink his pain away to escape the hurt, but everything in his house was a reminder of his wife's infidelity and two boys that weren't even his.

He opened the bottle, took it to the head, and guzzled down a large amount of the liquor. He dropped into a chair, still drinking, and sat in the dark, waiting for Wendy to come home. He was eager to confront her and see what type of lie she would come up with.

Two hours later, Wendy's car pulled into the driveway. From where he sat, AZ could hear every movement she made outside. Everything was off in the house, and the place was dark. He heard one car door shut. She didn't have the kids with her, which was for the better. There was about to be hell in his house.

Wendy marched toward the kitchen's back entrance. She was in a wool trench coat with a faux fur collar, shielding her from the bitter wind. She strolled inside looking like a million bucks, long black hair flowing, eyes glinting, because at that moment, life was good. She had secured a guilty verdict from the jury. It was another notch on her record, bringing her closer to a judgeship.

The lights came on in the kitchen, and seeing AZ seated in the dark with a liquor bottle in his hand she jumped back and placed her hand over her heart.

"AZ, you scared me half to death."

He didn't respond. He simply sat there frowning.

"You okay?" she asked him.

He remained silent.

It didn't take Wendy long to find out what was eating at AZ. She glanced at the kitchen island and saw the paperwork. She walked to it with nosiness and picked it up. Her eyes quickly scanned over the writing and the paternity results. She gasped at what she was reading. Her mouth was wide open.

"AZ—"

The moment she turned around to speak, he was standing right behind her. He snatched the papers from her hands and pushed them into her face. "You cheating bitch!" he screamed.

Then he pounced on her. His straight right to her face sent her flying across the island and almost blacked her out.

Wendy scurried toward the kitchen drawer and went for a knife. She looked fiercely his way, her eye blackened and droplets of blood coming from her nose.

"You wanna play with me, bitch?" he shouted.

"Get the fuck out my house!" she screamed.

"Your house? You better drop that fuckin' knife."

She gripped it harder and pointed it at him, but he wasn't fazed by her threat. He was drunk, angry, and ready to spread vengeance.

He pulled out something much more threatening—his loaded black

Glock 19—and pointed it at her. Wendy stood wide-eyed. AZ looked like he was ready to kill her dead.

"All this time, and they're not my kids," he griped.

"Of course, they're not your kids!" she admitted boldly. "You never fucked me!"

"What?"

"You don't know how to fuck me right, AZ! Because you don't like pussy, muthafucka! You think I don't know about you? You're a fuckin' faggot!"

AZ kept steady aim at her head. He was tempted to squeeze the trigger and blow her fucking head off. Hearing his wife holler that he was a faggot made his skin crawl. What made her assume he was gay? He had always been careful.

He lunged at her and smashed the butt of the gun against her face. She screamed and fell to the floor. AZ stood over her and shouted, "I'm no faggot!"

Wendy was shaking with fear. Her mouth and nose started to bleed more. She hugged the kitchen floor and cried.

He pointed the gun at her head. Every fiber in his body told him that she deserved to die. "I should kill you for lying to me. You played me for a fool all these years."

"You never loved me," she cried out.

"Because you're a fuckin' whore!"

The damage had already been done. Her face was bruised and broken apart. Her blood was dripping on the kitchen floor. She was on her hands and knees, and she expected to die by his hands.

"You think I didn't know about that white boy?"

"I'll kill you, bitch! Keep talking."

He threatened to kill her if she got him arrested again. There was no way he was going back to jail.

"I'm not the man you think I am, bitch! I'm somebody you do not want to fuck with. I will personally see to it that not only you but your family die too," he said through clenched teeth.

It was hard to tell what was coming more from Wendy, blood or tears.

AZ gave her one hour to pack whatever the boys needed and to leave his home. The kids had to go too. He didn't want to be anywhere around them. He couldn't bear to look at them. AZ knew that the mere sight of them would break him. It would be too painful.

Wendy knew not to take his threat lightly. The look on his face was ominous.

He nonstop pointed his gun at her, threatening to take her life. He told her to leave the car keys, the clothing, the furs, diamonds, and everything he'd bought her. She was to leave with the clothes she had on her back and the boys' items. In fact, he was tempted to have her strip down to nothing and kick her out butt naked in the cold. The faster she left the house, the better.

AZ sent his wife flying out the front door, in the cold, her face anguished with dismay and horror. He slammed the front door and then fell to his knees. He felt ashamed, embarrassed, and outraged. It was moments like this that he missed Aoki. He wished she was still alive so he could confide to her about his wife. She was the only friend he could talk to, the one who knew everything about him and from whom he hid nothing.

But Aoki had made her own bed, and she had to suffer for her choices. Oscar had told AZ that he'd murdered Aoki and asked if he had a problem with it. At the time, he was pleased with his decision. Oscar had done his dirty work for him. He and Aoki were at odds, and it was inevitable that one was going to kill the other.

But when the dust settled, AZ realized that Aoki didn't deserve to die the way she did. She had been gunned down and her body thrown in some dirty marsh to never be found. There had been no proper funeral, nothing at all. Aoki and her crew had taken a contract that was way over their heads, and it was a death sentence for them. There would have been no way Aoki and her crew would have come out of that nail salon alive.

A small part of AZ felt responsible for setting her on the path that ultimately led to her death.

*

On a 53-meter luxury yacht with six cabins, an outdoor bar, and a Jacuzzi, Oscar emerged from his master suite cabin and stepped onto the deck port-side. Dressed in a pair of white linen pants, barefoot, and shirtless, he stared up at the sun and smiled. It was a beautiful day in January. The temperature was 85 degrees, and the dazzling blue waters were calm and soothing. His yacht was anchored in the Atlantic Ocean, three hundred miles away from Miami, Florida. In fact, he could almost see Cuba in the horizon.

He lit a cigar and inhaled the smoke, his eyes stuck on the ocean. The stillness of the sea was therapeutic. The earth, the sea, and their beauty was his medication. A loss of eight hundred kilos with a street value of fifty million dollars would have crippled any organization, but not his. He was a big fish, able to swallow a massive loss like that and still swim faster and deeper than the other fish.

That didn't mean the people responsible for the loss wouldn't have to pay. There had to be retribution. He had to make a statement. The DEA knew exactly which trucks to target, and where and when. Oscar was angry about the seizure, but he kept his cool.

He puffed on his cigar and made his way toward the back of the boat. The deck wood felt easy on his feet. There was nothing better than being barefoot on a yacht in the Atlantic Ocean on a bright and sunny day. There was nothing to interrupt his blasé mood for miles. He walked farther toward the back, and then he went from stepping on a smooth wooden deck to plastic lining that was spread everywhere across the stern.

Oscar smiled and looked at the five naked, beaten men on their knees, their heads lowered to the floor, their wrists tied behind them. Four of his henchmen held them hostage at gunpoint.

"Gentlemen, I'm sorry it had to come to this," Oscar said.

"Oscar, look, we had nothing to do with Texas. I swear," one of the men cried out.

"Fifty million dollars is a lot of money to lose, Hector. And though I'm still a very rich man, I hate to lose that kind of currency, especially to the States."

"I know, but we didn't talk. We didn't tell anyone anything about your shipments. I swear it wasn't us."

Oscar took another pull from his cigar and walked closer to the men. He stood directly in front of them. He could either be their savior or their Grim Reaper. All five men were shivering with fear. He hadn't brought them deep into the Atlantic just to have some friendly chitchat.

Oscar's eyes didn't show any empathy. He squatted down, looking into their frightened eyes. "If you didn't do anything, then why ask for my forgiveness?"

The men were all shaking, and one had peed on himself.

"*Usted elige la manera que quieres morir, el cuchillo o la pistola*," he said, giving them the choice to die by the knife or the gun.

"Please, I have a family!" one cried out.

Once again, in a deadpan tone, Oscar said, "*¿Cuchillo o la pistola?*"

They couldn't decide. Either way, their choice would lead to their deaths.

Frustrated that the men were crying out and not choosing their deaths respectfully, he stood up and exclaimed, "Fine. I'll decide for you all."

He looked at the first man and uttered, "¡*Cuchillo!*"

Quickly, one of his henchmen reacted, placing a Bowie knife to the man's throat and carving into his neck, spilling his blood. He gagged and choked and then collapsed face down against the plastic lining. His blood pooled underneath him.

Oscar looked at the second man and uttered, "¡*Pistola!*"

A Desert Eagle was placed to the back of his head and his brains were blown out. He dropped dead.

Three men remaining were quivering and crying.

Oscar said, "¡*Pistola!*" and a round was fired into the back of the third man's head.

For the last two men, Oscar said, "¡*Cuchillo!*" and their throats were cut viciously like the first man's.

The plastic lining soon turned crimson with their blood. Oscar stepped back from the pool of crimson, not wanting to get their blood on his feet, and stared down at the bodies.

"Clean this up," he instructed his men, and he turned and walked away.

His goons wrapped the bodies in body bags before weighing them down with dumbbells and tossing each man overboard. Each body went sinking slowly down to the Atlantic floor.

Oscar went back inside his yacht and went to his bar. He needed a drink. He poured himself a glass of Richard Hennessy Cognac, priced at $4,800 a bottle. He needed to taste the good stuff. He was still warring with another cartel, and the pressure was building in the United States. The DEA, FBI, ATF, and Homeland Security were all gunning for him. They wanted to lock him up in an American prison, throw away the key, and let him rot away. He wasn't going to allow such a grim future. He would rather die in Mexico than be imprisoned in America.

He was retreating to Mexico, his mother's homeland, where he had the protection of his Gulf cartel. He had to pack up his organization in the States and flee. He didn't want to, but he refused to be captured by any authority.

Oscar walked toward the window, glass of cognac in his hand, and stared outside. He took a few sips. Then he called for one of his top lieutenants to see him.

Pena soon walked into the room and stood there coolly, waiting for orders from his boss.

Oscar turned and looked at him. "It's time to clean house, my friend."

Pena nodded. "Who?"

"I want a five-million-dollar contract on three names—AZ, Heavy Pop, and most importantly, Mateo."

"Consider it already done."

"I can't afford to take any chances. It's time to rebuild and restart. We take out the old and re-erect with something new. I want all three men dead by month's end."

Pena nodded.

Oscar told him, "I have a bad feeling about them, Pena. Make sure it happens quickly."

Pena pivoted and left the room, leaving Oscar to drink his cognac and relax on his yacht. The hammer started to swing, and soon three nails would be pounded.

TWENTY-SEVEN

AZ had called several times, but still not a word from Oscar. He couldn't help but to worry. Despite the busts in Texas, AZ was sure that Oscar had other methods of shipping kilos into the States and supplying him with the large amounts he needed to deal with Mateo. He had a fleet of minivans ready and half a dozen mules prepared to transport his cocaine from the pickup to the drop-off locations. But he couldn't reach Oscar. It seemed like it was all falling apart. Everything he had built was crumbling brick by brick.

He paced around his office downing vodka. Lately, he'd been drinking like a fish. The alcohol was his only reprieve. His wife was a disappointment, and his sons weren't his. He had to keep himself busy to keep from going insane.

Mateo was calling, arguing about his shipment, and AZ gave him excuse after excuse why it was late. Mateo was pushy and desperate for the kilos. He seemed nervous about something. He said really needed the cocaine—people were depending on him. It should have raised red flags with AZ, but he wasn't thinking rationally at the moment.

AZ also had other concerns. What if Wendy decided to go public with everything, revealing his homosexuality and press charges against him? He had threatened her if she did, but there was no telling what a woman scorned might do. But his threat was real. He was going to kill her if she tried to embarrass him or come at him legally. Though his sons weren't his, he did miss them. They had grown on him, but the pain was still fresh in his heart.

He tossed back another glass of vodka down his throat and rumbled from the taste. Where was his mind taking him? Where was his sanity going? He was thinking too much, worrying too hard about so many things. But he couldn't help it; both his livelihood and his reputation were in danger.

Just then his cell phone rang. He answered. It was Pena. Hearing one of Oscar's lieutenants on the other end at once brought him some relief.

"Pena, damn, it's good to hear from you. I'm trying to reach Oscar."

"I know, but I call to tell you to just sit tight and we'll get to you."

"When?"

"Soon. There's been a drought, so business is slow."

AZ sighed. It was news that he didn't want to hear. He'd been waiting for weeks now, and not only he, but his clientele was growing impatient, including Mateo.

"Oscar says not to worry; you'll be taken care of," Pena said.

He hung up.

AZ frowned and cursed. "Fuck me!" He didn't want to hear about any drought. He had to make moves on his own. He couldn't depend on Oscar. His connect was running scared, but he wanted to make money. Oscar couldn't be his only lifeline. He decided to make another call and push things through on his own. No matter, business had to continue to keep spinning like the earth. If it stopped, then he would die.

✳

AZ and Heavy Pop managed to scrape together fifty kilos from another connection and keep their meeting with Mateo. The meeting was set in Sunset Park, Brooklyn, at one of Mateo's storefronts on 2nd Avenue that doubled as a drug depot. AZ walked into the building first, followed by Heavy Pop. This time they came with armed security. The storefront was closed for the day, and the only occupants were drug dealers and goons. The minivan with the fifty kilos pulled into the alleyway of the storefront, and one of their workers climbed out and tossed Mateo the keys.

"Fifty kilos? I asked for five hundred," Mateo griped to AZ.

"I'm sorry, but there's a drought, Mateo, and shit is slow right now."

"I don't care about no drought, I care about my kilos."

"Look, you'll get what you asked for. You just need to be patient."

Mateo feigned disappointment. He stood in front of AZ and Heavy Pop dressed sharply in Armani, alligator shoes, sporting a Rolex and diamond rings, looking like a pretty boy. Things became tense in the room. AZ and Heavy Pop kept their cool.

Mateo started bitching. "If y'all niggas are too small-time to fulfill my order, then maybe I need to take my business elsewhere."

"You're going to play that card with me, Mateo? After two successful runs we had? You're the one that upped the order last-minute," AZ said gruffly. "We're the ones that took a chance with you when nobody wanted to touch you."

"I respect that, but business is business, and I'm four hundred and fifty kilos short."

"And you'll get your shipment. It's just gonna take some time."

"I don't have time."

"Why not?" Heavy Pop chimed. Suddenly there was something about Mateo he didn't trust.

"I don't like when people make promises to me they can't keep," Mateo said.

"Our word and our product are still good."

"What about your connect?" Mateo asked.

"What about him?"

"Where is he? I want to meet with him. I want a face-to-face. I want him to tell me about this drought."

AZ laughed. "It's not happening, Mateo."

"I'm not some dime-store hustler. I move a lot of weight, and I deserve a sit-down with the man. I deserve that much, don't I?"

"Why? Heavy Pop and me, we ain't good enough for you? We never wronged you. We kept fair and accurate count with each shipment every time. So why would you want or need to meet with our connect? You think we're fools?"

"I simply like to know who I'm dealing with. Look, there's been a lot of noise in the streets lately. I heard about that raid in Texas, and I've been under fire and under pressure and in this game for too long to feel comfortable with all my eggs in one basket. I simply want to know that who I'm dealing with won't come back on me."

"It won't."

"Is your man connected to that shit that happened in Texas? That's why you tell me about this drought. Why I can't get my five hundred kilos? Do I need to move on from y'all?"

AZ dared him. "And go where?"

"I have the money, and I have the clientele."

"And you also have a bad name in the game, Mateo. People don't trust you. I took that chance with you."

"And because of that chance, my name is back out there again."

"Our guy won't meet with you," AZ repeated, adamant.

"Why not? Huh? What's his name?"

Mateo was wired up, so everything was being recorded. He needed the name. Mateo was facing two life sentences. For his cooperation in the federal case, the prosecutor had worked up a deal, and once the case ended, he would do twenty years with the possibility of parole. But if he was able to help nab the big fish, then the prosecutor was willing to lighten his sentence to ten to years. And with a federal sentence, he would be required to do eighty-five percent of his time, providing he was on his best behavior inside. Mateo needed his name, the kilos, and the convictions of the major drug traffickers.

"Don Esposito, that's who you're dealing with, right?" Mateo said.

"Don Esposito? You think we would get into bed with that fuckin' nut? Nah, Os—"

AZ quickly uttered, "Heavy Pop, chill! It don't matter who he is, Mateo, as long as you get your product."

Mateo frowned. He tried to outsmart AZ, coming at him with a few more tactics, but AZ didn't give Oscar up, not because he was on to Mateo's betrayal, but because there were rules to the game. One primary rule was to never let other dealers know who your connect is because they'll cut you out and go straight to the connect for a much better price.

AZ and Heavy Pop exited the storefront and climbed into Heavy's Escalade.

"What the fuck was that about?" Heavy Pop said.

"I don't know."

"That nigga was acting all weird and twilight and shit. You don't think—"

"Nah, don't go there, Heavy Pop."

"I'm saying, he already got a bad reputation. What if he's working with the feds?" Heavy Pop said what they both were thinking.

"But I vetted that nigga."

"I don't care, AZ. Something's up with that nigga, and I don't like it. He got me nervous now."

Mateo had AZ nervous too, but he refused to show it. AZ sat back in the seat. He had to think. What if Mateo was working with the feds? What if it all had been a fraud from the beginning? The consequences would be severe. The feds were savvy enough to falsify Mateo's information. AZ had hired the best hackers in town to vet Mateo's criminal record, to make sure the cocaine bust the hood was whispering about didn't happen and he wasn't working with law enforcement. But what crack did he miss? What hole didn't he look through?

It didn't matter now. If Mateo was working with law enforcement, AZ knew they were fucked.

TWENTY-EIGHT

Cristal got off the bus in Maryland behind the other passengers at the Greyhound station on Haines Street. She blended in with the daytime crowd coming and going from the bus station, dressed in blue jeans, black sneakers, a North Face coat, and a baseball cap and carrying a duffel bag filled with guns, cash, and knives. She felt ambivalent searching for Daniel. It was more than likely he was dead and her efforts to save him would be in vain. However, she was also flooded with memories about Daniel, the places they used to eat, the things they used to do together, and the love they had.

There was no doubt that The Commission had people already planted in the city and were waiting for her to show her face. If they had tracked her down in New Orleans, it would be easy to track her in Baltimore. Cristal didn't care anymore. Daniel was in trouble, and she needed to help him, even if it meant trading her life for his.

She climbed into a cab and told the driver her destination. She checked in to a motel on Wilkinson Boulevard, west of the city. It was an outdoor motel in a not too busy area. It wasn't the perfect place, but it had to do. Then it was time to go to work.

Her first stop was at Daniel's school. There she was able to break into the admissions department, locate his files, and find his new apartment.

She arrived at his place, and the moment she walked inside, she knew something had happened. The signs were there. A knocked-over chair, papers tossed around, and his school books opened. His apartment looked like it hadn't been lived in for weeks. He was a clean person, but his bed was unmade, there was dust in the rooms, and his bedroom look disturbed. He had definitely been snatched. Cristal knew it was her duty to find him. She felt guilty. It was her fault. If she hadn't come into his life, kept in contact with him, then he would still be around, going to school to become a doctor soon. He didn't deserve a grizzly fate. He didn't deserve to die, or to be tortured. The man was kind and smart and had a bright future.

A deep wave of anguish washed over Cristal. It was the closest she ever felt to him in months.

She went on to observe the rest of his apartment. Her gaze lingered on a few pictures of him. She managed to smile, thinking how handsome he was. She picked up a few of his books and skimmed through them. She carefully walked around his apartment and absorbed the way he lived. He definitely was a single man. And he lived alone. There was nothing to tell her where he might be. Whoever took him was quick and stealthy. His knapsack and laptop were still left in the apartment. She picked them up to take with her. There were no other clues for her to pick up.

She left the apartment covered in a black hoodie and dark shades. Each step she made was a cautious one. She carried a .45 and several knives. The knives had saved her life in New Orleans. She had to worry about more gunmen coming her way, another lone assassin ready to earn her stripes, or a sniper perched on a rooftop yards away ready to put a bullet into her head.

She climbed into a cab and headed back to the motel.

Cristal had what she needed from his apartment, and now it was time to go analyze his laptop and the contents in the knapsack. Seated at the desk going through his laptop and being online for several hours, she was able to track his phone to a location right outside of Pittsburgh. Why was he in Pennsylvania? She didn't have time to linger; it was time for her to go. She packed her things and left the motel room. This time instead of taking the Greyhound, she planned on taking a car. It was a risk driving in a stolen car, but time was of the essence. She needed to be in Pennsylvania yesterday.

*

It was four in the morning when Cristal arrived in Pennsylvania. I-79 was covered with falling snow and some ice, and it was biting cold, with the temperature below 25 degrees. Pittsburgh felt arctic, like the next ice age was coming soon. Driving in a Ford Taurus, she had the heat on blast and the radio playing. Cristal downed cups of coffee and kept focused.

Her GPS took her off the interstate and onto Rochester Road, a two-lane main road bordered by trees and shrubbery on both sides. The road was icy, winding, and dark, so she had to take her time driving. Close to her destination, she turned right off the road onto a narrow dirt road.

Her final stop was an isolated farmhouse nestled deep in the woods. The snow was profuse, and the land stretched for miles. This was where Daniel was being held. She knew it.

She climbed out of the car and opened the trunk. She went through the duffel bag filled with guns and knives and readied herself with multiple weapons.

Cristal knew it was a trap, but she had to do this. She was tired of running, and if going into the farmhouse meant she would die, and die with Daniel, then so be it. She knew that whoever took him hadn't done it to let him go. It was like that psychic Ida had prophesized.

She sheathed her knives, holstered several guns, and trekked through the snow carrying a Heckler and Koch machine gun. If it was an ambush, then she was determined to take a few out with her before she met her

Maker. From a distance, she staked out the place with her binoculars and looked at every angle. The farm was dilapidated and seemingly untouched since its occupants had left years ago. The snow-covered remains of a dismantled tractor sat in the field of the farm. She didn't see anything else—no threat, no shooters, no life—around the farmhouse. She looked for footprints in the snow. Nothing.

She took a deep breath and proceeded toward the house cautiously. Each step to the farmhouse was a nerve-wracking one. Her eyes darted everywhere. She kept the gun poised in her arms. She had an eerie feeling as she slowly walked into the place. It was a mess and it was dark, with dusty shelves, broken-down furniture, spider webs everywhere, and moldy walls. The rank smell was insufferable.

Cristal went room to room, until finally, her heart dropped with dismay and grief. She had found him. He was bound to a chair with his throat cut open. Cristal immediately ran to him and scooped his body into her arms.

Overwhelmed with grief, tears streamed down her face. "Daniel!" she cried out.

A range of emotions flooded her body—sadness, rage, guilt, and anger all went through her. He was a good man and didn't deserve dying in some filthy, abandoned farm.

She released him from the chair, and his stiff body fell into her arms. The frigid weather had slowed decomposition, but she could tell that he had been dead for some time. Cristal held him close. She was on her knees and so deep in pain and grief, she didn't hear the threat approaching from behind.

Suddenly she felt the silencer placed to the back of her head. Aoki had gotten the drop on her. Cristal didn't flinch; she didn't care anymore. She wanted to die.

"Me thought yuh would be a challenge," Aoki said.

Cristal remained on her knees and continued to hold Daniel in her arms as best she could. "You didn't have to kill him," she said.

"Him die cuz of yuh," said Aoki. "There's no room fah love."

Cristal calmly and slowly turned her head toward Aoki. She wanted to look the bitch in the eyes.

Aoki gave her the pleasure. She wanted to see Cristal's eyes too before she killed her.

"I know you," Cristal uttered.

"Yuh don't know me."

Cristal knew Aoki was the female assassin that people were praising on The Farm. She'd secretly idolized this bitch for years.

Still locking eyes with Aoki, Cristal smirked. Her tears had stopped falling, and now she seemed focused again.

Aoki still had the gun pointed at her head. She would do what others failed to do, kill this bitch Cristal and move on with her life. She thought she'd hesitated for too long, though. She simply wanted to look into Cristal's eyes, see into her tortured soul before ending her life.

"Gudnite," Aoki uttered.

Her index finger squeezed the trigger, but not before Cristal reacted precisely, and in a split second, knocked away the gun from Aoki's grip and it simultaneously went off.

Bak!

The bullet whizzed by Cristal's ear, and she leaped at Aoki and plunged a knife into her leg.

Aoki hollered and stumbled backwards. Now it was an equal battle between them.

"Yuh fuckin' bitch!" Aoki hollered.

Cristal unholstered her own pistol and fired at Aoki rapidly, four shots in succession. *Bak! Bak! Bak! Bak!*

Aoki swiftly took cover behind a dividing wall as bullets tore into the old walls of the farmhouse. Aoki wasn't down and out yet. She had a little surprise for Cristal. She had weapons stashed everywhere in the place.

She reached for an UZI and opened fire back at Cristal. The machine gun fire splintered the walls and shredded everything in the surrounding area.

Cristal had to duck and take cover, her own fierce weapon, the Heckler and Koch, out of her reach. She shot back with her pistol, but was overwhelmed with bullets coming her way from the UZI.

The farmhouse had turned into a World War III battleground.

"Yuh gon' die tonight, bitch!"

Cristal took one final look at Daniel's body lying on the cold, dirty floor and sulked. She had to leave him. Though she had injured Aoki, there was no telling what kind of booby traps and weapons she had stashed elsewhere, or if she had reinforcements coming. She couldn't chance it. When the opportunity came for her to escape, she seized it. She bolted from the farm with Aoki shooting at her and disappeared into the woods and darkness.

Aoki cursed loudly. Now, it was likely that Cristal would be hunting her, wanting payback for Daniel's death.

TWENTY-NINE

AZ was elated when the call from Pena finally came. Pena told him that another shipment had come into the States. A thousand kilos had arrived in Miami, and half of that was heading toward New York and would be in the city early the next day. Every kilo was his. Pena gave him the location of the pickup point.

But there was one thing that worried AZ, and that was Mateo. Heavy Pop was right—there was something off about him. He was asking too many questions and seemed nervous. What if Mateo was working with the feds? Just the thought of it being true made AZ sick to his stomach. If true, how would Oscar take the news? It was a worrisome issue that he needed to deal with right away.

The house was quiet. Since he'd kicked Wendy and the boys out, the home felt like a ghost town. There was no laughter or quarreling, just one empty room after another. AZ barely stayed home. He spent his nights in the bar or in New York. He had gotten word that Wendy and the kids were staying at her sister's place in Glen Burnie. He didn't miss her at all. In fact, he was glad she was gone. AZ relished time alone in his home. He needed to think. He needed to take care of a few problems.

AZ got on the phone and called Heavy Pop. Two rings later, Heavy picked up and AZ said, "We're on for tomorrow morning. I'll be in town." He kept their phone conversation brief. There was no telling if the feds had their phones tapped.

AZ hung up and poured himself another shot of vodka, his liquid healing. He walked toward the window and stared outside. With February right around the corner, the winter was still significant in Maryland. The weatherman had forecasted more snow, up to six inches this coming weekend. AZ was tired of the snow. He was tired of walking in it, driving in it, and dealing with it. Maybe after this deal in New York, he would take a trip somewhere warm, Miami probably, or Las Vegas. He would enjoy the warm climate, spend some money, and have casual sex with different men. If he went to Vegas, he would get a luxury suite and gamble. If he decided to go to Miami, he would take in the nightlife and prowl their lengthy white beaches. It was time for a vacation.

His trip to New York was hours away. Until then, he wanted to escape sexually. Of course, Baron was on his mind. It'd been a while since they'd linked up. He was in the mood to see him. He called, and Baron answered.

"I really need to see you tonight," AZ said.

"I'm with my family," Baron replied.

"Can you break away from them for a moment? It's important."

Baron sighed. "I'll try."

"Two hours. You know where."

After their called ended, AZ poured more alcohol down his throat.

*

It was eight thirty and AZ sat in the parking lot of the Quality Inn on Security Boulevard in Woodlawn, Maryland. He sat in the driver's seat of his Benz truck smoking his cigar and waiting patiently for Baron to arrive. After his rendezvous with Baron, he was going to jump straight on the interstate and drive to New York. His idea was to leave tonight, beat the traffic, and settle into a hotel in the city.

He watched a pair of headlights turn into the parking lot of the motel from his rearview mirror. The closer they got, he could see it was Baron's silver Benz coming toward his truck. AZ could feel his erection growing in his pants. Baron parked next to him and stepped out of his Benz dressed sharply in a black three-piece suit and white tie. AZ smiled.

Baron climbed into the passenger seat of AZ's truck, and the two kissed for a moment.

"It's good to see you again. I missed you," AZ said.

"I missed you too."

AZ lit up when he was around Baron. The man was handsome and smart. His head game was fierce and he was endowed.

"What's important?" Baron asked.

"I'm leaving for New York tonight on business. I don't know how long I'll be gone. I had to see you before I leave."

"How long is long?" Baron asked.

"Maybe a month, maybe two."

"That long, huh?"

He nodded. "And I'm no longer with my wife."

"Why not?"

"Infidelity issues."

"She knows about us?" Baron asked, sounding worried.

"I know about her. I caught her cheating."

"Ironic, seeing that you're seeing me."

"Our business is cool . . . it's safe," AZ assured him.

Baron sighed profoundly. It looked like he had something on his mind.

"What is it?" AZ asked.

"I love my wife, and I love my kids," Baron told him.

"And?"

"And this sneaking around coming to see you, it's taking a toll on me. My wife is starting to become suspicious. She's starting to ask questions. She thinks I'm having an affair."

"You are."

"Yes, but she thinks it's another woman."

"You don't want to continue seeing me?" AZ asked.

"I do, but I feel we need to slow things down."

"Well, I'll be away for about a month, will that slow things down enough?"

"I want this, AZ, but I have to think about my family too. And my father, I told you about him. He's a frantic homophobe. If he ever finds out about us, you know what he will do to me."

"We've always been careful, Baron."

"I know. It's just I can't afford to have our business get out."

"It won't. I promise you that, Baron. But since you're here, let's have some fun. Give me something to remember you by while I'm gone."

Baron managed to smile.

AZ unzipped his pants and showed his erection. His heart was pumping fast, and he could feel the blood rushing inside of him. The way Baron made him come was unbelievable. He was better than any bitch at sucking dick.

Feeling Baron's thin lips wrap around his erection, AZ closed his eyes and leaned back into his seat. This was the perfect remedy that he needed. Sex. Baron's head bobbed up and down sprucely, manifesting pure perversion in the front seat of the Benz truck.

"I wanna come in your mouth," AZ said, breathing harder. He moaned and wanted to explode.

As AZ felt himself swimming in paradise, the passenger door suddenly flew open, and a man shouted, "What the fuck!"

Everything stopped. Both their heads spun in the direction of the voice, and there was Baron's father glaring at them. He grabbed his son roughly and snatched him out of the truck. Baron stumbled from the seat and fell to the ground, landing on his side.

His father started to kick him vehemently. He cursed, "You fucking faggot! You shame our family's name with your blatant homosexuality! How dare you!"

He was going to kill his son. He kicked and stomped Baron. Seeing his son committing a homosexual act in a motel parking lot, and on a black male was an abomination. "I'll kill you for sucking that nigger's dick!" his pops shouted angrily.

Baron's wife had called and poured her heart out to her father-in-law, suspecting something was off with her husband. Baron's father decided to get to the bottom of what was going on. His father used his clout and had a tracking device placed on Baron's car. When Baron left his family suddenly, she called the father. The tracking device led him to the motel in Woodlawn.

Baron could hardly defend himself from the vicious attack by the man who'd raised him. "I'll fucking kill you! You fucking faggot!"

AZ had to do something. He quickly fastened his pants, reached for his gun, and hurried toward the beating. He aimed his pistol at the man and shouted, "Get the fuck off him!"

Baron's father stopped kicking his son and shot a wicked look over at AZ and growled, "You know who I am, you nigger? I will have you destroyed for this. You turned my son into a faggot!"

"I didn't turn your son into anything, he's just being himself."

"You lying nigger!"

AZ was getting tired of hearing the word *nigger* spew from his mouth. He wanted to shoot this homophobic racist so bad, but he didn't need that kind of heat on him. The man was an aristocrat with connections all through D.C.

AZ shouted, "Back the fuck up, old man, or I swear, you won't leave this parking lot alive."

The man clenched his fists. If he became any redder, he would have turned into lava and scorched the place.

"Baron, you okay?" AZ asked him.

Baron was hurt badly. He managed to slowly pick himself up from the concrete. He pressed his hands against his ribs, and they felt broken. He was curved over in pain. His father had definitely done a number on him.

"Let's go, son," his father said with authority.

Baron looked saddened. His whole world had been suddenly turned upside down. The cat was out of the bag. He had been caught sucking another man's dick, and by his father no less.

"Baron, you don't have to go. Fuck him!"

"You mind your damn business, you black faggot! You have already done enough damage to our fucking family. Baron, get in your damn car, and let's go."

Baron glanced at AZ briefly with a sad, broken look, and then he did what he was told. He went to his Benz and got inside. The door shut. He couldn't look back at AZ. His father stood near AZ and continued to fume. AZ lowered the gun from the man.

"I'm not done with you, you fucking nigger! I swear I will end you. What you did to my son, I won't forget. You will regret this day." He pivoted and marched away.

AZ watched them both leave. He sighed heavily. *What the fuck just happened?*

AZ couldn't do anything else but climb back into his vehicle and leave for New York. Business still needed to be taken care of.

*

AZ arrived in New York before midnight. He checked into a Hilton in downtown Brooklyn and called Heavy Pop the moment he settled in.

An hour later, Heavy Pop came through, and the two went out for drinks at a bar nearby. AZ had a lot on his mind. With Heavy Pop listening, he cried the blues about his marriage and fake kids. Heavy was a good ear. The two shared stories about the good, the bad, and the ugly—about bitches and the streets.

As AZ continued to throw back shots, Heavy Pop was starting to become concerned about his drinking. The men managed to laugh despite what was going on around them. Mateo was still a grave concern.

"I think about her," AZ suddenly blurted out.

"Think about who?"

"Aoki."

"I told you, AZ, you need to get her out your head. She's gone. She's dead."

"I know, but we were cool peoples, and if I needed something, she was there."

Heavy Pop told him, "I'm here for you, nigga. You need to stop thinking about her. That was a long time ago."

Then, out of the blue, AZ looked across the room and he could see her. Aoki. She was standing in the distance, and they locked eyes. It had to be her. She winked and smiled at him, and AZ erupted from his chair and went after her. Then she suddenly disappeared from his sight. It had to be her. There was no way his mind was playing tricks on him again.

Heavy Pop was caught off guard by AZ's sudden movement. He chased behind him and asked, "Yo, where you going? What happened?"

The only thing AZ could say was, "She's here!"

"Who?"

"Aoki!"

Now he really thought AZ was losing his mind. He followed AZ out into the street. AZ stood on the sidewalk swiveling his head around the area, crazily looking for her. But he saw no one.

"It's cold out here, AZ. You're losing it. She's dead!"

AZ shook his head. Maybe he was losing it.

"We need to stay focused on tomorrow," Heavy Pop reminded him. "I don't need you tripping out on me, AZ. Don't do this! We came too far for you to start having hallucinations. That bitch is dead. Let her stay dead."

"You're right. I don't know what came over me."

"You're going through a lot. I understand. But let's get these kilos and take it from there. And we need to figure out what to tell Oscar if Mateo is working for the feds."

Now that was going to be harsh. What would they tell him, and how? AZ didn't want to think about it right now. It was getting late. He was tired. He needed some sleep.

They started to walk back to Heavy Pop's black Escalade, the cold wind pinching at their faces under a full moon. New York City was a wintry metropolis, but that didn't stop folks from coming out to enjoy the bars, the clubs, and the city.

AZ squeezed into the passenger seat of Heavy Pop's truck. The moment he settled in his seat, he lit a cigar and leaned back.

Heavy Pop started the ignition, and before he put the vehicle into drive, he turned and looked at AZ and said, "We're gonna get through this. You hear me? We done been through worse, nigga. It doesn't stop now. We're a duo, and we gonna continue being a duo. I love you, man."

Suddenly, gunfire from machine guns exploded into the Escalade, shattering glass and piercing the doors, and both men were hit with a barrage of bullets from both directions. Their bodies shook violently in the front seat as hot, sharp slugs tore into their flesh and bones. It was a brazen public assassination. The gunfire echoed for blocks, and people in the area quickly ran for safety. The three dark shooters hurried away in a white H3.

AZ lay slumped in his seat, leaning against the door, and Heavy Pop lay slumped near his partner in crime. They were a duo no more, but died together as friends.

THIRTY

The murders of AZ and Heavy Pop not only shocked Mateo, but the entire community. Brooklyn was saddened. The media was all over it. The shooting had made the evening news and was plastered across the front page of every New York newspaper. One newspaper article wrote in part: "AZ and Heavy Pop, alleged to be two of the biggest drug dealers in the city, were viciously gunned down last night as they left the JBL bar in downtown Brooklyn."

There were many witnesses to the shooting, and each individual told their own horrifying account of what they saw that night.

*

The news of AZ's murder was only the beginning of the end for Mateo. The feds had to shut down their operation, and the deal between him and the government fell through. He would now have to do his full sentence, since his agreement with the government was on the contingency that they arrest AZ, Heavy Pop, and the connect, and that he testify against them. Since AZ and Heavy Pop had never revealed the name of their connect, the feds had nothing to go on. Just like that, Mateo was thrust into a nightmare situation.

When they informed him that the deal was off, he flipped out. He cursed and acted a fool. He felt the feds had fucked him. It was assumed that AZ and Heavy Pop were killed because of his asking around about their connect.

Mateo became frantic. He was a marked man also. If or when Oscar found out he was a snitch, Oscar would want him dead too. He was looking at life in prison, and if incarcerated, he could easily be murdered inside by anyone on the drug lord's payroll.

Mateo sat in the federal office looking aloof. The handcuffs were too tight, and he hadn't showered, shit, or shaved in days. His pretty boy image was fading fast. He lowered his head and tried very hard to keep his tears from falling. His freedom was gone, and so was his life. The only question was, Which one would come first? Would Oscar have him killed before he saw the inside of a prison?

"Mateo, it's time!" one of the federal agents shouted from the hallway.

Mateo sulked. He didn't want to go anywhere. He stood up slowly and marched toward the agent dejectedly. Soon, he would trade in his thousand-dollar suit for prison overalls. There was no one left to snitch on, and he had no one to talk about. The streets didn't trust him, and the feds no longer needed him. So he was to be tossed away like trash and left to rot inside a federal jail cell for life. If he could have cut his own throat, he would have.

THIRTY-ONE

Aoki had to lay low for a while and tend to the stab wound in her leg. Cristal had put that knife deep into her thigh and twisted it. Luckily it didn't hit a major artery. She cursed Cristal, and then she cursed herself even more. She should have just pulled the trigger when she had the chance and ended it. But, no, she had to look Cristal in the eyes and stare into her troubled soul. That split-second hesitation cost her the hit. Now things had been prolonged. Cristal had gone deep underground and hadn't been seen or heard from in weeks. There was no telling where she was or what she was planning. With Daniel dead, Aoki's only lead to finding that bitch was gone. But she wasn't about to give up. Time was running out, but she had other tricks up her sleeve.

She peeled off her clothing and submerged herself into the hot, hot tub. The scalding temperature of the water alone would have sent the average body leaping from it and hitting the ceiling, but Aoki sat in the heat like it was a day on the beach. She put her body through rigorous pain to make it stronger. The heat felt like it could melt her skin off. She merely closed her eyes and meditated. Her leg was healing. Her mind and skills were growing sharper. She only had one thing on her mind—finding Cristal and killing her. Next time, she wouldn't hesitate.

After spending an hour in the tub with her eyes closed and her body healing, she lifted herself from the water and toweled off. In the bedroom she glimpsed the *Daily News* on the bed, and the headline grabbed her attention. It was about AZ and Heavy Pop getting murdered in downtown Brooklyn. The news was shocking to her; she couldn't believe it. Mixed emotions swept through her. Who had done it? And why? She wanted to take AZ out. He was hers, but somebody had beaten her to it. Once again, she'd procrastinated. She had spent years stalking him, watching him and his family, observing how his life had changed. She could have pulled the trigger any time, yet she allowed him to live.

Aoki stood in her bedroom in a daze. *The enemy of my enemy, is he my friend, or is he a larger enemy to me? Was AZ truly her enemy?* She felt the urge to kill whoever killed AZ.

*

Aoki stepped out of her building into the cool air and looked around. Where she lived was a bustling area with traffic, people, noise, and towering buildings crowded together from block to block.

The sidewalks were flooded with people coming and going from every direction. They were programmed to do the same thing day after day like zombies—off to work, then to their homes and families, and battling rush-hour daily to live paycheck to paycheck. They were like sheep on their way to the slaughter. How could anyone live so structured? Life wasn't fun unless there was blood, murder, money, mayhem, and power involved. These everyday people were trapped inside a small box and had no idea what the world really was about, and who was in control. The government? That's a laugh. It was the 1% organizations like The Commission who had godlike power to decide who would live or die, and had billions of dollars to finance wars and shake up countries. They altered nations and assassinated kings and presidents. Countries and people were like chess pieces on the board, whereas The Commission was like the queen, able to move anywhere on the chessboard while the other pieces were limited. Even the king was restricted.

These everyday people were content with their small lives and the way things were. They were the pawns.

Aoki stared at these passers-by, the same faces every day, and she wanted to pick them off one by one and take them out of their own misery. Death was better than living inside the law like these cowards, playing it safe. It was fun to kill, to hunt and to have control. Aoki lived a lifestyle that so many dreamed of. She got to travel the world, she wore the finest clothing, drove in nice cars, and she felt that she had power. Her skills in killing gave her the advantage over everyone. She had to go through hell to become the devil.

The night Oscar's men shot her down like she was some dog in the marsh and left her for dead was the night she was reborn. She had transformed into this vicious creature that felt unstoppable.

But there were consequences as well to this life she lived. The hunter could easily become the hunted. She had failed the hit, and now it allowed for her to be targeted by Cristal, a skilled assassin herself. Cristal could be anywhere and ready to strike at any time. Aoki's ten-week deadline to fulfill the assignment was creeping up, and she had no idea where the bitch was. If she didn't kill Cristal soon, then her life would be in jeopardy.

The Commission paid her for results.

Packaged snugly in her winter coat, and wearing UGG boots and a ski hat, Aoki lingered in front of her building for a moment and looked around. It was another cold day. She watched everything and everyone, her back to the wall. She was well armed and observant. She suddenly found herself paranoid. It felt like she was being watched, but by whom? Who would be stupid enough to stalk her?

She remembered how she'd made AZ feel. She'd made him paranoid too, playing tricks with his mind. Now, it seemed like someone was playing tricks on her. She had woken up this morning and swore someone was inside her apartment standing over her and watching her sleep. If she had woken up to some strange company, then they would have been met with a rude awakening. Aoki slept with two pistols. It would be them before they got her. But she checked the surveillance footage of her place and saw no one coming or going from her apartment.

She climbed into an Uber cab and told the driver her destination. It was a costly trip to Jersey City, New Jersey, but she didn't care. She wanted to sit in the backseat and relax. She exhaled and watched the city pass her by. Everyone was getting ready for Valentine's Day. There would be flowers, cards, and candy accompanied by long hugs and tender kisses. It was a day for love and romance, and the restaurants would be swamped with couples. Aoki cringed at such things. She hadn't loved anyone in years.

She briefly thought about AZ, then B Scientific. Then she thought about Emilio. Now all three men were dead. She felt like poison ivy.

The Uber cab glided through the Holland Tunnel into New Jersey. The ride was quiet. Aoki wasn't a talkative person. Soon it pulled up to her favorite place, Patti Joy, the Jamaican restaurant. She paid the driver and stepped out of the car. She strolled inside, took a seat at the window, and picked up the menu. Being early afternoon, the place was still somewhat empty. The lunch-hour crowd had just passed, and the next wave of folks would come after five p.m. Aoki liked it when the place was quiet. It was easier to keep track of everything.

She ordered her favorite meal, a large plate of oxtail with some rice and beans, and a sorrel drink. Her meal came quickly. Aoki dove into the oxtail. They always did them right. The meat was steaming and practically falling off the bone. One bite into the oxtail and Aoki almost had an orgasm. This was what she loved—some good Jamaican food. In Patti Joy, she was able to relax and eat her meal in peace.

She'd befriended the owner, a middle-aged lady named Ms. Louise from Kingston, Jamaica, who'd migrated to America thirty-five years ago when she was a little girl. She had opened Patti Joy twenty years ago, and it'd become a favorite since then. The place was named after her daughter who'd died in Jamaica from brain cancer. The restaurant was opened in her memory. Aoki respected the place, and she respected Ms. Louise. Though she was a silent and skilled killer, whenever Ms. Louise was in the restaurant, Aoki made it her business to converse with the woman, who was a kind and spiritual Christian woman. She believed in God and forgiveness, that there was good in everybody. Ms. Louise was one among the very few Aoki could talk to. Everybody loved Ms. Louise. Aoki did too. She wished Ms. Louise was her mother. Maybe her life would have turned out completely different.

"Me see yuh enjoying me oxtail again," Ms. Louise said, coming into the dining area.

Aoki smiled briefly and replied, "De best in town."

Ms. Louise was a thin, brown-skinned woman with high cheekbones, wrinkle-free skin, loving eyes, and long salt-and-pepper hair. She was beautiful at her age and epitomized the expression "black doesn't crack." She slid into the window booth opposite of Aoki, who didn't mind at all.

"Pickney, why yuh always come here with them sad eyes? Me know you have somethin' to smile about."

"Me wish me did, Ms. Louise."

"Valentine's Day is approaching soon. Yuh mean to tell me ah beautiful woman like yuh don't have nuh one in yuh life?"

"Me a workin' girl."

"Workin' girls still need love too."

"Yuh oxtail is all de love me need." Aoki took in another mouthful of food.

Ms. Louise smiled. "Me haven't seen yuh around in a while. Is tings okay?"

Aoki nodded. "Me fine." But she wasn't. There was a lot going on.

Ms. Louise was the kind of woman who read people easily, and Aoki's eyes paraded her pain. "Whatever issues yuh dealin' wit', put it in God's hands, pickney. Let Him handle yuh issues. Yuh can trust God."

There was never a conversation where Ms. Louise didn't bring up God and having forgiveness. Sometimes Aoki would be flooded with guilt around her, knowing she was the hell Ms. Louise talked about.

Aoki nodded, never having too much to say about God and religion. Did she believe in God? She believed in hell because, since she was born, she had been walking through hell, from her parents to the streets. Now she was the one giving people hell. It almost felt like an abomination sitting in front of Ms. Louise, a God-fearing Christian. Aoki felt like Satan, with the people she had killed and the lives she had destroyed. Too many to count.

"Yuh know me always pray fi yuh," Ms. Louise said.

"Yuh don't need to do dat, Ms. Louise. Me know how to handle meself."

"Yes, but dere's nothin' wrong fi prayin' fah yuh. Yuh need love, pickney. Yuh need to smile more, yuh understan'? Wit'out love in yuh life, then yuh have nothin'. Makin' money isn't everyting."

"Me tink 'bout it."

They both smiled.

"Me done talk yuh head off enough, pickney. Enjoy yuh meal. It was good seein' yuh again." Ms. Louise removed herself from the booth.

As Ms. Louise attempted to get up, she accidentally dropped her cell phone on the floor, and Aoki bent over to pick it up for her. While doing so, all hell broke loose.

The shots came through the window rapidly and abruptly—*Boom! Boom! Boom!*

Ms. Louise was hit in the chest and collapsed on her back, dying instantly.

Aoki ducked to the floor and took cover behind the booth, but the heavy-duty rounds were ripping the area apart. They were coming from a sniper's rifle; somebody wasn't playing around.

More shots were fired into the restaurant—*Boom! Boom! Boom! Boom! Boom!*

Aoki found herself scurrying for safety. She removed her pistol, but what good was it when she was outgunned and had no idea where the shots were coming from. The shooting sent employees and the few customers inside panicking as they ran for cover.

Aoki couldn't believe Ms. Louise was dead. She ached with sorrow, but now wasn't the time to mourn. She was sure they were aiming for her. If she hadn't suddenly bent over to pick up Ms. Louise's phone, then she would have been dead.

Aoki stayed low and glued to the floor. The shooting had stopped, but that didn't mean the sniper wasn't still perched somewhere nearby, waiting for her to peek out from her hiding spot and kill her.

People were screaming. They had no idea why Patti Joy was being shot up suddenly.

Aoki took one last look at Ms. Louise and puffed out. Her body lay twisted against the floor, and her blood started to pool around her, spilling across her floors painted green, yellow, and black. The hole in the woman's chest was astronomical. It had come from a very big gun.

Aoki needed a way out. Her eyes moved everywhere anxiously. The kitchen was her only haven for now. Quickly, she stood up and bolted toward the kitchen and dove into the narrow hallway and rolled back onto her feet. No gunfire. She still remained vigilant, crouched on the floor, gun in hand, and moved toward the rear exit. The stoves and ovens were burning unattended in the kitchen, since the cooks had run off scared. Just like that, Patti Joy had become a kill zone.

Aoki took a deep breath and went for her escape out the rear door. She burst into the alleyway preparing to lunge herself into firefight with maybe one, or several gunmen, but there was nothing. She heard the police sirens blaring in the distance. She hurried away from her favorite restaurant with deep regret.

As Aoki had predicted, she'd gone from being the hunter to the hunted. She assumed it was Cristal. It had to be that bitch. Cristal had gone invisible for weeks, and her return cost Ms. Louise—someone Aoki considered a friend—her life.

It was now cat-and-mouse between the two killers. And Aoki refused to be the mouse.

THIRTY-TWO

Wendy walked into her home with her two sons and looked around. She exhaled with gladness. It felt wonderful to be home again. The place was just how she left it. Her last memory there was AZ attacking her, belittling her, and threatening her life. Now he was dead. She was ecstatic. She'd smiled when she heard the news, but she pretended to be distraught around her coworkers. She had long ago activated a multi-million dollar life insurance policy on him, and being his wife, she was the beneficiary of all of his properties and investments.

Wendy had fallen out of love with AZ a long time ago. She'd only stuck around and stayed married to him for her and the kids' convenience. He was rich. He spoiled her. He took care of her kids, the children she knowingly had with different men. She loved nice things. The idea of being married to a wealthy businessman sat well with her, and it was a good look around the other ladies and her peers. She sat perched on her pedestal, looking down at the others. She was able to brag about her husband, show off her perfect family, and throw lavish get-togethers at her beautiful home.

When AZ had kicked her out of her own home, she and the kids moved in with her sister. Wendy had to tell a lie about her fight with AZ, and why she had to leave her home. She dared not tell anyone AZ wasn't the boys' father, that she was ghetto whore with a law degree. How would it look? They would criticize and judge her. She had to carry herself a certain way. She had to look and remain posh and have the best, drive the best, and be with the best. But inside, she was slumming, and had fallen in love with a gangster named Justice. Now he was dead. Did AZ kill him or have him killed? She would never know.

The coroner's office in New York City wanted Wendy to come and identify her husband's body, but she refused. It was too long a trip, and she had work to do. It left the coroner puzzled. Wendy pretended to be too distraught to travel anywhere. Instead, she sent one of her friends to identify his body, not wanting anything to do with AZ. He was gone, and she needed to move on with her life.

Wendy walked around the mini-mansion with a trash bag and, without the slightest hesitation, tossed away all items that belonged to AZ. There would be no reminders of him around her home. She walked into the bedroom, pulled open the doors to the walk-in closet, and threw every piece of his clothing into the trash bag. She would either sell them cheaply or give them away. She stood in the center of her bedroom, spread out her arms and shouted, "I's free at last, thank God Almighty, I is free at last."

She smiled and twirled around happily in the bedroom. For a widow, anyone watching would be scratching their heads and puzzled by her action. But Wendy was in the privacy of her home. She had no need to be concerned about prying eyes or intruders.

She plopped down on her bed and looked around. She had to admit, the memories with AZ weren't all bad. At times, he could be very playful and romantic. They sometimes did have good sex, but she could count those occasions on both hands.

For a moment, Wendy sat in the bedroom thinking. *Is it true what they're saying about my husband? Was he this big-time drug dealer in New York? Was he this violent kingpin?* She found it hard to believe. AZ seemed meek and clichéd. He was a smart and wealthy businessman, not this violent drug dealer. *Could this come back to haunt me?* She was married to the man, but she didn't know about his hidden life. He had kept it a secret from her, just like he tried to hide his homosexuality.

She shook off the fear of her husband's past and sighed. It was time to start over. It was time to have her fun, inherit her husband's businesses, collect on his insurance policy, and continue to advance her career by prosecuting the guilty.

*

It didn't take long for Wendy to bring a handsome thug into the bedroom she once shared with AZ. Sean was a six-two thug from Baltimore's East Side and nothing but muscles and a big dick. His tattooed, chocolate-covered skin and his long, stylish cornrows made her pussy throb.

Sean pounded his thick, fat, hard dick inside of the assistant state's attorney like it was his God-given right. He wanted to make her feel every inch, and his strokes were on point and fierce. Doggy-style sex made Wendy have multiple orgasms, leaving her breathless. She couldn't get enough of him. He was the total opposite of her late husband in that he allowed her to come several times before he even got his first nut. And when he did, he couldn't help himself. He tore off the condom and spurt his come all over her back.

She exhaled in his arms as they lay nestled in the bed. Her body felt content. She had the weekend to spend with Sean. The kids were with her sister, and work at her office had been put on hold until Monday morning. The only thing Wendy wanted to do was have sex with Sean inside her house. It was only Friday night, day one of their two-day weekend.

If only AZ could see the way Sean violated her body on the bed he bought. The nigga had spread his man juice all over the sheets and all over her—and once inside of her. She couldn't resist. The dick felt so good in her, she allowed him to come in her.

*

212

Wendy repeatedly called the insurance company to check up on her husband's multi-million-dollar policy. It had almost been a month since his death, and she hadn't received one red cent. She wanted to know what the holdup was. She had already liquidated all of AZ's assets, netting over three million dollars, and then she started to examine his paperwork. Shockingly, his paperwork was leading to an investigation not just from the IRS, but the feds too.

*

It was two months after her husband's death, and Wendy's life was good. Her sex life was even better. Sean was the truth. Why was she so attracted to that type of flavor? Shit, if she'd known about AZ's pedigree, she might not have strayed. Come to find out, her deceased husband was the biggest thug of them all.

She sat behind her large polished oak desk mulling over the extensive paperwork in a double homicide in Park Heights. The office was buzzing. Monday morning was always busiest, with people back and forth from court, clerks filing paperwork, and phones ringing off the hook. She skimmed through a few depositions from some key witnesses in her criminal case. Her glass doors were closed, and she was focused. Until she looked up and saw the commotion near the elevators.

She narrowed her eyes and could see several men marching her way. They wore flight jackets with FBI embroidered in the back in big yellow letters.

FBI? Her worrying eyes fixated on their approach, she stood up, befuddled by their presence.

They marched into her office forcefully and shoved some papers in her face and exclaimed, "Wendy Manson, you're under arrest for conspiracy and racketeering."

"This has got to be some kind of mistake!" she cried out.

One agent removed his handcuffs and took a strong hold of her wrist. Everyone in the office was watching the display, and the gossip started to flow.

"I'm an assistant state's attorney for Baltimore!" she shouted. "I did nothing wrong! This must be some kind of mistake!"

They handcuffed her and marched her out of her office like a regular perp.

Wendy lowered her head, her eyes glued to the floor, as two agents escorted her toward the elevator and out of the building. She could feel everyone's eyes watching her. She was embarrassed. She could feel the tears welling up in her eyes and fought hard to keep from crying.

Once outside of the building, it became an even bigger spectacle. Cameras flashed repeatedly, and reporters thrust microphones in her face and spewed out question after question. An assistant state's attorney, married to one of the biggest drug dealers in New York and arrested for conspiracy and racketeering was front page news and the night's banner.

Cameras continued to flash as she was shoved into the backseat of an unmarked car. Reporters swamped the car, but Wendy kept her head low and avoided eye contact with everyone.

This was it. She was ruined. Her arrest would soon go national and viral. Wendy couldn't hold back the tears any longer. Once the car started to drive away, she burst into tears and cried out hysterically.

Her marriage to AZ had come back to haunt her.

THIRTY-THREE

On the twentieth day on The Farm, the young recruits learned about computers—various software, hardware, spyware, encryption, and viruses. They were expected to pass numerous psychometric, psychoanalytical, polygraph, and aptitude tests. The rigorous instructors on The Farm taught the candidates the skill of espionage, covert operation protocols, and intelligence gathering techniques. The candidates were trained thoroughly in surveillance exercises; it was the perfect boot camp for assassins. Aoki graduated top of her class.

✳

Aoki put her skills in surveillance and computers to good use. She had gone underground; retreated to someplace far from the city to regroup. Ms. Louise's death had done something to her. She couldn't fight the guilt and regret. Although Aoki hadn't known her for that long, Ms. Louise was like a mother to her. There was an attachment and chemistry between them. The woman wanted better for Aoki, and she actually believed in her. To see her gunned down like that was jarring, but Aoki had shed her tears and continued to stay focused and alert.

Ten weeks turned into four months, which meant her deadline had completely expired. But she was still determined to execute the contract, no matter what. It was about pride.

It was mid-March, and the winter weather had started to thaw in certain areas. Where Aoki hid out, the snow and ice still covered many areas, and the trees remained barren. Alone with some much-needed solitude in the icy hills of northern Canada, she did some investigating. Through an experienced hacker friend she knew from The Farm, she was able to hack into sensitive files from The Commission. She was able to obtain covert information from their servers and transmit it to a thumb drive on a brand-new laptop, clear of any incriminating data.

Surprisingly, Oscar's name came up in their files. Why was he in their files? Reading through the documents, she learned that Oscar was once on The Commission's hit list, and was supposed to be assassinated years ago. Once a name was on The Commission's list, it was never removed until that target was dead. Yet this Mexican drug lord still remained breathing. Why so? They had lied to her. This man had almost killed her. He'd left her for dead.

Aoki continued to read on until it all started to go black. A virus was disrupting the documents, and at the same time revealing her location to them. They'd employed a backdoor Trojan virus to her setup, trying to identify the malicious program that'd given her remote access. They had no idea it was she who'd had hacked into their files, she assumed. She'd left no trace for them to finger her for any betrayal.

Aoki was simply being curious. She had done so much for The Commission and was one of their top assassins. But there was no telling who The Commission would send to the mountains to investigate the hack. She hurriedly packed her things and fled the area. She had what she needed.

*

Aoki still couldn't shake the feeling of being watched as she entered East River Park in Manhattan. The park was a 57-acre public location on the Lower East Side, with wide views of Manhattan, Williamsburg,

Brooklyn Bridge, the East River, and Brooklyn. With it being mid-March, the weather was still fierce in New York and biting like a rabid dog. She walked toward the promenade huddled in a black parka, a Glock 19 hidden on her. From her position she had a sweeping view of everyone, and she stayed clear of any open areas.

Soon Muriel strutted her way dressed in a mid-length Burberry trench coat and leather gloves. Muriel already seemed upset and standoffish about something.

Aoki didn't want to waste any time. She looked at Muriel and asked, "What make Oscar still breathe when him been targeted years ago by De Commission?"

"He is none of your business. You should have stayed in your place."

"Bullshit! Him tried to kill me ah few years ago," Aoki reminded her.

"I already know the details," she replied nonchalantly.

"Me want him."

"Little girl, you had one job to do, but yet that bitch is still alive," Muriel replied gruffly.

"Her very evasive."

"And you're supposed to be one of our best, but yet you have failed us."

"Me gon' bring her down. Me promise yuh dat."

"It's too late for that. You're dismissed from this assignment. We'll find someone more suitable for the job."

"Me suitable. Fuck you and fuck De Commission. Me don't give up!"

"You're just a stupid little bitch."

Aoki scowled at Muriel. She wanted desperately to slit her throat and spray her blood on the concrete. "Fuck you, bitch! You don't do dis to me!"

Muriel looked at her like she was second-rate. She stared at Aoki intently, cutting her eyes into the young girl's soul. She reached out and placed her leather-gloved hand on the side of her face, almost motherly like. She flashed a quick smile and then abruptly grabbed the back of Aoki's long hair tightly, yanking her neck back.

Aoki swiftly felt the cold steel blade against her throat. She squirmed in her grasp, but she was defenseless.

Muriel placed her lips closer to Aoki's right ear and uttered her reality. "You raw, little whore. I keep you around because I might want to fuck you one day. But don't test me. Don't test The Commission. You're good, but you're still our pawn. Remember that. We move you where we want to move you. And if you ever talk to me like that again, I will personally make sure you don't see your twenty-fifth birthday." She released her grip from Aoki's hair and took the blade away from her throat.

Aoki massaged her neck and continued to frown. Muriel had made her point loud and clear.

Muriel pivoted away from Aoki and marched out of the park, leaving Aoki with a bitter grudge.

✳

Aoki went back to her Manhattan apartment and did some counter-surveillance of her own. Someone was still following her. She felt them. She put eyes everywhere and rigged her apartment and the hallway and the outside of her building.

It took her only three days to find the culprit that had been stalking her from a distance. Shockingly, it was Rihanna. Crazy Ri-Ri. Only, crazy Ri-Ri wasn't really crazy at all. Or, she suddenly had regained her sanity. The entire time Ri-Ri was in the loony house, she sat stewing. She had grown a hard-on for Aoki. She strongly felt that if it had not been for Aoki, then her sister Tisa and her mother Gena would still be alive. Aoki stupidly had confessed everything to her during her visits, and Ri-Ri deduced all that confessing was for Aoki to clear her conscience. Aoki assumed Ri-Ri's mind had been completely gone. Both were wrong. It was hard for Aoki to swallow that her friend Ri-Ri might come against her. But why not? Everyone else was turning against her. She had no more friends, and her past was trying to come back to kill her.

It was late evening when Aoki walked into her apartment and flipped on the lights. Her place was still and undisturbed. For a moment, she lingered in the foyer and looked around. Her "spidey-senses" were going off. Though everything looked normal and in place, something was definitely off, and she knew exactly what it was.

She walked into the living room, and at once her intruder emerged from a room and trained a gun at her. Aoki turned carefully around to face her. She kept her cool and locked eyes with Rihanna.

"You killed my sister," Ri-Ri uttered with contempt.

"Tisa, she was a snitch."

"You destroy my family, Aoki. Why?"

"Me did what me had to do to survive."

Ri-Ri had tears trickling from her eyes as she glared at Aoki and held the gun to her head. "I trusted you, Aoki. I sat there in that fuckin' place listening to your confessions, and hurting. You know what you did to me?"

"Yuh need to calm down, Ri-Ri," Aoki said calmly.

"Don't fuckin' tell me to calm down!"

"How did yuh leave dat place?"

"I had to perform a few sexual favors on some staff."

Not surprising. They were bred to do what they had to do to survive and to get their way. Ri-Ri was determined to find Aoki and avenge Tisa's death.

Ri-Ri felt she had the drop on Aoki, but Aoki wasn't nervous at all. There was no way Ri-Ri could match her. Her skills were far superior. Ri-

Ri had no idea what treacherous ground she had stepped on. But because she was a friend, or used to be, Aoki decided to give her a chance to save herself.

"Leave now, Ri-Ri, and me will forget all dis."

"You were my friend, you bitch!"

Aoki stared into her eyes, and she could see the tenacity. There was no way Ri-Ri was going to leave without seeing bloodshed. Too bad it would be her own. Though Ri-Ri had killed before, back then they were complete amateurs to the game. Ri-Ri wasn't ready for what happened next.

Aoki read her signals and continued to remain cool. It was about timing. It was about body language, and the advantage would belong to Aoki.

Like a sudden flash of light, Aoki moved from out the line of fire.

The gun went off—*Bak!* But Ri-Ri missed.

Aoki tossed a blunt object at Rihanna's head, and it struck her. She winced from the pain, her forehead bleeding. For a split second she was blinded by pain. It only took a split second for Aoki to have the upper hand. She lunged at Rihanna with several punches to her head, causing her to wobble and then a fist thrust into her chest, and Rihanna found herself on the floor in pain and unarmed. The gun had slid across the room. Aoki stood over her friend now with a dagger in her grip.

Rihanna looked up sadly. She had been easily broken and defeated. "Fuck you, Aoki!" she snarled.

Rihanna was a threat, and Aoki couldn't allow for her to leave the apartment alive. "Me sorry, Ri-Ri." Aoki plunged the dagger into Rihanna's heart and twisted it. Then she held her former friend's hand while she bled out.

THIRTY-FOUR

There were days on The Farm when the trainees went with less than two hours of sleep and no meals. It was a military boot camp on steroids. There was no slacking and no retiring. Once on The Farm, the only way to leave was to kill or to be killed. The trainees were up before the sun. There was a five-mile run and cardio training in the morning. A killer should never become tired. A trained killer was a machine that kept on going. On the Farm, trainees were taught the fundamentals first before they advanced to the more technical things. There was endurance, survival, strength, and knowledge. They were educated—brainwashed—day after day and programmed to act like the Terminator in the fields. They were cultured to not have any compassion or empathy for their targets. They were taught how to become their targets, how to think like their victims, where to strike and how. The Farm was a breeding ground for killers like Aoki and Cristal.

*

"How did you find me?" Cristal asked Aoki.

Aoki smirked and responded, "Yuh can thank yuh grandmother fah dat. It's her birthday, right? I knew yuh would visit her grave. Like De Farm taught us, know yuh target, be patient, then strike. Me know yuh."

"You don't fuckin' know me," Cristal shot back.

The two females were at a face-off, guns pointed at each other's head in the Holy Cross Cemetery in Brooklyn in the middle of the night. It was cold. It was the only time Cristal could visit her Grandma Hattie's grave on her birthday without being seen by rivals. But she was wrong. It was a predictable move on her end.

"So how long we gonna do this?" Cristal asked. Her 9mm was steadied in her grip, and it was aimed at Aoki's head.

"Until me make yuh bleed and fall," Aoki answered with certainty.

Both girls stood steady and fierce. It was do or die for them both, like Bruce Lee against Chuck Norris in *The Way of the Dragon*. Their breathing was shallow and their attention transfixed with surviving the night. Their eyes locked. It would take one false move for one or the other to die.

Aoki knew this wasn't Rihanna she was going against. She would be equally matched in battle with Cristal. She smirked. It was either kill her or die trying.

Simultaneously, their guns exploded into the night. Cristal maneuvered sharply left with her arm outstretched, her feet moving like the Flash, and firing at Aoki.

Aoki maneuvered swiftly right, returning gunfire.

Bullets whizzed by them both, and then each took a gunshot to the body, collapsing against the ground, but still alive and still fighting.

Cristal, a bullet in her shoulder, hastily took cover behind a huge headstone. She reloaded her 9mm speedily.

Aoki, a bullet in her arm, took cover behind a tree.

Quickly they recovered and were ready for round two. They both peered out from their hiding sites and exchanged more gunfire. Slugs tore into the headstone Cristal took safety behind, and bullets splintered the tree that Aoki was crouched by.

Aoki was trying to reload when Cristal suddenly bolted her way and did a flying kick into her chest, sending Aoki staggering backwards, but she caught her footing and countered with a roundhouse kick that slammed into Cristal's side.

Fierce combat ensued with Cristal smashing her elbow into the side of Aoki's face. It was another staggering blow, but Aoki refused to fall. She crashed her knee into Cristal's ribs, and Cristal hammered her fist into her face with repeated punches.

Aoki propelled backwards and blocked several blows to her face and body, and then she banged Cristal's nose with her forehead, spewing blood. She then pushed her away and hit her with an uppercut, dizzying her.

It was pound for pound in the cemetery, one assassin trying to outdo the other.

Breathless and bruised, they stood poised with their fists clenched and their skillfulness shining. Aoki had to admit, Cristal was good. She was a brawler. She wasn't going down without a fight. Neither was she.

They stood close, scowling, circling each other.

Cristal abruptly charged with a high kick to her face, but Aoki read her move and dropped as Cristal rounded her kick. Aoki then executed a sweeping kick that lifted Cristal off her feet and sent her tumbling into the dirt. Aoki then threw dirt into her face, temporarily blinding her, and when Cristal recovered her vision, Aoki was already armed and ready to shoot.

Cristal shouted, "They'll kill you when you turn twenty-five! It's all a lie! The Commission."

Aoki hesitated again. Why? She had the drop on Cristal. This was it. She won. She defeated the bitch after five months of hunting. But again, Aoki glared at Cristal, not pulling the trigger and finally ending this.

"They won't pay you anything," Cristal said.

"Yuh lie to live."

"I know The Commission. You kill me now, and you'll be next on their list."

Aoki was ready to explode on her. She wasn't going to be able to talk her out of death. She didn't believe her.

"When is your twenty-fifth birthday?" Cristal asked.

Aoki didn't answer her. In actuality, it was in a few days.

"You're a dead woman. They use people like us. And whether you kill me or not, they'll still kill you."

Cristal figured that Aoki knew there was some truth to her story. If not, she would have been dead already. She went on to speak about GHOST Protocol, The Commission, and why she was being hunted.

Aoki was only listening because of the lie they'd told her about Oscar. But she had heard enough and hesitated too long. She still had a job to do. She aimed and fired—*Bak!*

THIRTY-FIVE

Cristal was dead, and Aoki went to Muriel, her only contact with The Commission and confirmed her kill with pictures of the body and a sample of her blood to test. Once again they met covertly at East River Park, where they stood side by side on the promenade.

Muriel said, "You're a stubborn little bitch, but you do well."

"Me tell yuh I would kill her."

"And her body?" Muriel asked.

"Disposed of."

Muriel stood expressionless to the news. The Commission had been chasing her for years, and now finally their headache had been erased.

"Me gon' turn twenty-five soon. Dat means me gon' age out. Me ready to put dis life behind me."

"You're ready to start a new life?" Muriel asked rhetorically.

"Me put in a lot of work fah yuh."

"We know."

"Me just want to live nice and slow."

"We understand. Your money will be available first thing tomorrow morning."

Aoki managed to smile. "Nice doin' business wit' yuh." She turned and walked away, leaving Muriel standing alone on the walkway smoking a cigarette and looking preoccupied.

*

At home, Aoki couldn't shake the feeling that something was wrong. All night she stayed alert. She couldn't sleep, although her apartment was booby-trapped from top to bottom. What if what Cristal told her was actually true? And Muriel was acting weird. Who could she trust? What if they sent assassins to silence her permanently? Paranoia swept through her once again. Aoki sat prepared and armed in her apartment, waiting for anyone to make that fatal mistake of coming for her. If they did, she was going to give them hell.

Morning came. It had been a long, slow, and quiet night. No one had come for her. No killers came through her window or kicked down her front door. Of course, Cristal was lying only to save her own life. She was desperate, and desperation made people into liars.

She went to her desk, sat down, and opened her laptop. She logged on to her online banking to check her overseas accounts. She was expecting a huge wire transfer in the millions to come through making her a very, very rich woman. The banks were open. She typed her information into the laptop, and her overseas account appeared. The money was there, but it had been red-flagged. It had been frozen. She couldn't transfer anything into her U.S. account. She didn't have access to anything. Even the large amounts she had previously in her other U.S. accounts had suddenly been frozen. It had to be a mistake. There had been some kind of confusion, and Aoki wanted to resolve the issues immediately. What kind of games was The Commission trying to play?

Frustrated and worried, she removed herself from the desk and walked toward a hidden room in her apartment. It was time for some answers, and she would get them. If not from The Commission, she knew where. As she was about to access the room, stealthily her end came intruding, unexpectedly, into the room and toward her—a large gunman dressed in black—definitely sent by The Commission to kill her. Aoki was stunned and speechless.

She wasn't going down without a fight.

✳

Cristal could hear the chaos happening on the other side of the door. It was an intense scuffle. She heard shots fired and furniture breaking apart. She could hear Aoki fighting for her life. Bound to a chair by heavy chains, she couldn't do anything about it. She couldn't move at all. She could barely wiggle her arms and feet. She fidgeted and squirmed, but Aoki knew how to secure her to the chair. She was a sitting duck trying to figure a way to escape her bondage. The hidden room was the size of a small bedroom with a swinging light bulb above. It was empty and it was cold.

Aoki had kept her alive for a reason. After their fight in the cemetery, Aoki fired into the ground near her head. She believed her. If she didn't, Cristal would've been dead. So Aoki kept her hostage alive momentarily. Now it looked like The Commission had sent someone to take care of Aoki, just as Cristal had predicted.

Phewt! Phewt!

It was definitely a silencer. There was a hard thump to the ground. The fighting had stopped. Someone went down. Was it Aoki or the other killer The Commission undoubtedly sent?

Cristal gawked at the door in trepidation. Who would emerge from the battle? Slowly, the door to the room opened, and Cristal could see the silhouette of the victor. Her eyes fixed on their every movement. It was Aoki. She wobbled into the room looking out of it. She was almost broken, her clothing was torn considerably, her face black and blue, blood trickling from her mouth. Behind her was a dead man sprawled across her floor in his pool of blood, shot twice in the head.

Cristal didn't know whether to be relieved or concerned. Was she still a dead woman?

Surprisingly, Aoki started to undo her restraints. Once they were off, Aoki stepped back and aimed her pistol at Cristal as she stood, stretching her legs and breathing out.

"I guess you believe me now," Cristal said.

"How me know yuh won't come fah me fi da murda of Daniel?"

"An eye for an eye. I took Ms. Louise from you, so consider us even," Cristal said. "Besides, there's been too much bloodshed already. If I was in your position, I would have done the same. Does that answer your question?"

Aoki didn't respond. She respected the truth.

Cristal's heart still hurt for Daniel, but it was the past and she had to put that behind her. She felt that it was something she should have done long ago. She lingered on her feelings and love, and it cost an innocent man his life. Whoever came into her life was at risk of being killed.

Though they weren't trying to tear each other's throats out, it still didn't stop them from being cautious and wary of one another.

"We need to keep a low profile, leave town, and never look back. I'm done with this life," Cristal stated.

Aoki looked reluctant to leave. She wasn't a runner. She wanted payback on everyone who wronged her, starting with Oscar. And she wanted her money. She was out of millions of dollars that was promised to her on her birthday.

Cristal noticed the reluctant look on Aoki's face and knew things weren't going to be that simple. She continued to tell Aoki about GHOST Protocol and The Bishop and how they had snuffed him out because of her. The girls actually had a heart-to-heart. They were two peas in a pod. They both grew up in the slums and ghetto of Brooklyn, made bad choices in life, and lost friends and family members.

"You know, one thing has been bothering me," Cristal said.

"Eh?"

"I remember you being, well, taller before."

Aoki laughed and looked down at her bare feet. "Me shoes came off when I killed dat fool."

Cristal admitted her envy of Aoki, and mentioned how she stalked her career through EP. Aoki had fueled her in killing and made her strive to become a better assassin.

Aoki went on to tell Cristal that she shouldn't be envied. She was a heartless killer, and it started when she was sixteen years old, when she took her father's life.

Aoki wanted the money owed to her from The Commission to help her buy forgiveness, which Ms. Louise always preached to her about. Her death had created an opening into her soul, and made her open to turning her life around. She even had an insane idea and thought about donating half of the money to the local church. Both girls had gone through the pits of hell, shoveled shit, and they were still around. They'd found each other, and now it was time to give 'em hell back.

They needed to leave the apartment and never go back. Aoki was sure that someone would call the police, and there was no time to clean the blood and remove the body. Though they were leery of one another, they realized that in order for them to survive, they would have to stick together.

Before leaving the apartment for good, both girls grabbed duffel bags of guns, cash, and knives. They were at war, and they would need an arsenal to fight.

Aoki felt her childhood home in East New York was the safest place to hide out. She figured they could hide in plain sight until they figured out how to win this battle with The Commission.

THIRTY-SIX

Aoki and Cristal experienced two weeks of peace at Aoki's childhood home. For Aoki, being back in East New York brought back sudden and harsh memories of why she'd left in the first place and never come back until now. There were more bad memories than good. Her parents were hell, her life was torment, and she could still smell their blood and feel their deaths haunting her. The place also reminded her of AZ, Rihanna, and Tisa; it was their hangout spot. The place was a home to her crew, but her crew was now dead. If only the walls could talk, what would they say?

Cristal told Aoki about Ida and the tarot cards, and how she predicted what would happen to Daniel and told her about the curse on her family.

Aoki listened intently. She felt that her family was cursed too. Growing up, her father was always dabbling in black magic on a small level. Maxwell would go on and on with that shit, especially when he was high off crack about voodoo dolls, hexes, and other chilling things. His Jamaican roots made him a believer.

Cristal wanted to go back to New Orleans to see Ida again. Though she had been spooked by the woman's foretelling, she wanted to know more about her future and her past. Aoki wanted to see the psychic too to ask her some questions. She wanted to know her future. She wanted some clarifications on her own life. Why was she like this? Why did she enjoy bloodshed and murder so much? Though she felt herself changing and wanting out of the murder-for-hire business, Aoki had always been a violent person and there was always some reason or someone pulling her back into killing. She wondered if she even had a future. Both girls needed answers.

The girls sat in the living room sipping hot coffee and talking. It looked like a slumber party, but they weren't talking about boys and music, but their techniques and survival. They were trying to formulate a plan to stay off The Commission's radar. They wanted to leave the country, but their money was low. Without a doubt The Commission would have the airports covered, and the moment they were spotted on surveillance, the goons would come gunning for them.

"Me have a plan," Aoki said. "Me know someone wit' a plane. But me gon' need yuh help to take him down."

"I'm down," Cristal said without hesitation.

They talked like they'd suddenly become sisters.

"We probably make better partners than we do rivals," Cristal said.

Aoki chuckled. She sat on the floor Indian-style. She was relaxed talking to Cristal, a female on the same speed as her, with the same nightmarish past. It was somewhat therapeutic. They somewhat started to trust each other.

Cristal stood up from the floor to get more coffee from the kitchen. The moment she stood though, she saw it—the tiny red dot moving around on the wall behind her. Then another red dot appeared suddenly on the wall, and a third—until there were half a dozen dancing red dots on the wall. It quickly dawned on Cristal and Aoki. Cristal shouted, "Shit, they found us!"

Right away intense gunfire exploded around them, blowing apart the windows, and high-velocity bullets ripped through the walls of the house.

Cristal hit the floor hastily, shielding herself from the debris falling around her. The girls kept low and scurried for their weapons. War had just erupted in East New York.

A group of assassins had converged and were approaching the house, spraying machine gun fire. They were in black fatigues, black boots, and tactical vests. They were from GHOST Protocol, and with them was the deadly black widow Natalia—The Bishop's ex-girlfriend and his murderer. She was leading the charge. She wanted Cristal's head on a stick—Aoki was the added bonus.

Cristal and Aoki were heavily armed and took cover behind a brick partition in the house. They kept low and readied themselves for combat.

"How many you think?" Cristal asked.

Aoki took a quick glance outside, almost getting her head shot off. "Me tink six!"

The girls took a needed deep breath and returned gunfire. Fuck it, they were ready to die today, ready to go out in a blaze of glory, but not before they killed a few men themselves.

All of a sudden, a shooter came crashing through the kitchen window like a maniac. Aoki spun around and impulsively took aim and shot him before he could shoot them. The head shot sent his body crashing to the floor.

Two more shooters fervently barged into the home, opening fire with their machine guns. The girls had to scurry for safety. They were outnumbered and outgunned, but refused to be taken out. The men's Heckler and Koch MP5 turned the living room wall into Swiss cheese. Bullets whizzed by them like rockets going off.

"I'll go high, you go low!" Cristal shouted.

Aoki hunkered down to the floor and slid herself from behind the wall, while Cristal stood erect and veered from behind the wall, and both girls simultaneously opened fire at the two shooters. One hit 'em high, and the other hit 'em low. Now three were dead, and they were still standing. But the threat was still coming at them strong.

Natalia wasn't going to let them live. It wasn't in her blood to fail.

She'd taken out The Bishop, but Aoki and Cristal were vicious and crafty. She and her three remaining shooters charged into the house determined to vanquish these two bitches.

Inside, Aoki and Cristal were waiting for them all, and they had that fire in their eyes to survive, or take everyone out with them in a bang.

And then the explosion happened. The ground shook violently, and the earth underneath their feet came apart. The billow of black smoke could be seen for several miles.

*

They had barely escaped with their lives in the shootout with GHOST Protocol. Cristal had rigged the oven with explosives and removed the gas line, so when the gunfire erupted again, everything went off, but by then the girls were dashing for their escape.

Cristal drove a stolen car. They needed to find a quiet, secure location. She needed to aid Aoki, who'd been shot in her side and was bleeding profusely. Cristal tried not to panic. They needed help. They needed a doctor without risking going to any hospitals.

Thinking on her feet, Cristal forced a doctor at gunpoint in a clinic parking lot while he was walking to his car at night back inside

"Save her, or you're a dead man."

He performed surgery on Aoki with the tools he had. She would live, but she would need to rest.

All of their friends were dead, and many of their enemies were dead too, and they both were going to be hunted until they were dead. Cristal knew it. They had both agencies hunting them. Agencies that they once held allegiance to were now their mortal enemies. And to stay alive, they were stronger together than apart.

But what worried Cristal the most was, Did Natalia die in that explosion? There was no telling. Natalia was a ruthless, coldhearted bitch.

She and Aoki were good, but Natalia was the best. If she could murder The Bishop, then they knew she couldn't be stopped. If Natalia had survived that explosion, then she wouldn't stop hunting Cristal even if it meant falling off the edge of the earth to succeed.

They needed to leave the country, and now!

THIRTY-SEVEN

Oscar puffed on his Cuban cigar as he stood on the tarmac of Opa-Locka Airport in northeast Miami. The place was a smaller relief airport for Miami International Airport, and offered Customs and refueling services for nine runways. It was a convenient private airport for Oscar and other wealthy men. Oscar's fifteen-million-dollar Learjet was fueled and ready to take off into the sky. He was leaving for Mexico dressed handsomely in his custom linen suit and white shoes, his gold Rolex and diamond pinky ring shining brighter than the Miami sun. He was accompanied by several armed henchmen, and along with their guns, his men carried two duffel bags of cash totaling six million dollars. It was time to leave America for good.

He walked toward his jet proudly. When he landed in Mexico he planned to have sex with many beautiful women, hire more killers to his organization, shield himself in his large mansion with his wife, run for public office, and continue warring with the Señor cartel. A powerful man with many powerful friends, Oscar felt untouchable.

He ascended the stairs and entered his jet. It was a beautiful plane—one of the best. The cabin held eight leather seats in a double club layout with plenty of room to swivel, recline, and track, several flat-screens, a mini-bar, and bathroom. The moment Oscar stepped into his plane, he could sense something wasn't right. His young beauty, Tamsin, wasn't there to greet him with her golden smile and gorgeous figure. Tamsin was his flight attendant and the only woman he trusted to have on his plane.

He walked toward the cockpit to greet his two pilots, but suddenly was met with a rude awakening and the shock of his life when Aoki appeared from out of nowhere and shoved a Desert Eagle in his face.

"You're dead!" he shouted.

"No, *you* are!" she exclaimed. She pistol-whipped him, and he fell to his knees, his nose broken and bloody.

When his henchmen tried to board behind him, there was Cristal taking them out with sniper fire, dropping every last one of them on the tarmac. Now Oscar had no protection. He didn't feel so untouchable anymore.

Aoki glared at him. This was her moment. She had done her research and found out that Oscar used The Commission a lot in his business and had given them millions of dollars to take out his competition. He had cheated death dozens of times, but today his luck had finally run out.

"You bitch!" Oscar growled.

"Yuh had AZ killed too, huh?"

"You think this is over? You kill me, and you and your entire family will suffer."

Aoki smirked. "What family? Me have no family left."

Aoki had heard enough. She blew his head off right there, and Oscar's body dropped backwards. Now his perfect linen white suit was covered in his blood.

Cristal grabbed the duffel bags and hurried onto the plane, carrying her sniper rifle and shouted, "We need to go!"

Aoki pointed her gun at the pilots and told them to take off, and they did what they were told. The plane started to move toward the runway. They wanted to be in the air and flying out of the country ASAP.

Cristal looked down at Oscar's mangled body and said, "So this is him."

Aoki nodded.

On the plane with them were the duffel bags of cash. The girls unzipped it, and they couldn't help but smile widely. It was totally unexpected. Aoki got her millions after all.

The Learjet lifted off, soaring into the clear blue sky. They would soon be out of the country and gone for good.

EPILOGUE

Rome Italy

One Year Later

The villa by the shoreline was beautiful, full of greenery, warm life, and tranquility. Aoki and Cristal took refuge in the small villa. There, they studied at a local college under assumed names and were trying to live normal lives for once. She and Cristal were both Catholics now and attended St. Mary's Basilica to continually repent for their sins. Both girls were content with their new lives. The Italian men were in love with the black women. Their place was full of life as they acquainted themselves with the locals.

In Italy, it seemed like everyone was family. There was lots of red wine, salad, and pasta. In their country home, the ladies chatted with their houseguests, laughed and enjoyed life the way it should have been from the beginning. Spread out on their reclaimed dining room table was a large meal of spaghetti and meatballs, spaghetti alle vongole, carbonara, linguini with clam sauce, risotto with lemon, and green beans.

Aoki looked around and smiled. She finally had a real family. She thought back to when she had gone to see the psychic Ida alone in New Orleans. It was risky traveling back to the States, but she needed to see this woman. Ida read Aoki's cards and told her that her future would be short-lived unless she killed the girl with the curse. The death card for Aoki could mean change, but Aoki had to set the stage. If she killed Cristal, the death card meant Aoki could live if she changed her ways. If she didn't kill Cristal, then death meant death. Aoki had listened intently to Ida's foretelling.

Aoki had every intention of killing Cristal to live, but traveling back to Italy, to her home, to where there had been no bloodshed in months and where there were smiles and family waiting for her, Aoki relinquished the thought and figured the psychic to be foolish. She couldn't do it. They'd come so far. She didn't want to do it. She told herself that she would rather die with Cristal by her side, and as a friend, than alone in the world without a friend.

The lively bunch of Italians and the girls continued to enjoy their meals and laughed like they'd never laughed before.

*

The Commission and GHOST Protocol's henchmen armed with a great deal of machine guns were advancing on the isolated home on the Italian land with rolling green hills and tall, leafy trees. Leading the assault was Natalia. Her killers dressed in black hurried toward the house they believed to be hiding Cristal and Aoki, and were preparing to slaughter them. Natalia was itching to kill them all. They had the house surrounded. This time there would be no escape; no explosion to distract her. Natalia was focused on murder, and with over two dozen armed soldiers on the land, Cristal and Aoki's lives would finally come to an end.

The front and back doors were kicked open all at once, and over two dozen shooters poured into the home and opened fire on the occupants inside. Bodies were sprayed with bullets, spilling blood, tearing limbs apart, and cutting the residents down to the floor.

When the smoke cleared, five people lay dead on the blood covered floor.

Natalia went looking for their bodies, but they weren't there. It wasn't Cristal or Aoki. It was the wrong home. Wrong tip.

Natalia screamed out of frustration. Where were they? Where did they go? She was going to hunt the two bitches to the end of the earth. Even God couldn't save them.

OH, BROTHER

MAFIO$O

PART ONE

NISA
SANTIAGO

LET'S BUILD.

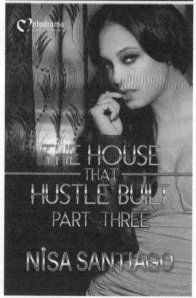

A Series by
**Nisa
Santiago**

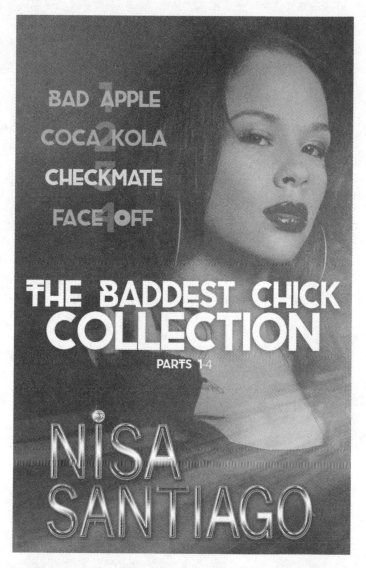